Just Passing Through

MARGARET TUTOR

Just Passing Through

Best Wishes
Michelle!

Love,
Margaret Tutor
Mat

TATE PUBLISHING
AND ENTERPRISES, LLC

Published by Tate Publishing & Enterprises, LLC
127 E. Trade Center Terrace | Mustang, Oklahoma 73064 USA
1.888.361.9473 | www.tatepublishing.com

Tate Publishing is committed to excellence in the publishing industry. The company reflects the philosophy established by the founders, based on Psalm 68:11,
"The Lord gave the word and great was the company of those who published it."

Book design copyright © 2013 by Tate Publishing, LLC. All rights reserved.
Cover design by Arjay Grecia
Interior design by Honeylette Pino

Published in the United States of America

ISBN: 978-1-62902-483-7
Fiction / Historical
13.10.10

Dedication

In loving memory of...Grandpa Ward with his quick wit. Grandma Ward with her cast-iron skillet skills. My mama, Mary Jane (Ward) Robinson, who had both a quick wit and a good aim. To my sister, Doylene and brother Bill; all my Ward aunts and uncles.

Special thanks to Jerry, Kim, and Karon Dru, my Robinson family. To Michael Tutor, my very own Grandpa Skippy. Thanks to Mrs. Mabel F. Tutor for her words of encouragement.

Chapter 1

Christmastime drew near, and as usual, the whole town was in a tizzy. Everyone was going about their holiday activities. Mary Jane wondered if Santa Claus would be able to find her house this year since he got lost the year before. She had to believe that *he just got lost* because the real reason for "no Santa" was just too heartbreaking for a little girl to understand.

This was the first time Mary Jane realized Christmas would be different for her and the family, but she was young enough to still believe in Santa Claus. There was no Christmas tree. The only Christmas tree Mary Jane could remember seeing was in a store window or in homes of other people, but never one in her home. This year, Mary Jane wanted to have a Christmas like everyone else. She wanted a tree with lots of gifts piled high underneath. She wanted Santa Claus to come to her house and leave her something special…something just for her.

This Christmas Eve filled Mary Jane with a heightened level of anticipation. She sat quietly with her brother, Jerry, on the couch looking through the catalog, talking about what they wanted more than anything else in the whole world. Out of the blue, Mary Jane looked up at her brother and said, "I wish we had a daddy like everyone else, don't you?"

Jerry smiled and said, "Me too."

Their daddy had died when Mary Jane was just a baby, so she never knew him. Jerry didn't remember much about him either. The older Jerry got, the less he remembered; although, Mama always said Jerry was the spitting image of his daddy.

"When Mama gets home from work, maybe we can talk about Christmas," Mary Jane said. "Maybe, this year, Mama won't cry."

When Mama came home with bundles in her arms, Mary Jane forgot all about having a talk about Christmas and Santa Claus. Mary Jane and Jerry rushed with excitement to help Mama with her bundles. *Bundles at Christmas!*

This was unexpected and exciting for the whole family. The children all rushed from their corners of the small house to see what the excitement was all about. Mary Jane and Jerry took the small bags, while the older children ran outside to help carry the remainder into the house. Mary Jane was so excited that she could barely contain her emotions! She danced around the kitchen with sparkles in her eyes. "This is going to be a good Christmas," she shouted.

Mary Jane watched the bundles being unpacked, *but these were not Christmas bundles*. Her little heart sank and her dancing stopped. The joyous sounds flowing through the house suddenly grew quiet.

Each of the seven children handled Christmas disappointment differently. One by one, the children drifted back to what they had been doing before Mama came home from work. Mary Jane went back to her catalog, what her Mama called the *wish book*. As she sat turning the pages to reveal treasure after treasure, she thought sometimes Santa Claus didn't come see her because she was bad. She *tried* to be good, but it didn't always work out that way. She was always getting into something or wondering off down the street to play without permission. Jerry could hardly keep track of her at times.

Mama had made preparations for their Christmas dinner and was ready for bed, but Mary Jane was too excited about Christmas again to sleep. She begged to be allowed to stay up a while longer. Mama was too tired to put up much of an argument, so Mary Jane got her wish. When all was quiet, Mary Jane and Jerry could hear their mama sobbing from her bedroom. "Why does Mama cry at night, when she thinks we can't hear?" Mary Jane asked. Jerry put his arm around his little sister and tried to explain in a way she could understand. Jerry was only seven, but he was very smart, at least to Mary Jane.

"When our Daddy died—" began Jerry.

"We became orphans!" Mary Jane blurted out.

"We are not orphans!" scolded Jerry. "Orphans don't have a mama or a daddy. We have a mama!"

Mary Jane settled down to listen as her big brother tried to explain what made Mama so sad at Christmastime. Jerry used words like *obligations, responsibility, hard work, and loneliness.*

Mary Jane looked puzzled by his big words. "Do you know what those words mean?" she asked.

"I heard Mama talking to Grandma Ward one day and she used those words," Jerry said. He never did tell Mary Jane that he didn't know what those words meant, but she seemed content with his explanation. If Jerry said it, it was good enough for little Mary Jane.

Jerry once again put his arm around Mary Jane; this time, he gave her a little hug. "I wish we could do something special for

Mama and the others for Christmas," Jerry sighed. Mary Jane's eyes lit up like a little Christmas tree; she had an idea.

"Mama is always telling us, we have to make do. Well, why can't we have a make-do Christmas?"

Now both Jerry and Mary Jane were excited about a make-do Christmas. Mary Jane was so excited she shouted, "We are going to have a make-do Christmas!"

Jerry quickly covered her mouth. "This is going to be a big surprise for the whole family," he whispered. "If Mama wakes up, we'll have to go to bed."

The house was small; the two little elves had to be very quiet. They quietly scampered around the house, gathering items to give as Christmas gifts. They searched every closet, every cupboard, every box, and every drawer to find items to wrap for Christmas. There was no wrapping paper, no tape, and no bows; but this was a make-do Christmas, so that's exactly what they did. They used brown paper grocery bags for wrapping paper. They made paste with flour and water, and they found some old string, in case the paste didn't hold. They even found some old broken crayons to give their packages some Christmas color. Mary Jane and Jerry were so busy with their make-do Christmas that they forgot all about everything else. They were going to make their mama happy for Christmas. Mary Jane's heart was full of Christmas joy and love for her mama. She knew Mama would be very pleased and proud to have a make-do Christmas.

For Mama, Jerry took an old photograph of Daddy and put it into a *newly found* old frame. He wrapped it very carefully, as if it were brand-new. Mary Jane took an old bottle of perfume, which had only a few drops and wrapped it for the prettiest Mama in town. Their sister, Doylene, received a tube of lipstick, which was almost all gone. Kim, the second sister, was too young for lipstick; she received a book. It didn't matter that she had already read the book; this was a make-do Christmas, and everyone would have a gift to open on Christmas morning. The older brothers,

Martin, Bill, and Eddy, received a brand-new comb and a pair of slightly used socks—*no holes*. The gifts were ready to go under the Christmas tree, but there was no tree.

Mary Jane and Jerry stood in the kitchen looking around at the mess they had made—now, they must clean up. Both had dried paste on their faces and hands, with little slivers of paper stuck to them. The kitchen was not the only thing that was a mess and had to be cleaned. However, that would have to wait; there was one more thing that had to be done before their make-do Christmas was completed. Mary Jane, still trying to be very quiet, began to hop, skip, and dance about the kitchen, whispering, "A Christmas tree, a Christmas tree, we're going to have a Christmas tree." Jerry watched Mary Jane do her little Christmas tree dance before he reminded her that they didn't have a tree, *just yet*.

"Is our Christmas tree going to be a make-do Christmas tree?" asked Mary Jane. "Oh how I would love to have a real tree," she softly begged.

Jerry would never say no to her, if he could possibly help it. He knew he had to at least try.

Jerry told Mary Jane, "If you will clean some of this mess, I will see what I can do." Mary Jane wanted to do another Christmas tree dance, but she restrained herself; instead, she gave Jerry a big hug. She wasn't sure how he was going to do it, but she knew he would try his best. Mary Jane was about to burst with excitement over all they had done and the big surprise the family would have on Christmas morning. Her pride made Mary Jane stand a little taller.

Jerry got his coat, which was a hand-me-down and still too big, and began to bundle up to go find Mary Jane a Christmas tree. Since Jerry did not have gloves, Mary Jane quickly ran and got a pair of socks for him to use as gloves. Jerry gave Mary Jane a slight punch to her little chin as a job well done. They both knew they were not allowed to go out at night, but this was an emergency. Mary Jane tried to keep her mind on cleaning up their mess, but curiosity was getting the best of her. She could see Jerry in the backyard, but she could not tell exactly what he was doing.

Mary Jane put on her coat and headed out the back door to see if she could help. Jerry scolded her for coming out into the cold damp air. As usual, it did no good. Mary Jane was outside, and she was going to stay out as long a Jerry stayed. Mary Jane went to the shed to find a bucket while Jerry tried to get control of the shovel. The shovel was so big and heavy that Jerry needed Mary Jane's help. Together they managed to get the shovel started into the ground.

"What are we doing, Jerry?" she asked.

"We are going to get us a real Christmas tree and put it in this bucket," he proudly told her.

Once again, Mary Jane started doing her Christmas tree dance. She worked and danced, danced and worked. This was going to be their best Christmas ever, she just knew it. Together the little elves walked to the edge of the property where there were some small cedar trees, if you could call them trees. Jerry was determined to get his little sister a Christmas tree. He found a little tree that he thought they could manage together; they went to work on the poor little tree. They pulled, pushed, tugged, and anything else they could think of to get the little cedar tree to let go of the ground. Together, they did it.

They got the little tree and were now ready to drag it back to their backyard. It was so cold and they were so tired, but they were proud of what they had been doing. The two half-frozen children got their Christmas tree, not a make-do Christmas tree but a real Christmas tree. The bucket for the tree was now ready for the dirt; Mary Jane called it Christmas dirt. Jerry just smiled and kept scooping more dirt into the bucket while Mary Jane watched and shivered from the cold. Once the bottom of the bucket was filled with the Christmas dirt, it was time to place their tree in the bucket and finish filling it.

Jerry stopped scooping dirt to ponder how to move the Christmas tree once is was completed. He instructed Mary Jane to stay with the tree; he would be right back.

"No," she said, "I want to go with you, Jerry!"

"We need the wagon to be able to move the tree when we finish it. It will be too heavy for us to carry," he explained. "You stay here and guard our real Christmas tree, please."

Jerry and Mary Jane managed to place the bucket of Christmas dirt in the wagon. Jerry continued to scoop the dirt while Mary Jane tried to keep the little cedar tree standing tall and straight. Once the Christmas tree was finished, Jerry looked at Mary Jane and said, "Merry Christmas."

Mary Jane threw her little arms around her brother and exclaimed, "This is the best Christmas gift I will ever get in my whole life. Thank you, Jerry." The little cedar tree was ready for its new home, and it would take all of Jerry and Mary Jane's strength to get it done. The tree was packed tight with plenty of Christmas dirt and loaded in their old rusty wagon. The wagon was so heavy they could hardly pull it, but they did manage to get it to the back door.

The steps to the house were another hurdle for them to overcome. There were only few steps, but with such a heavy load, it would be hard to manage. They were going to need muscles to get the tree inside. The two just stood staring at the steps as if there were hundreds. The task at hand seemed overwhelming for the two small children; Mary Jane began to quietly sob. Jerry took Mary Jane by the hand and helped her to sit on one of the steps. He brushed her straight, limp hair from her eyes and wiped her tear away. Jerry began to laugh out loud.

"What is so funny?" she snapped.

"The Christmas dirt on my gloves and your tears made Christmas mud on your face," he said with a big belly laugh.

"Jerry, please don't make me laugh. I am really sad." Mary Jane finally began to laugh about her Christmas mud. They looked like two little ragamuffins sitting on the steps; they were cold and dirty but full of the Christmas spirit. Despite the fact that Mary Jane and Jerry were from a poor family, living in a very small home with their mama and a total of seven children, they felt loved all year round. They were now becoming aware of what make do and the joy of giving to others truly meant. Never once while their make-do Christmas was being prepared did Mary Jane or Jerry think about what they wanted under the tree. There was no puppy for Jerry, and there was no baby doll for Mary Jane—that is all they wanted from Santa Claus. They never gave up asking Santa for a puppy and a baby doll. Every Christmas, the two would search the wish book for a special baby doll for Mary Jane and Jerry would sketch a picture of what he wanted his puppy to look like. Together they would huddle around the kitchen table and write Santa Claus a letter with Jerry's sketch of his puppy and a page from Mary Jane's wish book of baby dolls. In their letters, they never failed to ask Santa Claus for gifts for the rest of the family too.

After their letters to Santa was finished, each would receive a cup of hot cocoa to celebrate the start of the Christmas season. Then Mama would take the letters and gently place them in her purse to be mailed to the North Pole the next day on her way to work. No stamps were needed on letters going to the North Pole and Santa. For the next several days after their letters to Santa, Mary Jane and Jerry would ask, "Mama, do you think Santa Claus got our letters yet?" Without fail, Mama told them the same story about how the post office had a special postman that delivered all the mail to Santa without delay. The same story she was told by her Mama and Papa.

She told them that Mr. and Mrs. Santa Claus read each and every letter they received while sipping on hot cocoa. It was such a good story; Mary Jane and Jerry never grew tired of hearing it. Each Christmas season, something new would be added to the story, creating a little more excitement. This year, Mama told Mary Jane and Jerry while sipping hot cocoa and reading their Christmas mail that Mr. and Mrs. Santa Claus were wearing their Christmas slipper to keep their feet warm.

Mama said she had it from a good source… If Santa Claus caught a cold from not wearing his warm Christmas slippers, he would be too sick to work on Christmas Eve. This story soon became a Christmas traditions for Mary Jane and Jerry, a story they would pass on to their children.

Mary Jane and Jerry thought maybe Grandma Ward knew Mrs. Santa Claus because they both had rules about wearing warm slipper and not getting sick feet.

Grandma Ward was always reminding Grandpa to take care of his feet. She believed that if you caught a cold in your feet, it would travel to the rest of the body. If Grandpa Ward let his feet catch a cold, Grandma would put his sick feet into a pan of extra warm water. She would then fix Grandpa a hot toddy. It didn't take long for Grandma to figure out Grandpa liked his hot toddy, and if it meant doing a little play acting to get one, he didn't have a problem with it.

William Murphy Ward and Parthina (Dudley) Ward had been together so long Parthina could almost read his mind. According to Grandma Ward, Grandpa could be a grouchy old man; other times, he was like a cuddly bear. Grandma liked the cuddly bear best. If the grouchy old man showed up, Grandma would find something to do away from grouchy old Grandpa. When Grandpa was no longer the grouchy old man, he would find Grandma right away to say he was sorry. As soon as Grandma Ward accepted Grandpa's apology, he would kiss her forehead and promise to do better.

Chapter 2

Mary Jane and Jerry had no idea just how cold they were until the heat from the warm kitchen hit their little faces. They were cold and dirty from digging up their Christmas dirt. Jerry's make-do gloves were covered with dirt, and Mary Jane's face was streaked with mud, where Jerry had wiped her tears away. Their poor little cedar tree was still sitting at the bottoms of the steps. There had to be a solution, but they didn't know what.

The kitchen was a mess, they were a mess, and now they were caught. Not by their Mama but by Bill, their older brother. Bill came strolling from the bedroom and spotted what seemed to be the remnants of a small storm that hit the kitchen. All Bill could do at this point was to snicker at the two little ragamuffins standing in the middle of all the mess. Mary Jane immediately ran to Bill and begged him to please help them bring in their little tree—after she swore him to secrecy, of course. Mary Jane and Jerry each took Bill by his hands and almost dragged him to the back door. "See it! See it! That is our Christmas tree," squealed, Mary Jane.

Bill agreed to bring the poor little misshaped Christmas tree inside. Mary Jane and Jerry hurried to the living room to find the perfect place to put the tree. This was the most beautiful Christmas tree Mary Jane and Jerry had ever seen—beautiful because it was their very own Christmas tree, not a make-do Christmas tree, a real tree. Of course, Bill could see the tree was skinny, crocked, and full of holes; but he would never say that to the little ones. He was very proud and touched by all the hard work they had put into their make-do Christmas. The kitchen was still a disaster area and so was the backyard. Bill agreed to help them put things back into place before he went off to work. While his coffee was brewing, Bill went to the backyard to put away the wagon and shovel. In the middle of the yard was a big hole, the Christmas dirt hole. Bill just shook his head and went back into the house. Mary Jane and Jerry were still bundled, still shivering from the cold.

Bill inquired, "What is next for this make-do Christmas?" Mary Jane put her hand on her hip and gave all the details for decorating their tree.

As Mary Jane finished with all the details, Bill kneeled down and began to unbutton her coat. "Let's get you two unbundled and get you cleaned up before you start something else." Mary Jane watched Bill help Jerry get unbundled next.

"Since your so-called gloves are old, dirty, and have holes; I think we can throw them out," Bill said. So the make-do gloves went into the trash. Bill made a deal with the two little ones; he would start cleaning the kitchen while Mary Jane and Jerry washed their faces and hands. Two chairs were pulled up to the kitchen sink, and away they went washing, splashing, and laughing at each other. Bill had to remind them that everyone was sleeping and to please be quiet. They washed up with little being said.

The messy kitchen was much better, but it was time to make another mess: the Christmas decorations. Jerry took more brown paper grocery bags, paste, and crayons to make a chain to go around the tree. Mary Jane looked for anything that was shiny to hang on the tree. She spared nothing; she came back to the living room with all the old jewelry she could find. Jerry even offered some of his school pencils. White thread was tied around the pencil erasers and then hung on the tree. Together, Mary Jane and Jerry decorated their real Christmas tree and placed the make-do gifts under the tree. They stood and marveled over a job well done; they even did one of Mary Jane's little Christmas dances. Jerry was beginning to like *happy dancing*.

The little Christmas tree still needed something else to make it complete: a star. Jerry looked the house over for something to use as a star while Mary Jane just stood staring at the most beautiful Christmas tree she had ever seen. Her tree was prettier than the ones in Morrilton's store windows because it was her tree.

There was nothing to use for a star; the little ones would have to make do. Jerry and Mary Jane were so tired that could barely go on. They had worked so hard on their make-do Christmas, but they were just too tired to think about a star anymore. Once again, big brother Bill had come to the rescue; he suggested making a star from aluminum foil. Bill could see Jerry and Mary Jane were so tired they could do no more. He agreed to make a star for the tree if they would go to bed. Both Jerry and Mary Jane refused to go to bed until their make-do Christmas was completed. A compromise was agreed upon. Bill made both Jerry and Mary Jane a cup of warm milk. They were to sit quietly and watch him make their Christmas star. A blanket was draped over the bottom half of the children while they sipped their warm milk. They watched from the living room to the kitchen table with great anticipation, waiting for a star to appear. With each passing moment, Bill could see the little ones giving into their weariness.

The Christmas star was completed just as Bill had promised. Jerry and Mary Jane were still sitting up, but they were sound asleep. Bill placed the star on top of the Christmas tree; he was quite pleased with his creation. He watched Jerry and Mary Jane sleeping so peacefully and realized what a wonderful thing these two small children had done.

Before leaving for work, Bill gently nudged Jerry to wake up. It was definitely time for bed. As Jerry and Mary Jane were tucked into bed, each asked about the Christmas star. Bill assured each that the star was on their Christmas tree. Just as Bill turned out the light, Mary Jane's sweet little voice said, "Merry make-do Christmas."

On Christmas morning, the house was very quiet. Mary Jane sprang from her bed; she wanted to see if the make-do Christmas was still there. It was just as she remembered, except the tree had a big beautiful star, all shiny and sparkly. There was a small lamp sitting behind the tree, which made everything shine. Mary Jane slipped quietly into Jerry's room to see if he was awake; he was not. She stood staring at him for just a moment; she then leaned over and whispered, "Wake up, Jerry."

"Go away, Mary Jane, it's still dark," he growled. No matter what she said, Jerry was not getting out of bed. Finally, Mary Jane crawled back into the bed she shared with her sister Kim. It was hard for Mary Jane to stop thinking about the make-do Christmas and her real Christmas tree, but finally, she did go back to sleep.

It was now time to wake up, but Mary Jane and Jerry pretended to still be sleeping. They wanted to pretend they didn't know anything about the Christmas tree and all the make-do gifts. They could hear the other children talking about all they saw. Suddenly, they heard Mama yelling, "Mary Jane, Jerry, come quick, I think Santa Claus was here last night."

As Mary Jane and Jerry met in the hallway, they smiled at each other and knew their plan had worked. Jerry took Mary Jane's hand, and they proudly strolled into the living room with the rest of the family. They were as proud as two little strutting peacocks or roosters in a henhouse.

The two little peacocks walked into a living room full of Christmas. Under their crooked little cedar tree, packed in a bucket of Christmas dirt, was all kinds of wrapped gifts. Mary Jane and Jerry could not believe their eyes; Santa Claus really did come to see them. Mary Jane and Jerry danced in circles, singing "Santa Claus came to see us. Santa Claus came to see us." This was the first time in several years; the family had anything close to a real Christmas. Mama had tears streaming down her rosy little cheeks as she watched her babies be really and truly happy at Christmas. Mary Jane was somewhat confused; she had been up earlier and didn't see Santa's gifts.

"Mama, when did Santa Claus come to our house?" whispered Mary Jane. "I got up early and looked, but I didn't see gifts from Santa, only our make-do Christmas," she confessed. "When did he come to our house?" she asked again. Mary Jane did not give Mama a chance to answer her question. She just danced around the room, squealing, "Can we open them now? Can we open them now?"

"Not just yet," Mama said. "We have to wait until everyone is home."

Mama took a closer look at Mary Jane and Jerry; they were still wearing their clothes from the day before. They still had remnants of dirt, paste, and small slivers of paper on their little faces. Their fingernails were stained with Christmas dirt; they had slept in their clothes. As Mama finished her inspection of the two little ragamuffins, she gave each one of the children a chore to do. She explained to Mary Jane and Jerry that this was a very special day and things had to be made ready. "Grandma and Grandpa Ward are coming for Christmas," Mama proudly announced. Mama couldn't tell who was more excited, Mary Jane or Jerry; Santa Claus or Grandma and Grandpa coming for a visit. A visit from either was very scarce.

The first order of business was a bath for Mary Jane and then Jerry. The two older sisters, Doylene and Kim, took turns supervising baths and making the beds. Mama was in the kitchen making a Christmas breakfast, which consisted of homemade biscuits and rice, rice with milk, sugar, and lots of butter. Brothers Eddy and Martin flipped a coin to see who would peel potatoes or who would make the yard more presentable. Martin stayed in the kitchen with Mama and peeled potatoes. Eddy discovered the hole in the backyard; he called for Mama to come look. As soon as Mama stepped out the back door, she could see the hole and the mess left behind. All she could do was shake her head. "We'll have to fix that later," she said.

Mary Jane and Jerry were all clean and dressed in what Mama called their Sunday's best. Now they looked like Mama's little angels, and she wanted them to stay that way, at least until Grandma and Grandpa arrived. Mary Jane and Jerry were ready for breakfast. Mama tucked a dish towel under their little chins to catch any mess. The dish towels worked; their clothes were still neat, clean, and Mama was pleased. When Mama was pleased, here face sparkled.

Mama softly inquired about the hole in the backyard. Mary Jane and Jerry thought they were in trouble, so they just looked at each other and said, "The hole."

"The hole," Mama replied.

Mary Jane asked, "Are we in trouble?" When the two discovered they were not in trouble, Mary Jane explained all about the Christmas dirt. "Christmas dirt is special dirt." Everything seemed to be going smoothly. The house was in order, breakfast was over, and the children were ready for Christmas to begin.

Mary Jane and Jerry stood in the doorway of the kitchen and watched Mama making pie crust. Mary Jane asked, "Mama what kind of pie are you making?" Mama stopped rolling the dough and looked out over her glasses to say, "Chocolate, pumpkin, and pecan."

"Oh, Mama! This is the best Christmas we ever had, isn't it?" Jerry shouted.

With a slight sadness in her voice, Mama said, "Yes, the best Christmas since Daddy left us." Jerry put his arm around Mary Jane and softly explained, "Left us is a nice way of saying he died. Ain't that right, Mama?"

"Yes, Jerry," she replied.

Mary Jane put her hand on her little hip and said, "Okay." She was satisfied with the answer. Mary Jane didn't always understand the answers to her questions, but if she didn't get an answer—any answer she would—why, what, and where you until she got an answer.

Mary Jane had a streak of Parthina in her—just a little on the bossy side, at least that's what Grandpa Ward thought. Mary Jane took that as a compliment; she was happy to be like Grandma Ward. Mary Jane and Jerry soon became bored waiting for Grandma and Grandpa to arrive for the celebrations. To take their minds off what seemed to be a long wait, Mama asked about the make-do Christmas. Mary Jane and Jerry sat next to Mama on the couch and began their story. Each took a turn, telling how they got the idea and *everything* they did. Mary Jane had sworn Bill to secrecy, but she shared the secret with Mama. "Bill brought the Christmas tree inside for us," she whispered. "He made our brand-new, never-been-used star for our real Christmas tree too."

Mama waited until the children finished their story before asking about the hole in the backyard again. "How do you think we should fix the hole?" Jerry pondered and then suggested they could put the Christmas dirt back in the hole.

"Very good idea, Jerry," Mama replied. Mary Jane tried to say something, but before she could say anything, Jerry started talking again. He continued, "And we can plant our Christmas tree in the hole with the Christmas dirt. "We can always have a Christmas tree." Mary Jane thought it was a wonderful idea and began to bounce up and down, Singing, "Yes, Mama, can we? Can we? Please, Mama, let us keep our Christmas tree forever and ever?"

Mama agreed the Christmas tree and the Christmas dirt should stay together forever. "The family will always have a Christmas tree," Mama announced.

"Are Grandma and Grandpa ever going to get here?" Jerry asked. "It sure seemed a long time to wait before we can see what Santa Claus brought us."

"Yea, Mama, what Jerry said," Mary Jane groaned. Mama had to remind them; Bill had to drive to Birdtown to pick up Grandma and Grandpa. He couldn't do that until he got off work at eight o'clock.

"What o'clock is it now?" Mary Jane asked. Jerry and Mama laughed out loud. "They should be here anytime now, it is nine o'clock."

Grandpa Ward opened the door with a big "Hohoho" and scooped Mary Jane and Jerry up with a big hug. Grandma was right on his heel; she got in on the hugs and kisses too. Mary Jane took Grandpa by the hand and led him over to the Christmas tree. "Look, Grandpa, we have a Christmas tree, and ain't it the most beautiful Christmas tree ever?"

Jerry joined in the conversation by announcing, "Santa Claus came to our house, Grandpa."

Grandpa had heard about the hole in the backyard and wanted to see it firsthand. "Get your coats, kids, let's go look at that hole."

While Grandpa took Mary Jane and Jerry out the back; the others went out the front to bring in more food and gifts. Grandpa walked around the hole, shaking his head and mumbling about the size of it. The weather was still quiet chilly, but the little ones didn't care—they were with Grandpa. While examining the hole, Grandpa decided to smoke his pipe. "That must be a mighty big gofer to dig a hole that big," Grandpa decided.

Jerry laughed. "Grandpa, a gofer didn't dig that hole, we did."

Mary Jane added, "We needed Christmas dirt for our Christmas tree."

Grandpa gave them a big chuckle and a wink; he was just teasing them. Mary Jane and Jerry laughed along with Grandpa. Grandpa and the kids came through the back door and in through the front door came Bill. He was carrying something big, all wrapped in foil. In unison, Mary Jane and Jerry asked, "What is that?"

Grandma took charge right away. As Bill placed the bundle on the table, Grandma quickly revealed a turkey—a big, golden brown turkey. Mary Jane and Jerry watched with eyes wide open. Mary Jane looked at Mama in amazement and exclaimed, "Mama, that sure is *a big chicken!*"

"That is the biggest chicken I have ever seen," added Jerry.

"That big chicken will be ready to eat soon," Grandma replied. "But first, we have a make-do Christmas and a real Christmas to attend."

Mary Jane began her Christmas dance and Jerry just jumped up and down. "It's time, it's time, everyone. Come to the living room, it's time for Christmas!" Jerry yelled. All the children gathered in the small living room.

Mama and Grandma took their time. The faces of the children were priceless. Both Mama and Grandma wanted to savor the moment, *a moment long past due.* This was a good Christmas; the family was together, the house smelled like Grandpa's pipe, there was plenty of good food, but most of all, there was plenty of love to go around.

"If you ladies are going to have Christmas with us, ya'll better hop to it!" Grandpa shouted. "These youngsters are tired of waiting," he added. Mama and Grandma *finally* made their way to the living room to join the celebration. Grandpa removed the pipe from his mouth, cleared his throat, and gave thanks for all their many blessings. Grandpa could hardly get *amen* out of his mouth before Mary Jane began jumping around, yelling, "Okay, Grandpa, let's have Christmas."

Grandpa agreed it was time to have Christmas. "Which Christmas? A make-do Christmas, a family Christmas, or Santa Claus Christmas?" he asked.

Jerry looked at Mama in disbelief. "We have three Christmases?"

Mama just smiled back and replied, "I guess we do, and I think we should start with your make-do Christmas." That was all Jerry and Mary Jane needed to hear. Everyone found a place to sit to receive their gifts. Mary Jane stood tall and proud next to the tree as Jerry gathered the make-do Christmas gifts. Mama proudly told their story to the rest of the family with great pride. Mama was about to cry with pride. Jerry read the names from the gifts while Mary Jane proudly presented them. Each gift came with a "Merry make-do Christmas." Since Mary Jane and Jerry had no idea that Grandma and Grandpa Ward were coming for a Christmas visit, there was no make-do gift for them. As Mary Jane handed out the last gift, she became a little sad for Grandma and Grandpa. It was like having candy: either everyone got candy or none got candy.

Holding hands, Jerry and Mary Jane strolled over to Grandma and Grandpa Ward. A humble explanation was given as to why there was no make-do gift for them. Grandma and Grandpa were touched by the kindness and gentle hearts of Jerry and Mary Jane. Grandma had little tears on her face. Grandpa was a little misty-eyed, but nothing rolling out. The sound of a big sigh came from Mama; she too had little tears, just like Grandma. Mary Jane looked at her brothers and sisters, who were just staring at them, and sternly said, "Well, it's true!"

Mary Jane stood there with her hand on her hip, trying to make her point. Her actions caused everyone to burst out with laughter, which seemed to lighten the moment. Grandma and Grandpa gave Mary Jane and Jerry big hugs and kissed their foreheads.

Grandma sniffled, "This is the best make-do Christmas I ever had." Jerry sat next to Grandpa, but not Mary Jane. She went back to the Christmas tree. She stood there just a moment before making a little curtsy. "Okay, what's next?"

Chapter 3

Mama and Grandma Ward were in charge of the next Christmas, the family Christmas. Grandma would hand out the gifts since she said she had creaky knees. The gifts were as beautiful as those wrapped in downtown Morrilton's store windows. Everyone had a gift under the little Christmas tree, *even Grandma and Grandpa.*

The family Christmas consisted of items that were more essential rather than desired. Some items were handmade and others were store-bought. Each grandchild received a hand-knitted scarf from Grandma and a shiny half-dollar from Grandpa. Mama received a brand-new pair of comfortable work shoes, along with five of Grandma's handmade quilts.

Grandma greeted each grandchild with a "Merry Christmas" as she presented them her gifts. Mary Jane and Jerry patiently waited to hear their name called. Jerry was still hoping for his puppy, and Mary Jane was still hoping for her baby doll. *There was no puppy for Jerry and no baby doll for Mary Jane.*

Mama had planned all year for this one day, but never did she dream it would be so wonderful. With the help of Bill, her dreams of a special Christmas did come true. Earlier in the year, Bill dropped out of school to begin working to help support the family. Each payday, Bill would turn his earnings over to Mama for food and other necessities. From their two combined paychecks, Mama put aside a little bit for Christmas. The children knew nothing of Mama's plans, only Grandma and Grandpa knew. It was a hard-to-keep secret, but Mama did keep her secret all year long. Mama was quiet pleased with herself.

Perhaps the older children suspected Mama was keeping a big secret, but they never let her know of their suspicions. Mama always seemed to be sewing, mending torn and tattered clothing for the children. They never realized she was making something special for Christmas. No matter the time of the year, something new to wear was always a special treat. Mama had reconstructed two of her own dresses for Doylene and Kim. She made a new pinafore and two new hair ribbons for Mary Jane. The four boys, Bill, Martin, Eddy, and Jerry, all got a brand spanking new shirt—handmade by Mama.

The living room was all a buzz with laughing, talking, and sounds of crinkling Christmas paper. Mary Jane was bouncing around the room, showing off her new pinafore and ribbons. Jerry strolled around the room showing off his new warm hat with earflaps—flaps up, flaps down. He was so proud of his new hat. Mama even let him wear it inside. Grandma decided to join the fun and show off her new slippers while Grandpa tried out his new pipe. Grandma walked around the room, getting a good feel for her slippers. Grandpa stood in the middle of the room for all to see him with his new pipe.

Grandma and Grandpa could always make the grandchildren laugh. Grandma Ward was a good storyteller; she used funny voices with her stories. Grandpa Ward made funny faces—with or without a story. Sometimes he would stick his tongue out at the kids.

As Grandma started to tell one of her funny stories, Mama, Grandpa, and Bill slipped away to bring in the Santa Claus Christmas. Grandma was doing a great job entertaining and distracting Mary Jane and Jerry. They never noticed the others were gone. Upon their return, Mama, Grandpa, and Bill took their seats and listened to the rest of Grandma's story. Grandma finished her story, curtsied to her audience, and waited for the applause. Her story was a big hit, especially with Mary Jane and Jerry.

Christmas morning was beginning to turn into Christmas afternoon. Mary Jane's little stomach was beginning to talk to her; she was hungry. Mary Jane smiled at Grandma and asked, "Are we going to eat that big chicken?" Grandma pointed over to the Christmas tree where gifts from Santa Claus were all on display. Mary Jane quickly forgot all about her hunger and the big chicken. With a skip and a hop, Mary Jane headed for the Christmas tree. This was the first time Santa Claus had ever made Christmas on time, and Mary Jane didn't know exactly what to do. With her hands behind her back and her eyes wide with excitement, she looked for a baby doll. Jerry soon joined Mary Jane at the Christmas tree; together they carefully looked for their special gift from Santa Claus. There was no baby doll for Mary Jane and no sign of a puppy for Jerry.

Mama called to the children, "Come see what Santa brought you." Mary Jane and Jerry, with heavy hearts, seemed to just back away from the Christmas tree. They watched their brothers and sisters gather their gifts and squeal with excitement. Everyone seemed to get exactly what they had secretly wanted. The excitement of Santa's gifts soon spilled over to Mary Jane and Jerry. They joined the others as they opened and showed their gifts.

Kim received her very own sewing basket filled with all she would need to follow in Mama's footsteps, sewing. Doylene and Martin both received drawing pencils, colored chalks, and special drawing paper. Eddy, the fix-it brother, received a small red toolbox with more tools than he had ever seen. Bill showed off his new boots and a crisp five-dollar bill. Mary Jane and Jerry soon realized all of Santa's gifts were gone. With his sad little heart, Jerry took Mary Jane by the hand, and together they sat on the couch. As they watched the others enjoy their gifts, Mary Jane began to softly sob. Jerry comforted her in his usual way, his arm around her shoulder. The living room soon grew still. All eyes were upon Mary Jane and Jerry.

Without a word, Mary Jane and Jerry walked over to comfort Grandma who seemed just as upset. Mary Jane patted Grandma on her leg and asked, "Did Santa Claus forget you too, Grandma?"

Grandma pulled out her hanky and wiped her tears. With a big smile, she said, "No, child, he didn't forget me, and he didn't forget you and Jerry either."

Mary Jane and Jerry once again began looking around the room for a special gift from Santa Claus. There were no more gifts under the Christmas tree. *Where could it be?* They looked high and low, even behind Grandma and Grandpa.

Mary Jane and Jerry seemed to make a game of trying to find their gift from Santa Claus. As they moved around the room, the other children yelled out "hot or cold" to help guide the way. The house was full of excitement again. Mary Jane and Jerry were so happy, just knowing that Santa Claus did come to see them. While the older children played hot and cold with Mary Jane and Jerry, Mama and Grandma slipped away to the kitchen. Grandpa could see Mama and Grandma in the kitchen, laughing, crying, and hugging with happiness. He gave them a few minutes to savor their joy.

Grandpa casually strolled into the kitchen waving his empty coffee cup. Mama filled Grandpa's cup as he lit his new pipe again. Puffing his pipe and trying to steady his coffee cup, Grandpa slowly walked back to the Christmas celebration. Mary Jane and Jerry were still having fun searching for their gift from Santa Claus. However, they were beginning to become somewhat weary. Mary Jane's face was all red. Jerry was beginning to sweat; he was still wearing his new hat, earflaps up. Jerry liked saying "flaps up, flaps down."

Patiently, Grandpa watched Mary Jane and Jerry search for their Santa gifts, but it soon became clear they needed help. Grandpa, without saying a single word, tried to get their attention by clearing his throat. After several tries of clearing his throat and a few fake coughs, Grandpa *finally* got the attention of all the children. Grandpa just pointed to the little Christmas tree in the corner of the room, but Mary Jane and Jerry still did not see any Santa gifts. Mary Jane and Jerry were looking for gifts wrapped with pretty paper and bows, but their Santa gifts were sitting on a scrawny little branch of the Christmas tree. No pretty paper, no bows, and no ribbons, just two white envelopes with their names written on the outside.

With her hand on her hip, Mary Jane stomped her foot and said, "We give up, Grandpa!"

"Those are the magic words!" Grandpa replied. With a big smile on his face, Grandpa gently lifted Mary Jane to the little branch of the Christmas tree holding the envelopes. She took both envelopes and exclaimed, "I found them, Jerry, I found them!"

The family gathered around to watch Mary Jane and Jerry opened their envelopes. This was a thrilling moment for the family. Mary Jane received a page from her wish book. The exact page she mailed to Santa Claus. Jerry got his drawing of the puppy he, too, had mailed to Santa Claus. Jerry sat all quiet, holding his drawing. He had big tears ready to drop from his eyes. Mary Jane yelled, "This is not funny! Where is Jerry's puppy?" Jerry smiled at his bossy little sister, and the big tears came rolling down his cheeks.

Grandma stood and announced, "You two come with me now!"

Grandma was using her "you're in trouble now" voice. Slowly, Mary Jane and Jerry followed Grandma into Mama's bedroom where Grandpa stood holding a black furry puppy and Mama was holding a brand-new baby doll. Now it seemed the whole family had big tears.

As happy tears rolled down Mama's face, she gently handed Mary Jane her new baby doll. Mary Jane cradled her new doll in her arms as her own happy tear rolled down her little cheeks.

Mary Jane kissed her new baby doll and whispered, "Oh, Hannah Polly, you're beautiful!" Mary Jane instantly loved Hannah Polly.

Mary Jane skipped over to Jerry to show off her new baby doll, Hannah Polly. Jerry was sitting on the floor with Grandpa, inspecting his new puppy. With Hannah Polly still cradled in her arms, Mary Jane carefully sat next to Jerry on the floor. As Jerry played with his puppy, Mary Jane removed the blanket from her new baby for her own inspection.

Hannah Polly was perfect. She was dressed in a white T-shirt and a real diaper, but smaller. She even had little pink booties to keep her cubby little feet warm. Her eyes were blue and her hair was brown, and best of all, she smelled like baby powder—*like a real baby*. In all her dreams of having a baby doll named Hannah Polly, Mary Jane never dreamed it would be so wonderful. "I'm the happiest little girl in the whole, big, wide world."

Grandpa gave special instruction for taking care of a pet as he watched Jerry play with the new puppy. Grandpa would talk, the puppy would lick, and Jerry would laugh. Grandpa's instructions would have to wait. Jerry was having too much fun to listen. "Grandpa, can we take my puppy outside?" Jerry asked.

Before Grandpa could say a word, Mary Jane yelled out, "I want to go outside with your new puppy too!" Grandpa agreed that it was time to take the little fur ball out for a walk, but only if Jerry and Mary Jane would help him up from the floor. Sitting on the floor made Grandpa all stiff; he needed a little help getting up. Jerry used both hands to grab Grandpa's hand. Mary Jane used only one hand to help pull Grandpa up from the floor. She was not going to let go of Hannah Polly, the most beautiful baby doll in the whole big world. Hannah Polly was Mary Jane's *first ever* baby doll. Grandpa sprang to his feet with cracking sounds coming from his bones; Mary Jane and Jerry giggled with delight.

"Grandpa, your bones are talking to us again," snickered Jerry. Grandpa gave a big belly laugh and grabbed the two for a hug.

"Let's get bundled up and take this fuzzy dog outside for a walk." Grandpa laughed.

"Fuzzy Dog is a good name for him, Grandpa!" Jerry shouted.

Bundled and ready to take Fuzzy Dog for a walk, Mary Jane and Jerry skipped to the back door with big smiles on their faces. Grandpa tried to do the same. His skipping brought tears of laughter to the whole family. Grandpa looked more like he was walking on hot rocks instead of skipping.

"Come on, Grandpa, I will teach you how to skip!" Mary Jane giggled.

Mary Jane took Grandpa's hand and led him away. Grandpa looked back at the others and gave them one of his funny faces.

"Grandpa, you're so funny, I love you!" sighed Mary Jane. Grandpa snickered back, "I love you too and you're bossy! Who taught you how to be bossy? he asked.

Without hesitation, Mary Jane shouted, "Grandma! Grandma says I'm just like her, except not old." Grandpa nodded his head in agreement.

"Come on, little boss, teach me how to skip!" Mary Jane handed her baby doll, Hannah Polly, to Grandpa, and she skipped away.

"Wait…you're going to fast, slow down!" Slowly, Mary Jane skipped back to Grandpa. She gave instructions with each skip, and Grandpa watched carefully. "Now you try it, Grandpa." Grandpa gave Hannah Polly back to Mary Jane and went for a skip. Jerry and Fuzzy Dog watched with delight. "Hey, Grandpa, I think your britches are too long!" Jerry yelled. "Roll them up."

Grandpa, eager to please, did as Jerry suggested. He rolled his pants high above his boots, revealing his skinny white legs. "Come on, Mary Jane, let's go skipping," Grandpa said with a shiver in his voice. Mary Jane took Grandpa's hand and away they skipped. They skipped and sang songs while Jerry played chase with Fuzzy Dog.

"You're a good skipper, Grandpa," Mary Jane whispered.

"You think I'm ready to show the other what a good skipper I am?" he replied. Mary Jane began to dance around with excitement.

"Jerry, let's go show everyone what a good skipper Grandpa is. Hurry!"

Grandpa instructed Jerry, "Go to the house and get everyone to come outside." Jerry ran to the house with Fuzzy Dog right on his heels. Jerry scooped Fuzzy Dog up into his arms and calmly entered the house.

"Grandpa says everyone has to come outside and see him skip," Jerry announced. "He is a good skipper now," he added. Everyone began laughing as they grabbed their coats, especially Grandma Ward. Grandma knew this was going to be funny. Mary Jane and Grandpa patiently waited for their audience to arrive. Grandpa stood quietly, smoking his pipe with his britches still rolled high above his boots. Mary Jane was swaying back and forth, holding her baby doll. Once the family was gathered, Grandpa remained quiet as he puffed on his pipe. He wanted to give everyone time to finish laughing. Mary Jane didn't understand exactly what was so funny, but she stood proudly by Grandpa's side.

Mary Jane took one step forward. She shouted in her bossy tone, "Grandpa is a good skipper, now ya'll watch us!" Mary Jane and Grandpa turned and skipped away hand in hand. They skipped all the way to the end of the yard and back again. Mary Jane curtsied and Grandpa bowed to the sounds of applause. It was official—Grandpa was a good skipper. Mama and Grandma watched as the children congratulated Grandpa on a job well done.

"Papa should get an award for his fine skipping," Grandma mumbled. Mama and Grandma smiled at each other with pride. They knew Grandpa had worked hard on his skipping. Grandma took a deep breath before calling Grandpa to come in out of the cold. "Skippy, you need to roll your britches legs down and come inside! Bring the other kids with you." Everyone laughed out loud at Grandpa's new nickname, Skippy.

Grandpa Ward lead the way as a trail of happy grandchildren followed behind. Grandma waited inside the warm kitchen to greet Grandpa with a warm blanket. She gave him strict instructions to rest and get warm before lunch. This was one time Grandpa didn't mind being bossed by Grandma. He was too cold and tired to put up much of a fuss. Grandma watched and waited for Grandpa to get all settled before taking him a cup of hot coffee. Mary Jane and Jerry huddled around a small heater, trying to get warm. They watched as Grandma tenderly cared for Grandpa. She tucked the blanket tightly around his body, she rubbed his legs to get them warm, and she gently patted his hands. Grandma was worried about Grandpa's health, too worried to scold him for playing in the cold. Once she was sure Grandpa was feeling better, Grandma returned to the kitchen.

While Mama and Grandma made sure the Christmas feast was still piping hot, Doylene and Kim set the table with pieces from Mama's wedding china. The table was festive and elegant for the first time in many years. Mama was happy to see her china put to good use. Hannah Polly was put down for a nap in Mama's bed while Fuzzy Dog was sleeping back in his box.

Chapter 4

All faces and hands were inspected by Grandma before sitting down at the dinner table. Each passing inspection was rewarded with a kiss on their cheek. Even Grandpa passed the inspection and received a kiss on his cheek. "Grandpa Skippy got a kiss too!" shouted Mary Jane. Again, the sounds of laughter echoed through the once drab little house. Grandpa took his place at the head of the dinner table.

He quickly gave the blessing and declared what Christmas meant to him: "Christmas is the time to celebrate the birth of Jesus, a time for the family to gather around the Christmas tree, to huddle around the kitchen and take in the wonderful aromas, to overindulge in Mama's home cooking, and to catch up on the family news. Grandpa finished with a loud "Now let's eat this big chicken!"

"Merry make-do Christmas" came from little Mary Jane.

"Merry family Christmas" came from Grandma Ward, and "Merry Santa Claus Christmas" came from Jerry.

Mama added, "Happy Birthday, Baby Jesus."

Grandpa Skippy stood ready to carve the *Big Chicken*. The effortless way Grandpa carved was an amazing sight. The kitchen was full of chattering children...until Grandpa made the first cut, then all talking stopped. Mama and Grandma Ward helped Mary Jane and Jerry decide what they wanted on their dinner plate. The little ones didn't have a clue what was being put on the plate; they were in a trance watching Grandpa and his masterpiece carving.

Mary Jane and Jerry both asked for a drumstick. The drumsticks were almost as big as a dinner plate.

Little Mary Jane had to hold her drumstick with both hands while trying to eat. Jerry could hold his drumstick with one hand, but it was a wobbly hand. Grandma Ward suggested Jerry use both hands to hold his drumstick.

"If you use both hands with that drumstick, you'll have enough strength left for eating some pie."

Not having strength to eat pie was just what Jerry needed to hear; he started using both hands with his drumstick. Grandpa Ward said he agreed with Grandma. "The only thing you should be worried about is which kind of pie you are going to eat first."

Jerry asked Grandpa, "What kind of pie are you going to eat first?"

Grandpa replied, "Well, if I eat too much at dinner, I may have to take a break before I can eat pie. However, when I eat some pie, I'm going to have a sliver of all three kinds of pie." Grandpa didn't want to hurt any of the pie's feelings by choosing one over the other, so he would eat all three at the same time. Mary Jane and Jerry knew if Grandpa said it, it must be true.

Of Course, Grandpa was right about needing to take a break before eating any pie. Grandpa suggested he, the little ones, and Fuzzy Dog should go outside while the others cleared the table and put away the leftovers. Before getting completely out the back door, Grandpa asked Grandma to make a fresh pot of her fine coffee.

"Drinking a cup of Grandma's fine coffee will make the pies taste even better."

Jerry had a question for Grandpa. "Mama says I'm not old enough to drink coffee, how old do I have to be?"

Grandpa thought for a minute or so before giving an answer. "Boys have to be at least ten years old, and girls have to be twelve before they can drink coffee." Mary Jane felt that was not fair, and she let it be known.

"Ms. Bossy wanted to know where Grandpa got his information about drinking coffee."

"I read it in a book, and it talked about kids and drinking coffee."

Jerry didn't say anything else about drinking coffee; he sure didn't want to be in that argument. Just as Grandpa Ward thought he was off the hook, Mary Jane came back with "You can't read, so how did you read about kids and coffee drinking?"

Grandpa stammered, sputtered, and stopped in his tracks because he was caught in a big fib. "Oops, I meant to say Grandma read it in a book, and she told me what the book said. Ya'll know Grandma is a real good reader, so when she reads and tells me what she read, that is the same as me reading."

"Jerry reads us a story from his school reader. Does that mean I can read?"

Grandpa was now required to us his quick wit; he was about to dig a hole bigger than the one in the backyard.

"No, honey, that kind of reading only works for grandmas and grandpas."

Mary Jane was satisfied with Grandpa's explanation. Jerry never said a word about reading or drinking coffee.

Thanks goodness Grandma called out the back door. "Coffee is ready...come on in."

Jerry was happy to hear Grandma calling for Grandpa. Mary Jane was young, but she didn't miss much; she was always trying to listen to the adults to maybe learn something new. Sometimes she pretended to be looking at pictures in her wish book, but really, she was listening to the adults talking.

"Little elephants have big ears" was Mama's way of saying the children can hear you.

Grandpa Ward and the little ones came inside to a toasty warm kitchen. Grandpa was ready for his three slivers of pie with a fresh cup of Grandma's fine coffee.

Mary Jane and Jerry were ready for their pie too.

"What kind of pie do you want?" Mama asked.

"Can we have what Grandpa is having, but not the coffee because Jerry has to be ten before he can drink coffee. Girls like me have to be twelve before we can drink coffee."

Mama didn't know exactly what Mary Jane was fussing about, but she knew it had to do with kids drinking coffee. Mama just agreed with her and poured each a small glass of store-bought milk to go with their slivers of pie.

There was a knock at the door. It was Melissa Stratton and her two young boys, Cole and Garrett, dropping by with a little Christmas treat: homemade banana pudding. Cole and Garrett both got to ride the big yellow school bus with Jerry every morning. Melissa's husband, Sean, was an over-the-road truck driver. Mr. Sean didn't get home in time for Christmas because of the snow and ice on the roads up north. The Robinson boys were good about checking on Ms. Melissa and the boys. Eddy's new toolbox would be a big help to Mrs. Stratton. Mr. Stratton didn't get home as often as he would have liked, but the money was good and he was able to provide a good living for his family. Ms. Melissa had learned to drive a car right before Mr. Sean took the truck driving job. Bill Robinson helped Ms. Melissa with any car problems while Eddy, the fix-it brother, made little repairs on the inside of her house.

"Cole, you and Garrett want some pie?" yelled Jerry. The minute Jerry yelled and little pie crust crumbs flew out of his mouth, he knew he was in trouble. "Oh, Mama, I forgot," he said. Mama always told the children, "I'm not raising a bunch of heathens, and we don't yell across the dinner table." Mary Jane and Jerry quickly finished their pie so they could tell Cole and Garrett all about their Christmases.

"Mary Jane wanted a real Christmas tree, mainly because she had never had a real tree come from the woods, Christmas tree," Jerry explained. Mary Jane was eager to tell the boys about the Christmas dirt and the big hole in the backyard. Jerry asked Mama for permission to show the Stratton boys the Christmas dirt hole. If Ms. Melissa is all right with Cole and Garrett going back outside, it was all right with her. The children headed out the back door, and as soon as they saw the hole, they were almost speechless. Jerry was very proud of the big hole in the backyard. He also reported that Mama was going to let them plant the little Christmas tree in the Christmas dirt hole. "Then we will always have a Christmas tree..." Even if it was outside, it was going to be their forever-and-ever Christmas tree. Fuzzy Dog was playing outside while Jerry showed off the hole in the backyard.

Mary Jane even told about teaching Grandpa to skip, and now he has another name...Grandpa Skippy is his new name. "I think he likes his new name," said Mary Jane. Jerry asked the Stratton boys if Santa Claus came to their house. Cole told about their gifts from Santa, but the gifts from their parents were all wrapped and still under their Christmas tree. They were going to do Christmas as soon as their daddy got home. They were also planning to leave their Christmas tree up too. Their tree was an aluminum tree, and they didn't have to worry about it dying. The Stratton family usually left their Christmas tree and decorations up until New Year's Day anyway.

By the time the children came back into the kitchen, it was time for Ms. Melissa and her boys to head back home. Mama hugged Ms. Melissa and thanked her for the banana pudding. Mama thought the Stratton boys were nice young boys. When school was in session, she watched Jerry, Cole, and Garrett talking or playing while they waited for the bus. They didn't even mind when Mary Jane followed them or waited for the bus to come and take them to school. Cole was in the seventh grade; his homeroom teacher was Mrs. Caldwell. Garrett Stratton was in the sixth grade; Mr. Latimer was his teacher. The Stratton boys had already set their minds to what they wanted to be when they grew up.

Jerry was undecided, but he still had plenty of time to decide. Cole had his eyes focused on a military career—the United

States Marine Corp to be exact. Cole loved saying "Semper Fi," a Latin phrase meaning *always faithful*, which is also short for Semper Fidelis. "HOOAH" is a slang used by US soldiers to represent the acronym HUA, which stands for *heard, understood, and acknowledged*. Mr. Latimer loved teaching history, especially *the War Between the States*. He even had relatives who fought for the South. When Mr. Latimer was not teaching, he was doing what he called living history. Mr. Latimer and his living history buddy, Mr. Herron, were always dressing up in a Confederate gray uniform to honor their Confederate ancestors. Mr. Latimer dressed like a soldier in the infantry, which meant they marched and walked. Mr. Herron's uniform was also gray, but he had red around his sleeves and even on his hat. The red on a Confederate uniform signified artillery—big guns. Yellow on a Confederate uniform means cavalry; they rode horses. October was considered Confederate History Month. Mr. Latimer invited Mr. Lynn Herron and his cannon to visit his history class.

"Confederate history would not be complete without having a few ladies dressed in their Annabelle dresses," said Mr. Latimer. Of course, Mr. Herron was not allowed to bring his big cannon into the classroom, so the class went outside. The boys in the class really enjoyed what Mr. Herron had to say about his cannon. The girls in the class were fascinated with the ladies and their Annabelle dresses. The ladies were the epitome of Southern grace and Southern charm. Ms. Dorothy, Ms. Peggy, Ms. Patsy, and Ms. Shirley were true Southern ladies; they were very proud to show respect and honor for their Confederate ancestors. Some of the same ladies had Revolution War ancestors.

Garrett Stratton at a young age decided he wanted to be a chef. He loved it when his Mama let him loose in the kitchen. Even before Garrett was tall enough to see the tops of the kitchen counters, he wanted to cook. Ms. Melissa would let him stand on a little step ladder to watch her cook. Ms. Melissa didn't really know how to cook when she and Mr. Sean got married. By trial and error, she taught herself to cook, and Garrett learned how to cook by watching his mama. He had his own cookbooks, measuring cups, and spoons. The measuring cups and spoons were not used that much because Garrett could measure without the cups and spoons. During the holidays, Garrett and Ms. Melissa would work together, cooking, baking, and making decorated containers to hold the sweets they planned to give friends and family. Garrett enjoyed cooking, but his favorite thing to cook was desserts and sweets. Maybe he was destined to be a pastry chef. The banana pudding for the Robinson family was made by Garrett.

When Mr. Sean came home for two weeks before going back out over the road, Garrett was allowed to be in total charge of the kitchen for one night. Garrett called the one night he was in charge—Mama and Daddy's date night. Mama didn't have to cook, and she didn't have to clean the kitchen. Normally, Cole and Garrett were not allowed to eat in their bedrooms, but date night was an exception. Garrett did all the cooking, and Cole helped him set the mood for a real date night. Ms. Melissa had been given a white lace tablecloth from her grandmother; Cole sat the table with Great Mother's tablecloth. Date night was always with candlelight and soft music. Cole pretended to be a waiter in a fine restaurant while Garrett was putting the final touch to their dinner.

Garrett told Cole, "Don't call them Mama and Daddy. They're on a date."

"Dating people don't have kids, I think," said Garrett.

"We have chocolate mousse for dessert," said the waiter Cole. "If you need anything, just ring this little bell."

Cole and Garrett were having pizza for their dinner in their bedrooms. Date night was fun for the whole family; everyone got to pretend to be someone else. Cole was a waiter, Garrett was a chef, and Mr. Sean and Ms. Melissa were on a date. Once dinner was served, the boys didn't leave their bedrooms unless the little bell was rung.

Garrett had learned from his Mama that it was easier to clean the kitchen as you go. Otherwise, the mess in the kitchen could be overwhelming—that a messy kitchen can suck all the fun out of doing what he enjoys—cooking. Ms. Melissa praised

Garrett's cooking skills; she thought his skills had by far passed her cooking skills.

While Mr. Sean was off working, Ms. Melissa and the boys had their own routines, but when he came home, their routines were changed, at least two weeks. Now that Cole and Garrett were older, the changes in their routines didn't bother them much. The boys were happy to see their daddy. Their mama had a glow about her when Daddy was home. A glow is happiness on the inside coming out for all to see.

Mary Jane and Jerry waved bye to Cole and Garrett from the living room window. It didn't seem that cold outside, but Mama thought Mary Jane and Jerry had been in the cold weather enough for the day. The Stratton family lived just around the corner from the Robinson family. Cole and Garrett, even though older, were nice, even to a little tag along like Mary Jane. They knew Mary Jane had a bossy side, and they still liked her.

Chapter 5

Mary Jane and Jerry never imaged just how their Christmas surprise would touch the hearts of others. After having three Christmases, Grandpa and Grandma Ward were tuckered out and decided to get an early start for home in the morning. Grandpa Skippy had caught a chill and needed to rest. Grandma hovered as close to Grandpa as she could without getting on his last nerve.

Grandpa Skippy was stripped down to his long johns and wrapped in one of Mama's new Christmas quilts. As Grandma rubbed some stinky cream on Grandpa Skippy's chest, Mama placed his feet into a pan of warm water.

"If I'm sick, now would be a good time for a hot toddy," Grandpa snickered. Mary Jane didn't know what a hot toddy was, but if it was good enough for Grandpa Skippy, it was good enough for her. Mary Jane started her happy dance and sang, "It's hot toddy time. It's hot toddy time!"

"Now, Will Ward, look what you've started," Grandma scolded. Mary Jane looked somewhat bewildered.

"Who is Will Ward?"

Grandma tried to explain that Grandpa's name was Will Ward and that her name was Parthina Ward. Little Mary Jane just couldn't grasp the concept of Grandpa and Grandma having other names.

Mary Jane got very close to Grandpa's face and asked, "Which names do you like the best? Will Ward or Grandpa Skippy?"

"I like Grandpa Skippy the best, but if Grandma gets upset with me, she might call me Will Ward." Mary Jane snuggled close to Grandpa Skippy and promised to help keep Grandma's upset away from him. Mama had the teakettle whistling for her attention while Grandma was whipping up some of her yummy hot chocolate with tiny marshmallows. The house was beginning to smell like Christmas again. Each child had a Christmas mug from long ago. Grandma had the children lined up just waiting for the hot chocolate to be poured. Mama was in charge of the hot toddy for Grandpa Skippy and keeping his feet water warm. Grandpa Skippy welcomed his hot toddy with great delight, along with his feet water. Only on special occasions were the children allowed to eat or drink anything in the living room, and this was one of those occasions. The little lamp that gave the small Christmas tree its sparkle and shine was turned on. The children sat on the floor sipping their hot chocolate as they marveled the wonderfulness of the whole day.

Grandpa Skippy must have had a song in his head. He was swaying side to side, tapping his toes in his feet water, and holding his hot toddy with both hands. Grandma knew Grandpa Skippy was not far from being ready for bed. Since the house didn't have heat in the other rooms, Grandma fixed a hot water bottle to preheat the bed from Grandpa Skippy. Soon Grandma tried to entice Grandpa Skippy to bed.

Grandpa Skippy thought he needed just one more hot toddy, and he would be right as rain. Mary Jane watched Grandma get that "Will Ward" look on her face. Grandma had a way of saying "Will Ward" without really saying it. This time Grandma called him Mr. Hot Toddy and explained that Christmas was over, and he would have to wait for the New Year's celebration to have another hot toddy.

Mary Jane and Jerry giggled and snickered as they watched Mama and Grandma get Mr. Hot Toddy ready for bed. Grandpa Skippy, with a smile on his face, leaned back and let them take charge of his feet. Mama dried each foot and applied lotion. Grandmas put his newly pampered feet into fresh socks, but not before she gave each foot a big tickle. Grandpa Skippy looked very funny trying to get his feet from Grandma. The entire family was laughing by the time his last sock was put on. Grandma helped Grandpa Skippy to his feet and pointed him in the direction of the bedroom. "My name is Grandpa, Will Ward, Grandpa Skippy, and Mr. Hot Toddy and the four of us are going to bed now."

Grandma shook her head and rolled her eyes. "The four of you come with me." Grandma tucked the four grandpas into bed and returned to the kitchen to help Mama tidy up.

The Robinson house was all quiet and busting at the seams with happiness. Since there was a shortage of beds, Mama slept on the couch and Mary Jane and Jerry slept on a pallet in the living room. The little ones didn't mind sleeping on a pallet; the living room was the warmest room in the house at night. The small heater made the shinnies on the Christmas tree sparkle even in the dark. Mary Jane slept with her new baby doll, Hannah Polly; Jerry slept with his new puppy, Fuzzy Dog. Fuzzy Dog snored.

Grandpa Skippy and Grandma were early risers. Along with Mama, they sat in the kitchen drinking coffee. Mama had already fried some bacon and was patiently waiting for the biscuits to be ready. Grandpa Skippy was feeling much better, except for the cobwebs in his head. He had already taken Fuzzy Dog out to do what dogs do outside.

Just as the biscuits were taken from the oven, there was a knock at the door. It was Uncle Seaburn and Aunt Ruby. They lived at the other end of Maple Street with their ten children. Uncle Seaburn wore overalls like Grandpa Skippy, except Uncle Seaburn's had stripes. He had a deep raspy voice. Sometimes his voice was scary.... if you didn't mind him. Aunt Ruby was soft spoken and always had a smile on her face. Uncle Seaburn dipped snuff and always looked as if he needed a shave.

Aunt Ruby's hair was very long and always well-kept on top of her head. You rarely saw Aunt Ruby without her apron, unless she was taking the kids to church or going to town. In the hot summer months, Aunt Ruby used a big black umbrella to shade her face from the scorching sun. Her umbrella was big enough to shade some of her children too.

Besides being a brick mason and growing food for his family, Uncle Seaburn raised watermelons. He always had a watermelon party, as he liked to call it. All his children and all the nieces and nephews were invited to come to his watermelon party. If you were big enough to pick watermelons, you picked them. If you were too small to pick, you laid down old newspaper to catch the seeds and brought all the saltshakers from Aunt Ruby's kitchen. The freshly picked watermelons were still warm from the sun—just the way the kids like them. Uncle Seaburn had only a few rules for his watermelon party: Eat all you want, no wasting, save the seeds, and his favorite rule of all, he got to hose down each kid—to wash away any sticky that might be left. If Mary Jane (Ward) Robinson had not been little Mary Jane's mama, she would've liked to be an Aunt Ruby and Uncle Seaburn's kid.

Uncle Seaburn and Aunt Ruby along with three of their children came bearing gifts—fruits, and lots of it. The large brown bag that Uncle Seaburn held was full of apples and oranges. Before passing out the gifts to the children, they had to hug Mama, Grandpa Skippy, and of course, Grandma. Uncle Seaburn, Aunt Ruby, Harold, Kay, and Diana all stood next to each other with big smiles on their faces. The Robinson children lined up, one behind the other. Uncle Seaburn gave each kid an orange, Aunt Ruby gave each an apple, Harold gave each a peppermint stick, Kay gave each a brand new pencil, and Diana gave a large box of crayons for all to share. The grownups all went to the kitchen to visit over some piping hot coffee. Mary Jane and Jerry proudly showed off their little Christmas tree and told how the little tree came to be. "Do you want to see where we got the Christmas dirt?"

The cousins had never heard of Christmas dirt. Mary Jane and Jerry proudly showed off the big hole in the backyard, from which came the Christmas dirt. Mary Jane put her hand on her hip and announced, "Mama is going to let us plant our little Christmas tree in this hole with the Christmas dirt. And from now and forever, when Baby Jesus has his birthday, he will see that we still love him! Amen. Grandma said if we talk about or talk to Jesus we are to always say Amen. The five kids, standing around a hole in the backyard, all shouted "Amen." Grandma heard "Amen," so she said amen too.

While the kids were outside examining the big hole, Grandpa Skippy and Uncle Seaburn decided just what was needed to give the little Christmas tree a chance to grow and be strong. Together they agreed they needed one part compost, one part well-rotted manure, two parts original soil, and a little chicken wire for some good luck. The chicken wire would keep any animals from getting too close—that was the good luck part.

Grandpa Skippy had all the ingredients at his farm, but Uncle Seaburn's house was much closer. Grandpa Skippy agreed that it would be wise to get the ingredients from Uncle Seaburn's and get the little Christmas tree in the ground while it still had a chance to live. Mary Jane and the other children didn't even notice that Grandpa Skippy and Uncle Seaburn were gone until they returned, eager to save a little Christmas tree. Before the official planting of the little tree, Uncle Seaburn needed a hot cup of coffee; Grandpa Skippy wanted coffee and again to try out his new pipe that Santa had given him for Christmas. Mary Jane, Jerry, Harold, Kay, and Diana patiently watched and waited to see some empty coffee cups.

After what seemed like forever. Uncle Seaburn and Grandpa Skippy had finished their coffee down to the last little drop. Harold and Kay were twins; they were closer to Jerry's age. The older children didn't seem to get as excited about things as Mary Jane and Diana.

Uncle Seaburn stood up from the table and, with his raspy voice, announced, "It's time to save Baby Jesus's birthday tree." Mary Jane took little Diana by the hands, and they danced around in circles. Grandpa Skippy, Uncle Seaburn, and big brother Bill were in charge of planting the little tree. Somehow, Uncle Seaburn and Grandpa Skippy had managed to load a really big barrel into the trunk of Uncle Seaburn's car. Bill and Uncle Seaburn unloaded the barrel while Grandpa Skippy supervised. Grandpa Skippy was a very good supervisor.

The barrel was being rolled to the backyard, and Grandpa Skippy was still making sure it was being done correctly. While the big hole in the backyard was being prepared with a barrel of stinky stuff, the children inside were removing their homemade Christmas decorations. The only thing that was left on the little tree was the big shiny star. Mama had to explain to Mary Jane that the cold night air would destroy the paper decorations. Grandma agreed, and said leaving the star on the tree might not be a bad thing since it was made from aluminum foil.

The items that were on the little Christmas tree were now in one of Mama's saving boxes. A saving box was where things were tucked away to be gazed upon or to use again at another time. Mama had a saving box for all seven of her children.

The morning frost was now gone, the sun was shining bright, but it was still bitterly cold. Grandpa Skippy, Uncle Seaburn, and Bill all came inside to get warm before taking the little Christmas tree to its new home. Grandpa Skippy got strict orders from Grandma that he couldn't go back outside until the tree was planted. "Once the tree is planted, we will all go outside and bless the little tree." Grandpa Skippy didn't put up a fuss at all; he was way too cold to fuss about the cold. Uncle Seaburn was concerned if the little tree had any roots still attached. He was pleasantly surprised when he removed the tree from the bucket that held it. The little Christmas tree had plenty of roots still attached. Uncle Seaburn looked at Bill and said, "Some things are here to stay while other things are just passing through. This little tree is here to stay.

Uncle Seaburn placed the little Christmas tree into the prepared soil. Bill shoveled the stinky stuff that had been mixed in with the Christmas Dirt. Uncle Seaburn and Bill looked very please with themselves. They shook hands and even gave each other a manly hug. Bill went to the house to gather everyone to come see the now planted little tree. The chicken wire made a little fence around the tree to keep animals away. Everyone came to see the little tree that now looked more beautiful than ever. The tree was still adorned with its own shiny star. Mary Jane and Jerry would never be without a Christmas tree, even if it was in the backyard. This little Christmas tree would always be special, just like this day would always be special.

The entire family members circled the little tree and joined hands. Aunt Ruby suggested, "Let's sing 'happy birthday, Baby Jesus.'"

Everyone sang at the top of their lungs, and afterward, they all yelled "amen." The little Christmas tree now had a real home, not just growing wild in the woods, and a family that would love it forever. Little Mary Jane, not being too shy about saying what was on her mind, took Grandpa Skippy by his cold hand and gave him her opinion about his singing. "Grandpa Skippy, you are a good skipper, a very good supervisor, but your singing sounds like you rocked on a cat's tail."

Grandpa Skippy already knew his singing was not the best and often hoped it was not the worst. Grandma looked at Grandpa Skippy and said, "Out of the mouths of babes!" Grandpa Skippy couldn't help but laugh—a big opinion from such a little girl. Grandpa Skippy had already decided that little Mary Jane was a smaller version of Grandma Ward.

"Well, so much for getting an early start this morning," Grandpa Skippy mumbled. The early morning had turned into lunch time. Mama and Grandma convinced Uncle Seaburn and his family to stay for some lunch, leftover Christmas lunch. There was plenty of the big chicken that Grandma cooked and brought from her house. It was really a turkey, but little Mary Jane had never seen a cooked turkey; she called it a big chicken.

Mama, Grandma, and Aunt Ruby got started warming everything up, while Kim and Doylene set the table. A smaller table was set up for the children to eat together. Mary Jane wanted to sit by Diana.

Grandpa Skippy was about to say grace when there was a sound of a car turning into the driveway. The sound of a car horn echoed through the house. Mama's rule was if they can't come to the door, it's not for you. Everyone stayed seated, waiting to see if there would be a knock at the door. The knock at the door came from Aunt Lizzy and Uncle Cloud. They were being chauffeured in style by their daughter Betty and son-in-law Charles Gray.

Aunt Lizzy and Uncle Cloud (his full name was Cloudy Night Williams) had four children; Betty was their only daughter. Charles, her husband, was a postman; he walked everywhere, giving everyone their mail. Betty was a secretary for a local car dealer. This year as a Christmas bonus, Betty got the use of a brand new car for the whole month of December. As Grandma Ward would say, "They are in High Cotton." Betty and Charles left their four children at home with their other grandma, still playing with what Santa Claus had left for them. Aunt Lizzy was a Jehovah's Witness and didn't celebrate Christmas like most of the family. Since Christmas was over, she said they would be pleased as punch to stay for leftover lunch, but not leftover Christmas lunch. Once it was understood by all, lunch was just leftover lunch Aunt Lizzy presented Mama with a yummy cake with a big hole in the middle. It was a pretty cake—even with a hole in the middle.

While Doylene made more room at the table, Mary Jane whispered to Mama, "Did someone already eat the middle out of the cake?" Mama smiled at Mary Jane and told her, "Aunt Lizzy will tell you all about the cake with the hole in the middle when we are ready to eat the cake."

"Seems like everyone has their favorite kind of cakes to make," said Mary Jane. Grandma likes making her two tiers coconut cake; she uses Grandma Nancy's fancy cake plate to show it off. Aunt Ruby makes a tasty applesauce cake with white frosting, but her tiers are square. Uncle Sonny is not big on anything sweet; Aunt Dolly uses a small square pan for her yellow cake with chocolate frosting. For her children, Aunt Dolly makes chocolate cupcakes with chocolate frosting. All the children stayed close to their mama's kitchen so that when called, "Who wants to lick the bowl, or who wants to lick the beaters," they could be first to claim bowl or beaters, and sometimes there was a spoon to claim.

When Mama made a cake, she always made one little round cake with no frosting especially for Bill. His favorite way to eat his meals was with a slice of cake as his bread. Bill didn't care for cakes of any kind if it had frosting. Aunt Shorty had to make two cakes for her family. Trying to feed eleven children with one little cake was not possible, at least not at her house. Each cake had two tiers, but one cake was baked in round cake pans, the other was baked in square cake pans. The two cakes were exactly the same, other than the shape of the cake pans. "Make them the same, and there'd be nothing to squabble about."

Chapter 6

Aunt Lizzy was half Grandpa Skippy and half Grandma Ward. She told fun stories from her childhood days, and she also used funny voices. I guess Uncle Cloud had already heard all of Aunt Lizzy's stories 'cause he didn't have much to say. Once, Mary Jane heard Mama tell Grandma that Aunt Lizzy was a talker and Uncle Cloud was a listener.

When the families got together for whatever celebration, or even when there was no celebration, the women would end up sitting around the kitchen table talking, but only after the kitchen was spick-and-span. Most of the time, the men would go out to the front porch or just walk around talking about anything and everything. Grandma told Mary Jane, "There are two reasons men go outside after a good meal: (1) They're afraid you might ask them to help clean the kitchen, and (2) being outside, they can't see how much work the women do. Therefore, they don't feel guilty for not helping."

Mary Jane looked at each woman in the kitchen and asked, "Is that for real"?

Aunt Ruby replied, "Afraid so."

Aunt Lizzy added, "Happens all the time at my house."

Mama replied, "I guess it's a way of life."

Grandma replied, "You should see how fast Grandpa Skippy moves when his meal is over. I didn't know the old man could move so fast, but he can."

"Betty, why aren't you telling us about Charles and the mealtime at your house?" asked Aunt Lizzy.

"If I start talking or even thinking about this, he will be walking home, and the police might call it premeditated murder."

Mary Jane was always underfoot, as Mama called it, watching and listening to the women talk. She thought she might learn something new and important. A few times, Mary Jane tried to listen to the men talk; that was not a good idea. She just learned a few swear words that later got her in trouble for repeating them. Trying to be helpful, Mary Jane came up with a third reason why the men might go outside right after a meal. "Maybe they go outside to see who can fart the loudest."

The roar of the laughter echoed through the whole house. Mama had to wait until she and the others were finished laughing before she could ask, "Mary Jane where did you learn that?"

Mary Jane explained that when Aunt Dolly and Uncle Sonny come over, that was a game the boys liked to play. Mary Jane was the little tag along with the boys. Aunt Dolly and Uncle Sonny had five children. Gracie was Doylene's age, and they liked boys, music, and learning how to dance. Brenda was just a toddler not big enough to play with Mary Jane. If Jerry wanted to go play with the Smith cousins, he had to let Mary Jane tag along.

Mary Jane gave great details about what she had learned from Jerry and the Smith cousins. "We go down to the creek and learn to skip rocks on the water, see who could spit the best, how to whistle, who could fart the loudest and sometimes the longest. I didn't do the fart thing because Jerry told me that girls don't fart. Oh yea, if they had heard any new swear word, they said them, even if they didn't know what they meant."

As the men came in from the cold, Grandma asked if they had gotten all their farting done. They didn't seem to know what Grandma was talking about, much less what the wives were laughing about. Grandpa Skippy spoke up and asked for some of that fine cake Aunt Lizzy brought.

"The holy cake," Mary Jane shouted. Aunt Lizzy looked at little Mary Jane and told her it was an apricot nectar cake. Mama asked Aunt Lizzy to explain to Mary Jane why the cake has the hole in the middle. "Bless her little heart, Mary Jane thought someone had already eaten the center out of the cake," Mama explained.

Mary Jane climbed up in a chair very close to where Aunt Lizzy was getting ready to slice *the holy cake*. Mary Jane thought the holy cake was the most beautiful cake she had ever seen. The cake was tall with fluted sides; it was baked to a golden beauty. It had a golden sugary mixture dripping down each of the fluted sides and topped off with sprinkles of white, powdered sugar. Aunt Lizzy got so involved in the telling of how she made the cake, she almost forgot to tell Mary Jane it was the bunt cake pan that gave the cake its shape.

Holy cake and a piping cup of hot coffee was just what Grandpa Skippy needed. The cake went as fast as Aunt Lizzy could slice it. The hot coffee didn't last much longer than the cake. The last of the milk went to the children to have with their cake.

Mary Jane made a declaration for all to hear: "When I get big, I'm going to cook a big chicken like Grandma does, and I'm going to cook a holy cake just like Aunt Lizzy does."

Aunt Ruby wanted to know what she cooked that Mary Jane might want to cook when she gets big. "Chocolate fried pies," Mary Jane quickly replied. "And we will have lots of fun when I get big, just like we are having today."

Of course, the children were still having fun, but the adults were beginning to tire. Grandma and Grandpa Skippy lived at Birdtown, just a few miles from Aunt Lizzy and Uncle Cloud.

"Since we're going right by your place, Grandpa, how about hitching a ride with us?" suggested Charles. Mama was worried that Grandma and Grandpa Skippy might have a hard time heating their house since they had been gone so long. Uncle Cloud volunteered himself and Charles to get the wood burning stove toasty warm before leaving Grandma and Grandpa Skippy alone. Betty even suggested, "They could wait in the car with the heater going while Uncle Cloud and Charles got the stove going."

It didn't take Grandpa Skippy long to ponder Charles's invitation. "I always wanted to know how a rich man's butt felt while riding in style," Grandpa Skippy proudly said. Grandma, as usual, shook her head and rolled her eyes as she graciously accepted the invitation. Uncle Seaburn announced it was time for them to go too.

Mary Jane hated to see such a fun-filled day come to a close, but she knew everyone had to go home eventually. Before leaving the house, everyone had to hug everyone. Mary Jane watched all the different kinds of hugs. There were hugs with kisses on the cheek, hugs without kisses, shake hands and hug, hugs without handshakes, tight hugs, hardly-touch-you hugs, long-time hugs, and the short-but-sweet hugs. Grandma gave the long-time hugs. Grandpa Skippy gave the short-but-sweet hugs. It didn't matter to Mary Jane what kind of hugs she got; she just liked to be hugged.

As the last of the guest drove away, Mama took a quick look around the room to see what might need tidying up. She fluffed a few couch pillows, and then straight to the kitchen she went. The house was once again quiet and a little lonely for Mama. Little Mary Jane pointed out to Mama and the others, "If you listen really close, you can still hear all the fun we had today." Mama bent down to Mary Jane's level. "How did you get so smart?"

"Mary Jane looked into Mama's eyes and said, "From you, silly."

Mama gave Mary Jane one of Grandma's long-time hugs. That long-time hug was the best hug a little girl could hope for, and it was to never be forgotten. Mama had one happy tear roll down her cheek, and everything was right as rain again.

While Mama made the kitchen spick-and-span again, Mary Jane and Jerry pulled chairs to the windows to look at their little

Christmas tree. It was so dark they could hardly see the little tree. Mama agreed to turn the back porch light on just until she finished cleaning the kitchen. Even with the porch light, the little tree was still hard to see, but the star shone so bright and beautiful. Mama said it looked like a beacon in the night.

Mama called to the other children to come see the Christmas star in the backyard. They all came to see the bright star that seemed to be hovering. The star was a beautiful sight to see, and the day was a day to be cherished.

The kitchen was clean. Mama didn't say anything, and she didn't turn the porch light off. She stood with her children gazing at the beautiful star in the backyard. Mama hugged and patted each child before turning off the porch light. Mama's hugs always came with a pat on the back. Mary Jane and Jerry returned the chairs to the table. The older children went back to their own little corners of the house to finish what they had been doing.

Mama now had a few quiet moments to herself—so she thought. Mary Jane brought Hannah Polly, her new baby doll, and sat next to Mama. Mary Jane hugged her baby doll and patted her on the back, just the way Mama hugged and patted her own children. Mary Jane softly said, "Mama, we did a bunch of hugging today, didn't we?"

"I guess we did, Mary Jane."

Little Mary Jane had one more question for Mama. "Do other people like to hug as much as we do?"

Mama paused before answering. "If they don't like to hug as much as we do, they're probably not kin to us. Hugging is a way of saying things to each other without having to say it out loud. Sometimes a hug can be so powerful; you can feel your heart talking to their heart."

"Like Grandma's long-time hugs," Mary Jane quickly replied. "I wish Grandma and Grandpa Skippy lived close to us, and then we could get more of Grandma's long-time hugs," whispered Mary Jane.

"Mary Jane, can you keep a secret?" Mama asked.

"No, Mama, I can't keep a secret."

Of course, Mama already knew Mary Jane couldn't keep a secret. Letting Mary Jane know the secret just might help persuade Grandma and Grandpa Skippy to move to town. The little gray house right down the street, very close to Uncle Seaburn's house, was for sale; Mama wanted Grandma and Grandpa Skippy to buy it and move to town. Grandma Ward was ready to move to town and put down some roots as she called it, but Grandpa Skippy thought living in town might not agree with him. Mama said Grandpa Skippy had a streak of gypsy in him; he didn't like to stay too long in one place. They were always just passing through. Before moving to Birdtown, Grandma and Grandpa Ward lived most of their married life out of a cover wagon, going from cotton field to cotton field to make money. A few times over the years, they did some sharecropping, which gave them a roof over their heads, a warm dry place for the children to sleep, and even a chance to go to school.

Grandpa was a man of few words back then. He couldn't read or write, but he was good with numbers and money. Grandma once said nobody could ever cheat one red cent from Will Ward. Grandma could read and write and wanted her children to be able to do the same, but going to school regularly was not a luxury the Ward children could afford. Most were able to finish at least the third grade. Will and Parthina Ward's children may have been lacking in book learning, but they made up the difference in common sense.

"Without common sense, an educated man is worse off than an uneducated man," according to Will Ward. Some decisions didn't come easy for Grandpa Skippy. The Birdtown place was the only property Grandpa Skippy and Grandma had ever outright owned. He liked being a landowner even if he wasn't able to put it to good use anymore. Grandpa Skippy would not be pushed into making a decision. The little gray house on Maple Street was in pretty rough shape, but it wasn't anything that couldn't be fixed. There would be no more wood burning stoves for cooking or heating the house. It had all-inside plumbing, including an inside-out house, as Grandpa Skippy called it. There was enough land with the little gray house for a nice-size garden and enough room for Grandma to grow some flowers if she wanted.

All of Grandma and Grandpa Ward's children had been working on Grandpa, a little at a time, to consider moving to town. Now that the little house on Maple Street was for sale, they wanted to press him harder. Grandma explained to their children that Grandpa has got to think he is getting the best of a deal. As long as the little gray house looks the way it does now, Grandpa won't give it the time of day. Grandpa always said, "If you ain't get'n no boot, don't trade." He was a sly o' fox in his younger days.

Grandpa Ward was a proud man; he never much liked asking for help. Grandma Ward, on the other hand, found bartering to be a much better way of asking for help. Grandma and Grandpa were as different as night and day; however, over the years, their personalities seemed to have met in the middle. Grandpa would never admit that he had mellowed in his old age, but Grandma was very proud to say she had toughened up in her old age.

Little Mary Jane sat very still and listened to Mama's words very carefully. As Mama finished telling all about Grandpa and Grandma, she let out a slow and somber sigh. Mary Jane patted Mama's leg as if to assure her all would be all right.

"Mama is all that the secret? Maybe I can't keep a little secret, but this secret is too big for me. I'm just a little girl."

Mary Jane used the "I'm just a little girl" when she didn't want to do something she was told to do or if she didn't understand what was being asked of her. A few times it worked on Mama, but it always worked on Jerry. He was always there to bail her little butt out of trouble. Sometimes they would both be in trouble and sometimes just Mary Jane.

Mama was pretty smart; usually, she knew who was in trouble and who was trying to cover for Mary Jane. If the trouble was bad enough, Jerry was scolded for trying to cover for his little sister—just scolded, no switching. Mary Jane would have to go pick her own switch for her switching. Each time Mary Jane was sent for her switch, she would bring back something that looked more like a tree limb. Mary Jane knew Mama couldn't switch her with something that big; therefore, Mama would be out of the switching mood. The many times Mary Jane tried the big stick trick, it never worked. Mama would scold her and send her back for a real switch. Mary Jane was in no hurry to get her legs switched, so she just took her time there and back, but Mama was still there, patiently waiting for the switch. For little Mary Jane, the knowing of the switching was worse than the actual switching.

Uncle Seaburn used a belt on his in troubled children while Aunt Ruby used a switch that she always had handy. Aunt Dolly used a flyswatter when her children got out of hand. Uncle Sonny let Aunt Dolly be in charge of the flyswatters. She always had at least two swatters, one for the flies and the other for spanking the kids. Aunt Lizzy and Uncle Cloud could never agree on a method of punishment for their children. Uncle Cloud usually made them go chop firewood and fill the wood box. They always had plenty of firewood, and the wood box was never empty. If Uncle Cloud had enough firewood to last a while, he would send his boys to chop wood and fill the wood box for Grandma and Grandpa. Grandma would always reward them with a slice of her homemade coconut cake and a glass of milk for a job well done.

Aunt Shorty was a pincher, and her children were runners. The seriousness of the trouble determined the power of her pinch. She didn't mind if they ran from their punishment because she would be there waiting for them to come home. Aunt Shorty never forgot who did what, or when it was done. Uncle Marvin was pinched a few times for his trouble.

Aunt Effie and Uncle Isaac locked their children out of the house as their punishment. The children had to sit on the front porch until Aunt Effie was over being mad. Uncle Isaac would occasionally try to intervene, but he would end up on the front porch too.

Chapter 7

Early morning was Mama's favorite time of the day, with the exception of wintertime mornings. Mama did everything fast on cold winter mornings. The little heater in the living room was turned up, and Mama would stand very close to the flames to keep warm. She would warm her front side then she would turn around and warm her back side. While she still felt toasty warm, she would go to the kitchen and turn on a couple of burners on the stove. Waiting for the kitchen to get warm, she would go back to the little heater in the living room. She would get herself all toasty warm again then back to the kitchen to start a pot of coffee. By the time the coffee was ready, the chill in the air had become nice and warm.

The hot coffee in Mama's cup kept her hands toasty warm. The early morning quietness gave Mama some time for her own thoughts. It was her time to give thanks for all her blessings, ask for forgiveness, and ask the Lord for strength to do his will. *Amen.*

Mama wondered how the newly planted Christmas tree faired overnight. The Christmas star was still on the little tree, and it was shining bright in the early morning light. Mama's thoughts took her back to how the little Christmas tree came to be, all the hard work Mary Jane and Jerry had done to make a Christmas for the family. Mama was very proud.

Mama heard the pitter-pat of little paws. Fuzzy Dog seemed to be an early riser too. Mama quickly bundled herself and threw on some old shoes to take the puppy outside.

While Mama and Fuzzy Dog were outside, Mama noticed something new about the little Christmas tree. The little tree was wearing a winter scarf attached just above the last of the branches. On the ground was an old, tattered blanket lovingly wrapped around the bottom of the little tree. Mama smiled from ear to ear. The Robinson family had the best dressed tree in town—possibly the best dressed tree anywhere. Mama had never seen such a sight, a tree dressed with a winter scarf and a blanket while wearing a shiny star as a hat. Of course, Mama knew who had dressed the little tree. Mary Jane and Jerry had sneaked out again.

Despite how cute the dressed-up tree was and how hard they worked on that special Christmas. Mama had to scold the little ones for sneaking out after dark.

Since the last of the store-bought milk had been used, Mama decided to fix some powdered milk and let it get nice and cold before the children got up. They didn't much like the powdered milk, but this was all they had. Sometimes, Mama would mix some powdered milk with store-bought milk to make it last longer. If the children noticed, they never said a word. Just plain powdered milk they knew right off—it was powdered milk.

Once a month Mama would go to a place called the Care Center to get a box of what was called commodities. Most of the time, everything fit into one box, but sometimes it took two boxes to carry it all. The two-box days were usually around the holidays and were filled with a few extra items such as cocoa, sugar, a cake mix with frosting, and maybe a few pieces of hard candy. Once in a while, a box would have a loaf of bread; the bread was usually smashed. Mama said, "Smashed bread tastes just as good as un-smashed bread."

A few times Mama would drive to Birdtown to get Grandma so Grandma could get some commodities too. The first time

Grandma brought home some of those commodities, Grandpa Skippy had a hissy fit. He huffed, puffed, and even threw out a few new-swear words that Mary Jane had never heard before.

"That food is for the widows and orphans," he yelled. "I'll not have the whole county thinking I can't put food on my own table!"

When Grandpa Skippy had gotten over his hissy fit, Grandma started taking items from the box. As much as Grandpa Skippy hated to admit it, there was some good food in that box. After the hissy fit about the commodities, Grandma never brought up the subject again. However, she continued to go every month or so to get a box of commodities. Grandpa knew she was still getting commodities, and Grandma knew that Grandpa knew she was still getting commodities. They knew what they knew, but they didn't talk about it.

In the early years of their marriage, Grandpa often threw hissy fits, and Grandma threw whatever she could get her hands on at him. As the years went by, and Grandma's aim got much better, Grandpa stopped having so many hissy fits. With a gun, Grandma couldn't hit the side of a barn, but with a flying skillet, her aim was right on.

Grandpa would tell the grandchildren stories about his covered-wagon days. He made his stories sound like great adventures. "Living off the land, sleeping under the stars, being free to go when and where he wanted," Grandpa said.

Grandma was the best thing to ever happen to him in his covered-wagon days. "She has kept me on the straight and narrow with her wisdom and her flying skillet skills," he jokingly said.

Grandpa and even Grandma never wanted the grandchildren to know that life had been hard, cruel, and even vicious at times. The Ward children knew all too well that life could be hard because they had lived through it...just like Grandpa and Grandma Ward.

The many years together, Grandpa and Grandma used humor to cope with the sadness from their younger years. Sometimes

Grandma would talk about when each of her children was born. Grandma told how her Aunt Julia, who was a midwife, would come galloping on horseback, carrying a medical bag to help in the delivery of each child. According to Grandma, families moved where work could be found but were never too far from their kinfolks.

"Having a baby is the hardest job a woman will ever endure, and with it comes the most amazing joy and love at its purest, Julia Jinks Green, midwife."

Mama was running on automatic. The whole time she was remembering Grandpa's covered-wagon stories, his hissy fit days, she was making breakfast for her children. The powdered milk was all mixed and chilling in the refrigerator. Her homemade biscuits were baking in the oven, the milk gravy would be ready, just as the biscuits were removed from the oven. Mama had an added treat to go with breakfast; they still had some of the commodity butter and a jar of Grandma's homemade blackberry jelly.

Back in the summer, Mama, Mary Jane, and Jerry went to Birdtown and helped Grandma pick wild berries to make jelly. They walked the countryside searching for berries and had such a fun day. Grandma had packed peanut butter–and–jelly sandwiches and a big jug of water. When they got hungry, they just sat right down on the ground and had lunch. After lunch, they finally found a berry patch—blackberries. Mama had brought little metal lard buckets to put their berries in—if they found any. Grandma used the basket she had packed lunch in for her berries. The little berry patch had totally been missed; it was busting at the seams with ripe blackberries. Mary Jane and Jerry ate as much as they put in their buckets. Of course, Mama and Grandma had to taste the berries too.

The blackberry jelly that the children were having with their breakfast was from the same blackberries they had helped Grandma pick. Mary Jane and Jerry were so excited to be eating jelly they helped pick. During the berry picking outing, Mary

Jane had gotten into chiggers. Now she wanted to know, "If I eat this jelly, will I get chiggers again?" As Mama smiled at Mary Jane, she assured her that Grandma had washed all the chiggers off the berries before making the jelly.

"Grandma makes the best chigger-free jelly in the world," Mama announced. Since there were no chiggers in the jelly, Mary Jane asked for two buttered biscuits with chigger-free jelly for her breakfast. Jerry was big enough to butter his own biscuit, but Mama put the jelly on his biscuit. Jerry only wanted one buttered biscuit with jelly because he wanted another biscuit topped with some of Mama's milk gravy. Mama had even fixed a saucer of her milk gravy for Fuzzy Dog, and his little plate was cleaned just like ones on the table. When all the food was eaten at breakfast, Mama would always say, "It's going to be a fair day." That was one of Grandma's sayings, too, so it must have meant something good.

Mama's milk gravy was mostly for breakfast, and it was white. Her water gravy was for other meals, and it was always brown. Her milk gravy was everyone's favorite.

Mama only had two kind of gravy. Aunt Ruby had four kinds of gravy; she had chocolate gravy, one she called red-eye gravy, and of course, she had white and brown gravy. Eating Aunt Ruby's chocolate gravy was almost like eating one of her chocolate fried pies. Her chocolate gravy had to be eaten inside, at the table, but her chocolate fried pies could be eaten sitting under a shade tree if that's where you wanted to eat.

Aunt Ruby cooked on a wood-burning stove and rarely did she burn anything. She cooked enough at breakfast, and there were always leftovers. The leftovers were placed in small containers in the middle of the kitchen table and covered with a clean tablecloth. If any of the children got hungry before suppertime, they had leftovers from breakfast for lunch.

Uncle Seaburn was a wheeler and dealer, like Grandpa Ward use to be. Aunt Ruby was the rock her children could always count on. If you found Aunt Ruby sitting down, she was churning milk to make their butter. Before going to school, the cow had to be milked, and after school, the eggs had to be gathered. Weather permitting, Saturday was laundry day. It was an all-day job, and without help from the older girls, Aunt Ruby would never finish.

Mary Jane was very happy when Jerry got big enough to walk down the street to play with the Ward cousins—that meant she got to go play too. It was still a little cold outside the first time Mama allowed Mary Jane and Jerry to go down the street to play with Harold, Kay, and Diana—the Ward cousins. Jerry had to promise to hold Mary Jane's hand until they got to Aunt Ruby's house. They were to thank Aunt Ruby for letting them play at her house.

Besides having lots of toys, Aunt Ruby and Uncle Seaburn lived right across the street from an elementary school for the colored kids. Those colored kids had the biggest and the best playground Mary Jane had ever seen. She played on everything except the big slide. The big slide was too tall and looked like the top was up in the clouds. Mary Jane wanted no part of that slide; it made her dizzy just looking up at it.

After a while of hard playing, all the kids heard Aunt Ruby calling them to come home. They all knew if they didn't come a running when called, they would get in big trouble. Aunt Ruby was putting more wood in the living room stove when the half-frozen kids finally arrived. The kids didn't realize how cold they were until the warm air touched their faces.

Aunt Ruby had all the kids take their coats off and huddle around the wood-burning stove. She had apple cider warming on the kitchen stove just waiting to be poured. Aunt Ruby told the kids, "When ya'll feel thawed out, come to the kitchen and drink some warmed apple cider to warm your insides too." One by one, they thawed. They all drank a cup of warmed apple cider with a cinnamon stick poking out of the cup. Aunt Ruby was right; the warmed apple cider did warm their insides.

Now that Mary Jane was all warm, inside and out, she didn't want to get back out in the cold. Jerry helped Mary Jane get all bundled for the walk home. Mary Jane looked at Jerry and said, "I'm just a little girl, and it's too cold outside for me." Just as the words came out of her little mouth, Uncle Seaburn walked in and totally agreed. "On my way home, I believe I saw a polar bear wearing a blanket." He could see the little eyes grow bigger and bigger.

"How about I give you kids a ride home, and maybe we'll see that polar bear?" Uncle Seaburn yelled. "Come on, kids, let's take Mary Jane and Jerry home. Ya'll be on the lookout for that polar bear wearing a blanket."

Uncle Seaburn and a car full of kids were headed down Maple Street looking for a polar bear wearing a blanket. Uncle Seaburn told the kids, "Give out a big shout if you see that polar bear wearing a blanket." "If it's cold enough for a polar bear to need a blanket, he just might need a ride home too." Mary Jane gave a big shout, but it wasn't a polar bear, it was the little gray house Mama told her about. "Look everyone, that little gray house is where Grandpa Skippy and Grandma are going to be living.... just as soon as they can trick Grandpa Skippy into moving to town." Since it wasn't a polar bear wearing a blanket, the other kids didn't pay much attention to what Mary Jane was saying. But Uncle Seaburn heard her loud and clear. "Oh Boy," was all Uncle Seaburn could say.

Mama met Mary Jane and Jerry at the front door as soon as she heard the car turn into the driveway. Mary Jane and Jerry thanked Uncle Seaburn for the ride home; they had lots of fun even if they didn't get to see the polar bear. Jerry wanted to know, "If you see the polar bear wearing a blanket, are you going to give him a ride home?" Uncle Seaburn quickly replied, "I will for sure give him a ride home because it's too cold even for a polar bear."

Mary Jane and Jerry were both very excited about their day of playing with Harold, Kay, and Diana. Mama helped them unbundle and hang their coats in the closet. Mama was so pleased the kids had a good play day. She finally had to ask them to take turns telling about their fun day. Mary Jane told Mama all about the colored kids' big playground and how she and Diana played on everything except the big slide. Jerry told Mama about how Harold, Kay, and he had a contest to see who could swing the highest. Before Mama could ask who won the swinging contest, Jerry said, "We all went really high... It was a tie."

Aunt Ruby called us to the house to get warm, and then we drank warmed apple cider with a cinnamon stick to warm our insides.

He continued, "Oh yea, Uncle Seaburn said he thought he saw a polar bear wearing a blanket…that's why he brought us home in his car."

"Mama, we didn't see a polar bear wearing a blanket. Shoot, we didn't see any polar bears at all," Mary Jane sadly said. "But we did see the little gray house that Grandpa Skippy and Grandma are going to live in when they move to town." Uncle Seaburn wanted to know when they would be moving to town.

"As soon as Grandpa Skippy is tricked into moving to town," that's what Mary Jane told Uncle Seaburn. Tricking Grandpa Skippy wasn't exactly what Mama meant; Mary Jane just put her little spin on the situation.

Mama had written her sister's Effie Shiflett who lived in Fresno, California, and Velma Cochran who lived in Pine Bluff, Arkansas, and her other brother Don Ward who also lived Fresno about the possibility of getting Grandpa and Grandma Ward moved to town.

Aunt Shorty and Uncle Marvin lived by Lake Atkins. Uncle Marvin worked as a crop duster. "If Marvin Young is not crop dusting, he's out playing music somewhere," according to Aunt Shorty. Aunt Shorty saved every penny she could get her hands on to get a car for her and the kids. She and the kids were always visiting some of the family once she got her car. Sometimes she would leave a note for Uncle Marvin, letting him know who they were going to visit, and sometimes she didn't. That car gave Aunt Shorty a feeling of freedom.

Mama wrote letters because she didn't have a telephone. Mary Jane thought Aunt Dolly and Aunt Velma were rich because they had a telephone and a television. She thought Aunt Effie and Uncle Isaac must have been double rich because every time they came back to Arkansas for a visit, they were driving a brand spanking new car, plus they had a telephone and a television too.

When Aunt Effie and her family were planning a trip back home, Aunt Dolly would make sure everyone got the news. Grandma Ward said, "Aunt Dolly could make a big splutter out of anything." Grandpa Skippy never let her big spluttering bother him. He once said, "Dolly is Dolly, and there ain't nothing you can do about it."

When Aunt Effie and Uncle Isaac would come for their visit, only two of their four kids came with them, Barbara and Ronnie.

Bobby and Betty Shiflett were all grown up and had grown-up things to do in California. Uncle Don would hitch a ride back to Arkansas with Aunt Effie and Uncle Isaac in their new car, of course. They would stay a whole week.

Uncle Don answered one of Mama's letters instead of having Aunt Dolly deliver a phone message. He asked Mama to get any and all information about the little gray house on Maple Street, including the owner's name and a phone number if he had one.

"Finally it looks like someone has a plan, and they're ready to get started," Mama said as she put the letter back into the envelope. Since Mama was laid off from her job, she would have the time to dig through the land records at the Morrilton Courthouse, at least until she found another job.

The holidays were over. The schools were back in session. Bill was back working at the cotton mill on the night shift. While Bill slept during the day, Mama and Mary Jane had use of the car. Mary Jane thought she was big stuff because she got to ride up front with Mama in the car. Mama had plenty of work to do around the house; she didn't need a list to remember that. However, she did need a list of thing she was to do for Uncle Don.

The weather was confusing. Some days it might be warm if you stood in the sunlight, but cold if you were in the shade. Mary Jane was dressed according to what Mama thought the weather was going to be for the day. Mama was smart about the weather. In Grandpa Skippy's covered-wagon days, he learned to look for signs of changing weather and to read the sky for the weather. Grandpa Skippy taught all his children to do the same, just like Grandpa Skippy's papa, Seaburn James Ward, taught him.

Mama had a small notepad with her list of things to be done. Mary Jane got to hold the pad and be in charge of checking things off the list as they were completed. Of course, Mary Jane couldn't read yet, but Mama could show her which to check off.

Mary Jane couldn't wait to tell Jerry and the others that she had been in charge of the check-off list.

The first on the list was to inspect the little gray house inside and out. Mama tore a page from the little notepad to write down all that needed fixing. She had to write on both sides of the paper because she didn't want to forget anything. The kitchen had a gas cook stove, and just past the back door was a little room for washing clothes. The washroom had a secret panel where the hot water tank was hidden out of sight. The living room had a tall gas heater, and the bathroom had a small gas heater. There was no front porch, just concrete steps, but they were in good condition according to Mama. The screen door on the front of the house was full of holes. The other screen doors were in pretty good shape. Most of the windows were busted out, and the roof would have to be replaced.

Mama thought the little gray house had possibilities, but only if all agreed to do their part to help make it happen. The children of Will and Parthina Ward were all in agreement to make life easier for their mama and papa. There wasn't much money to go around, but there were plenty of skilled workers to make repairs to the little house.

"Lord, please let this happen for Mama and Papa," Mama prayed. "Amen."

Chapter 8

Mary Jane was still holding the little notepad, and she was ready to start checking things off the list. Mama sat at the kitchen table with Mary Jane to inspect the list. Mama read the list then pointed at the line for Mary Jane to put a check mark. They had inspected the house, taken inventory of what was inside the house, made a list of work needing to be done, and Mary Jane got to check off three things on the list.

Mama pulled some leftover pinto beans from the refrigerator to reheat for supper. She peeled several potatoes and one big onion for making fried potatoes, then she whipped up some of her buttermilk cornbread. The kitchen was toasty warm and smelled like suppertime. The house was full of chattering children; they all seemed happy and content. These were the sounds that let Mama know all was right with the world.

Supper was a time for the children to share the events of their day, a time to get to know each other as people, not just as siblings. Mama so hoped her children would continue to love and respect each other, and they would learn to like each other in their adulthood.

After the kitchen table was cleared, Mama would help Jerry with his homework. Jerry was in the first grade, and he liked school just fine. He didn't like reading out loud at school, but he enjoyed reading his books to Mama and Mary Jane. Mama was patient, and she helped him sound the words out when he needed help. As long as Mary Jane was completely quiet, she was allowed to sit and listen to the stories. She watched Jerry use his finger to point at the words as he read. It was very exciting when Jerry finished reading a book. The next day, he would always bring home a new book with new stories to read. Mary Jane wished she could read.

Mary Jane already knew she was going to like going to school. She wanted to ride the big yellow school bus with the other kids. The kids just stood outside, and the bus would come to give them a ride to school. The big kids rode the same bus as the little kids.

As the doors closed on the bus, the happy kids could still be heard. Almost every day, Mary Jane wanted to know, "When can I go to school?"

Mama always gave Mary Jane the same reason: "You're not big enough." When the weather was really cold, Mary Jane would watch from the living room window as Jerry and the other kids got on the school bus. If the weather was nice, Mary Jane was allowed to go stand at the bus stop with Jerry and the other kids. Sometimes, Jerry would let Mary Jane hold his lunch box, and she felt just like one of the school kids. Of course, Mama was watching the kids from the living room window.

Little Mary Jane stood waving at the kids on the school bus until Mama called for her to come inside. Mary Jane asked, "Mama, did you see me holding Jerry's lunch box? Holding that lunch box made me look big, didn't it, Mama? When I get big enough to go to school and ride the big yellow school bus, I would like to have my very own lunch box." Mama patiently waited for Mary Jane to calm down and finish all her questions before giving an answer.

Mama agreed; holding the lunch box did make Mary Jane look just like the other school kids and every little girl who goes to school should have their very own lunch box.

Conway County Court House, Morrilton, Ark.

"It's going to be a fine day, Mary Jane. Do you still have your check-off list?" Mama asked. Mary Jane, smiling from ear to ear, went to the kitchen and brought back her little notepad. Mama thought it would be a good day to go to the courthouse and go through land records. Mary Jane and Mama were going on an adventure—the courthouse.

Mama drove to downtown Morrilton where the courthouse was located. There were lots of people going in and out of the big building, and the parking spaces were mostly taken. Mama found a parking space on the side of the building, but she had to move fast because someone else wanted to park there. Mama got the parking space just in the nick of time, and the man that didn't get the parking space had a sour look on his face.

Mama held Mary Jane's hand as they walked into the basement of the courthouse. The floors were marble, and you could almost see yourself; they were so shiny. All down the hallway were offices and then more offices. The office doors had their own names written right on the glass part of the door. The land records were on the second floor, and there were lots of stairs to get there. The handrails were black wrought iron to keep you from falling down. Everyone seemed nice; they all said "good morning." Mama said "good morning" too.

The courthouse had a smell about it, an old smell. Mama told Mary Jane that the building was very old; many of the records were just as old. Mama said, "The old smell was the smell of history." Mama and Mary Jane were there to get some history on the little gray house at 502 Maple Street, Morrilton, Arkansas. Mama was right about the address on the house.

A very nice lady showed Mama and Mary Jane the room with all the record books. The books were so big and heavy Mama had a little trouble getting them off the bookshelves. The record books were all bound in red leather and had numbers stamped on the spines. There were no chairs in the record room, just a few long and very tall tables. Mary Jane wanted to see what was in the big red books; she was lifted a couple of time to see all the fancy writing in the books. Those red leather books must have been full of old history because the room was full of that old history smell. Mary Jane was beginning to like the smell of old history. While Mama was working on her check-off list, Mary Jane kept herself entertained. She strolled around the big room, touching the beautiful red leather books she could reach. Mary Jane touched the books with one finger only. She was told by Mama that old history was very fragile. Mary Jane was extra careful with her little touch.

Mama found some history on the little gray house. The little gray house was located on Lot nine (9), block one (1), Scroggins Addition to the town of Morrilton, Arkansas, according to the resurvey of S. G. Davies, civil engineer, made on May 16, 1936, of W. O. Scroggins Addition[1]; the correct address was 502 Maple Street, Morrilton, Arkansas.

Mary Jane was still in charge of the little notepad, and Mama needed another page from the little pad. Mary Jane carefully took the little notepad from her coat pocket and handed it to Mama. Once the blank page was torn from the little pad, it went right back into Mary Jane's coat pocket for safekeeping. Mama wrote all the information listed in the big red book about the little gray house. The nice lady, Barbara Davidson, came to see if Mama needed any help with her search. The records in the courthouse were like puzzles.

Mama still needed to know the current owner and how to contact the person. Mrs. Davidson took Mama and Mary Jane to another room to see who paid the taxes on that property. Mrs. Davidson saw that Mr. W. O. Scroggins still owned the property. She also knew Mr. Scroggins had been using the property as rental property for several years.

Mrs. Davidson had worked at the courthouse for many years. She knew just about everything there was to know about everybody in Conway County—if it had to do with property records and taxes. She was happy to provide Mr. Scroggins's contact information.

Mama and Mary Jane had a very productive day. Mary Jane was going to tell Jerry and the others all about the courthouse, the smell of history, and the really big red books. She would also get to put check marks on the check-off list. She might even have to remind them that she is still in charge of the check-off list. Mary Jane didn't mind telling anyone that she was doing a fine job being in charge of the check-off list.

Mama and Mary Jane got home just in time to see Jerry and the other kids get off the school bus. The school bus didn't have as many kids as it did in the morning time. Jerry was excited to see Mama and Mary Jane standing at the bus stop to greet him after his day at school. He was so excited to show off his new book.

"Look, Mama, I got a new book for us to read," Jerry proudly announced. Getting a new book to read was like a reward for doing well in reading, and Jerry was pleased as punch to get his reward. Mrs. Jackson was his teacher, and sometimes she would send a note home to give to Mama. Mrs. Jackson sent Jerry home with a note, telling Mama that Jerry's reading was very much improving.

Jerry's first and most important chore was to take Fuzzy Dog outside for a potty break. Jerry took Fuzzy Dog out before school, after school, and any time he went to the door to let us know he needed a potty break. Fuzzy Dog was still just a little thing, and the weather was still too cold to make him an outside dog, just yet.

Mama would remind Jerry, "When Fuzzy Dog gets bigger and the weather get warmer, he will have to be an outside dog."

Grandpa Skippy promised to help build a doghouse for Fuzzy Dog. Jerry and even Mary Jane were not going to let Grandpa Skippy forget his promise. Eddy was just itching to try out his new tools he got for Christmas. Jerry knew Fuzzy Dog would have the best doghouse any dog could ever have because it would be built by Grandpa Skippy and Eddy, with lots of loved thrown in.

Suppertime was over; the kitchen was all spick-and-span. Bath time was over, and now it was time for Jerry to read a story from his new book. This time, Mama wanted to sit on the couch with a blanket over their laps to hear Jerry read his story. The house was nice and quiet; it felt like Jerry was reading the whole family a bedtime story.

The children were all fast asleep; the house was quiet as a mouse. Mama decided to write a letter to her brother Don to let him know all the information she had found about the little gray house and its owner. At the kitchen table, she sat with a blank piece of paper, trying to gather her thoughts. The thoughts in her head were all riddled with worry and doubts.

Grandma and Grandpa and her own family worries had all been mixed together. While she sat all alone trying to untangle all the worries, Mama prayed for guidance and the strength to know what was expected of her. When Mama finished her prayer and just as she said "amen," a complete calmness covered her from head to toe. The Heavenly Father had wrapped his arms around her and calmed her worries. Mama put the teakettle on to brew herself a cup of hot tea. A cup of hot tea was one of life's pleasures Mama still enjoyed.

As a child, she had learned to appreciate a cup of hot tea from her own grandma, Nancy Elizabeth Jinks Dudley. Grandma Nancy and her sisters Julia Jinks Green, the midwife, Rosannah Jinks Fisher, and Sally Jinks Davidson all enjoyed, as they called it, a soothing cup of tea. The Jinks sisters were taught the comforting effects of different teas from their mother, Epsa Catherine Foster Jinks. Sassafras tea seemed to be their favorite.

There weren't many pieces left of Mama's fine wedding china, but she used a cup and saucer from the set to drink her hot tea. Grandma Nancy once said, "A proper teacup with saucer is required to enjoy a cup of tea." As Mama sipped from her proper teacup, she thought of Grandma Nancy and her prim-and-proper ways.

Mary Jane kept her little notepad secretly stashed in a kitchen drawer under the dish towels. Before going to bed, Mary Jane whispered to Mama where she had stashed the check-off list, just in case she might need it. Mama wrote the letter to her brother Don and included copies of her notes and her check-off list. After using the little notepad to copy her notes, Mama put it right back where it had been stashed. The letter was ready to be mailed.

A buttered biscuit with very little jelly was the only thing Mama had to feed the children before sending them off to school. Jerry's lunch box contained a peanut butter–and–jelly sandwich and his little thermos contained powdered milk, not store-bought milk. The older children were able to work in the cafeteria at school and were given lunch for their work.

Mama had very little money to spend at the grocery store. Mary Jane and Mama sat at the kitchen table and made another list; this time, it was a grocery list. Mama felt a sigh of relief when she realized it was the day she could pick up some commodities.

"Thank you, Lord, and amen," Mama said.

Mary Jane repeated what she heard Mama say. "Thank you, Lord, and amen."

Mama told Mary Jane the letter to Uncle Don was ready to be mailed. "I told Uncle Don what a big help you had been and that you had been in charge of the check-off list."

Mary Jane was very pleased that Mama had bragged on her to Uncle Don. "Since you have been such a big help with the check-off list, how about you lick the stamp and then you can drop the letter in the mailbox at the post office?" Mama asked. Happy, happy dance!

The new check-off list included, the post office, pick-up commodities, and then to the grocery store. The first stop on the new list was the post office. Mama purchased a four-cent stamp. As promised, Mary Jane got to lick the stamp; Mama gave Mary Jane a boost to reach the outgoing mailbox. Just to make sure the letter went down the mail shoot, Mama took a quick look.

"Did our letter go down to the bottom with all the other letters"? Mary Jane asked Mama. Mama gave Mary Jane a little smile and assured her their letter was on its way to California to Uncle Don. Little Mary Jane asked Mama, "Why does Uncle Don call me Little Mary Jane?" Mama explained they both had the same name—Mary Jane. "When I was a little girl growing up, everyone called me Mary Jane. Uncle Don still likes to call me Mary Jane, and to him, you're Little Mary Jane." Mary Jane was just wondering, and she seemed satisfied with Mama's answer.

Since the long and narrow sidewalk back to the car was deserted, Mary Jane skipped all the way to the car. Mama had going-to-town rules and skipping rules too. As long as Mary Jane didn't skip too far ahead of Mama, she was allowed to skip on the sidewalks. If the town and the sidewalks were all busy with people, Mary Jane was not allowed to skip. When the town was all busy, Mary Jane had to walk holding Mama's hand. Walking slow and holding Mama's hand gave them a chance to view the beautiful window displays. Mama called it window shopping, and window shopping was totally free. Mama liked window shopping.

Sometimes on commodity days there were people standing in a line that went to the end of the sidewalk. Mama was very smart; she always made sure they got to the care center early to avoid the long lines. The holidays were over and commodities were back to one box now. Mama had no problem carrying the one box back to the car where she locked it in the trunk of the car.

They then walked down the street to the grocery store. Mary Jane was excited about going to the grocery store; she knew they were going to get some store-bought milk. Store-bought milk was a treat for all the children; powdered milk was just make-do milk. Mama always said, "Sometimes we just have to make do."

Mary Jane and Jerry's idea of a make-do Christmas came from Mama's own words: "Sometimes we just have to make do.

Mary Jane and Jerry discovered "just have to make do" is not always a bad thing. When you take what little you have and turn it into something special for others, it's called love.

The commodities were placed on the kitchen table along with the grocery-store food. With everything displayed together it looked like a lot of food. Seeing all the food on the table reminded Mary Jane of all the food they had at Christmas and all the fun too. Mama, with a little help from Mary Jane, put away all the food. Mama decided to make some homemade yeast bread and some homemade cinnamon rolls. Mama thought by the time schools out, the bread and cinnamon rolls should be coming out of the oven. When Mama made her yeast bread and cinnamon rolls, the whole house smelled like a bakery. The children would know what she had been making as soon as they came through the front door.

Besides making the bread and cinnamon rolls, Mama made a pot of her homemade vegetable soup, which would go great with the fresh bread. Mama could make a meal out of almost nothing, but when she had all the ingredients, she could really make a feast. Grandma taught Mama to cook like that and Grandma Nancy Dudley taught Grandma to do the same.

While Mama was busy in the kitchen, Mary Jane was allowed to take Fuzzy Dog outside. As Fuzzy Dog did his dog stuff, Mary Jane inspected the little Christmas tree that was still wearing a winter scarf wrapped in a blanket and still wearing a shiny star as a hat.

Grandma once told Mary Jane, "If you talk to your plants, they seem to grow better." Mama took a peek out back to make sure Mary Jane and Fuzzy Dog were still there and doing fine. Mary Jane was standing in front of the little tree talking up a storm. She was telling the little tree all about what she and Mama had been doing, the places they had gone, and as soon as the weather was better, she would take the scarf and blanket away. When Mary Jane finished talking to the little tree, she said, "Bye. I will come talk to you some more later."

Mary Jane had remembered what Grandma told her about talking to the plants. She was going to do everything she could to make sure the little tree grew up big and strong. This little tree was going to be their *forever* Christmas tree. Mary Jane and Jerry would never forget how that one little tree brought so much joy and happiness to their once drab little house. The little tree was now planted in the backyard, but the joy and happiness it brought still remained in the little house and the hearts of those who lived there.

Mary Jane and Fuzzy Dog came in from the cold just in time to see Mama punching the bread dough. Once the punching was done, Mama divided the dough into two really big bowls and covered them with a dish towel. One bowl was for loaves of bread and the other was for her homemade cinnamon rolls. Mama's cinnamon rolls were always topped with a glaze of powdered sugar. At dough rising time, Mary Jane was asked to play quietly and not to jump around. Mary Jane brought Hannah Polly to the living room where they could sit still together. Mary Jane talked to Hannah Polly like she had talked to tree in the backyard. After Hannah Polly was all caught up on the news, Mary Jane was fast asleep on the couch. Mama covered Mary Jane and her baby doll with a blanket. Mama was sure that Mary Jane would go to sleep if she sat still long enough, and Mama was right.

During the resting time for the bread dough and Mary Jane, Mama watched over the vegetable soup on the stove. She brewed herself a cup of tea and relaxed while she had the chance, and yes, she used a proper teacup with a saucer for her tea. Mama wasn't sure if drinking the tea was what relaxed her or was it the fond memories that came from dinking the tea in a proper teacup with a saucer. Maybe it was a combination of both. Mama's tea time gave her a chance to gather her thoughts and put things in perceptive.

Chapter 9

*O*f all times for someone to come a calling, Mama thought as she heard a knock at the front door. She had just taken two loaves of bread from the oven and was ready to put the first batch of cinnamon rolls in to bake. Mama always took a quick peek before opening the door even though she always kept the screen door latched. The car in the driveway read, "The Morrilton Headlight Newspaper." The woman introduced herself as Charlotte Miller, a reporter for the newspaper. Mama couldn't imagine why she would be coming to her house.

Ms. Miller's niece Karon Dru was in Jerry's class at school. Jerry was heard telling some of his little friends about all that happened during his Christmas break. Ms. Miller thought the story and how it came to be would be a wonderful story to share with her readers.

Just as the reporter was invited to come in out of the cold, Mary Jane and Hannah Polly awoke from their nap. Ms. Miller pulled a big notepad from her briefcase to take some notes. Mama told the story as she knew it but suggested Jerry and Mary Jane could give more details about how they made a special Christmas for the whole family. Ms. Miller wanted to know about the hole in the backyard and about the Christmas dirt.

When Mary Jane heard Ms. Miller asking about the hole in the backyard and the Christmas dirt, she spoke right up and said, "We don't have a hole in our backyard now, we have our very own forever-and-ever Christmas tree growing in our backyard." Mary

Jane sounded a little like Grandma Ward, with that matter-of-fact tone in her voice. Mary Jane offered to show Ms. Miller the little tree, but Ms. Miller wanted to wait until Jerry got home from school. She also wanted to take a picture of Mary Jane and Jerry with the little tree. She wanted to tell the whole town about the little Christmas tree and the Christmas dirt. Ms. Miller didn't even know what Christmas dirt was, but Mary Jane thought her eager to learn. Mary Jane told the reporter how they had planted the little tree and sang "Happy Birthday" to Baby Jesus. Mary Jane even told about Grandpa Skippy, Uncle Seaburn, and Bill mixing the stinky stuff in with the Christmas dirt to make the little tree grow strong.

Mama had been right in the middle of making bread and cinnamon rolls. She invited Ms. Miller to come sit in the kitchen while she continued her baking. Mama sent Mary Jane to wash her face then bring back a hairbrush so Mama could tidy her hair. Ms. Miller watched and waited as Mama placed here first batch of cinnamon rolls into the oven.

Mary Jane heard the school bus; she knew Jerry would be walking through the door very soon. Just like clockwork, Jerry came through the door with his schoolbook, his school papers, and his now empty little lunch box. Jerry knew from the car in the driveway there was company in the house. Normally Jerry would quickly open the door and be all excited about his day at school, but today, he calmly came into the house because there was company.

Mary Jane was so excited she was about to jump out of her skin, and Mama was as nervous as a cat in a room full of rocking chairs. Ms. Miller was pleased to meet Jerry and wanted to know more about the little tree and the Christmas dirt. Jerry looked a little puzzled; why did Ms. Miller want to know about the little tree, and how did she even know about it?

Jerry waited for Mama's approval before he started telling all about the special Christmas he and Mary Jane had done for the family. He told about their struggle to get the little tree to let go of the ground and how they planted it in a bucket with Christmas dirt. "Where did you get the Christmas dirt?" asked Ms. Miller.

"We dug a hole to get the dirt to plant the little tree, and since the dirt was for our little Christmas tree, Mary Jane said it was Christmas dirt."

Feeling comfortable talking to Ms. Miller now, Jerry told her about the other two Christmases they had all on the same day.

"Santa Claus even brought me my new puppy, Fuzzy Dog, and he brought Mary Jane her very own baby doll, Hannah Polly."

Ms. Miller had now heard the little tree story from three different points of view. Her big notepad was now on page two; she was a fast writer. Mary Jane watched as Ms. Miller put her big notepad away; she then brought a camera from her bag. Finally, she was ready to see the little tree and take some pictures too. Mary Jane enjoyed having her picture taken, but this picture was going to be in the newspaper; everyone would see it. Jerry was more excited about his interview with the newspaper lady. Mama helped the little ones get all bundled to go outside again. Jerry took Fuzzy Dog to show him off to the newspaper lady.

Mama stayed in the kitchen to watch over her cinnamon rolls, but she watched Mary Jane and Jerry from the window. The newspaper lady was just as surprised as Mama and her first glimpse to see the little tree dressed for the cold weather. Jerry pointed out to the newspaper lady; the shiny star was made from aluminum foil and the cold air wouldn't hurt the star.

Ms. Miller asked, "Why is the little tree wearing a winter scarf and a blanket?"

Mary Jane looked at Ms. Miller and said, "Because it's cold out here." Ms. Miller had to chuckle. "Uncle Seaburn and Grandpa Skippy told us, if we didn't take good care of our little tree, it might get sick. Grandma said plants seem to do better if you talk to them. I talked to the little tree today already," explained Mary Jane.

"I can see you're taking good care of the little tree," replied Ms. Miller. She began taking pictures of the little tree from all sides, some with Mary Jane and Jerry, and some without Mary Jane and Jerry. She even took a picture of Jerry holding Fuzzy Dog but not next to the little tree. After the pictures were taken, the newspaper lady returned to the warm kitchen with Mary Jane, Jerry, and Fuzzy Dog. Mama had just put the powdered sugar icing on the first batch of cinnamon rolls. When Ms. Miller left with the story of the little tree and how it came to be, the pictures she had taken; she also left with one of Mama's fresh from the oven cinnamon rolls with icing. Mama invited her two little superstars to a cinnamon roll and a glass of milk. Jerry already knew the milk was going to be store-bought milk.

On the days that Mama made homemade bread and cinnamon rolls, there was always store-bought milk to drink, not powdered. Mary Jane and Jerry hung their coats up while Mama poured each a small glass of milk and placed a warm cinnamon roll on a little plate for each. Grandma Ward called Mama's cinnamon rolls heavenly good.

Mama could tell by the lack of talking, Mary Jane and Jerry were enjoying their treat. They knew Mama thought the day was extra special because she didn't normally give them such a big snack before suppertime. Mama made different sizes of cinnamon rolls, and today she had given Mary Jane and Jerry each one of her big cinnamon rolls with extra icing. Mama didn't even mind when they licked their fingers just a little bit.

Snack time was over. Mama help the children wash their little milk mustaches away and any sticky left on their fingers. Now they were ready to tell each other all about their day. Mary Jane started telling Jerry about the post office: how she got to lick the stamp, and even better, she got to drop the letter to Uncle Don down the mail shoot. "I got to skip all the way back to the car, there was no people on the sidewalk." Mary Jane told Jerry every little thing she and Mama had done all day; she didn't leave anything out.

"Today we played kick ball, and it wasn't even recess time," Jerry said. "Everybody got a turn to kick the ball and then run around some bases. Kick ball is like baseball, except the ball is a big rubber ball and you don't use a bat, just kick it with you feet and run. We still got our recess after lunch too!" Mary Jane could tell Jerry had enjoyed the kick ball game.

The older children started trickling in one by one. The smell of Mama's freshly baked bread led them straight to the kitchen for a taste. Some wanted to taste bread, some wanted to taste cinnamon rolls, and some wanted to taste the bread with the vegetable soup. Mama took her cue to move from the path of the hungry children, a time to rest a few minutes.

By the time the older children had tasted everything, it was time for Mary Jane and Jerry to have their supper. Mama's suppertime schedule had been changed, and she wasn't sure if she was behind or ahead of schedule. Mama felt blessed to even have a suppertime schedule. *Tomorrow we'll be back on our suppertime schedule*, Mama thought to herself.

The evening meal was the families time to be together...as a family. Mary Jane and Jerry had almost forgotten about the newspaper lady. They had gotten a little sidetracked, listening to the others talk about their day. The girls talked about books and boys while the boys talked about sports and cars. Mary Jane and Jerry thought they might learn something new.

"Guess who is going to have their picture in the newspaper?" Mama asked. Mary Jane and Jerry pretended they didn't know what Mama was talking about, just like the rest of the children. Jerry put his arm around Mary Jane and they shouted, "It's us, it's us!" The floodgates of excitement were now open. Jerry talked about the newspaper lady and his interview with her. Mary Jane talked about getting their picture taken in front of the little tree.

"The newspaper lady never heard of Christmas dirt," Mary Jane said. By the time the newspaper lady left, she knew all about Christmas dirt, the little tree, how it came to be, and how good Mama's big fat cinnamon rolls with extra icing tasted.

"What did the newspaper lady think of the best dressed tree in town?" asked Kim.

"I don't think she had ever seen a tree like ours," replied Jerry. We told her what Grandpa Skippy and Uncle Seaburn told us: "Take good care of the little tree, and it will grow big and strong."

Just as the newspaper lady had promised, Mary Jane and Jerry's story was in the newspaper as well as the picture of them standing by their well-dressed little tree. She made one story from the three points of view she had been given. To show her appreciation Ms. Miller brought four copies of the newspaper to Mama; she could do whatever she wanted with the copies. Mama knew exactly who would be getting a copy of the newspaper: Uncle Seaburn and Grandpa Skippy. Uncle Seaburn had provided the stinky stuff to make the Christmas dirt better, and Grandpa Skippy had supervised the planting of the little tree.

Mary Jane and Jerry each had their own copy of the newspaper. Mama fixed the pages in the newspaper so the picture of Mary Jane and Jerry was right there to see. They didn't have to turn the pages after Mama fixed them. Jerry's reading was getting better, and he could read what the newspaper lady had written. Mary Jane couldn't read the newspaper, but she knew the story by heart. At times, Mary Jane would go talk to the little tree; she would take the newspaper and pretend to read the story. She was sure the little tree enjoyed the story.

It was easy to remember to talk to the little tree; Fuzzy Dog went out every day. Jerry would just say hi to the little tree as he watched over Fuzzy Dog. Mary Jane didn't pay as much attention to Fuzzy Dog as to the little tree. Fuzzy Dog was showing signs of growth, but the little tree still looked the same. According to

Mama, the little tree was not showing any signs of being sickly, and that was very good. A slow-growing tree she called it.

On occasion, Uncle Seaburn would drop by to drink coffee with Mama; he would get caught up on any news from Uncle Don concerning the little gray house. Uncle Seaburn always asked about the little tree. Before leaving, he would take a quick peek; he thought Mary Jane and Jerry were doing a fine job taking care of the little tree. Spring was just around the corner; Mama said she could feel it in the air. The little tree was no longer wearing a winter scarf and a blanket. The shiny star was still atop the little tree, but it was beginning to look worn and tattered. Mama allowed the not-so-shiny star to remain.

Saturday was going to town day for Aunt Lizzy and Uncle Cloud. Aunt Lizzy might visit with Mama and the children while Uncle Cloud went shopped around for bargains at the local flea markets or yard sales. Uncle Cloud never paid the bargain price on any of his finds. He enjoyed a good haggle, especially if it was something he could turn into a profit. Uncle Cloud was good at working with wood, repairing and refinishing furniture. Of course, Aunt Lizzy got first dibs on any of his finished work.

Aunt Lizzy had volunteered Uncle Cloud to make new window frames for the little gray house when it was time. She agreed to provide Grandma and Grandpa with a newly refurbished dresser with mirror for the little gray house. Aunt Lizzy and Uncle Cloud were proud of how they were going to help Grandma and Grandpa Ward and their move to town.

Uncle Seaburn and his sons William, Daniel, and James would provide the labor for the new roof on the little gray house. Aunt Ruby volunteered herself to feed the workers and have plenty of cold water on hand. Harold, Kay, and Jerry were volunteered by Uncle Seaburn to drag any rubbish away from the house, including the roofing rubbish.

Aunt Dolly and Uncle Sonny committed to the installation of the vinyl floor covering for Grandma and Grandpa's little gray house. The installation of the new floor covering would be the last of the repairs; hopefully the move to town would soon follow. Until everything had been agreed upon, the move to town for Grandma and Grandpa Ward was still in the planning stage. The repairs to the inside walls still had to be done, along with the painting of the walls. New screens for all the windows and doors were still needed.

Mama and Kim were happy to commit to making curtains for Grandma's new windows. Grandma Ward never liked naked windows; that was the difference between living in a house or barn. Grandpa Ward thought curtains to be frivolous. In addition to curtains for the windows, a curtain for the bathroom was needed; there was no door. Aunt Shorty and Uncle Marvin choose the painting and wall repairs for their contribution to help with the move to town. Aunt Velma and Uncle LG agreed to new screens for the doors and windows.

Uncle Seaburn and Uncle Cloud shopped around for the best prices on the materials needed by all. Uncle Cloud haggled for the prices, and Uncle Seaburn insisted their deal be put into writing; there would be no reneging on their deals. Uncle Seaburn was impressed with Uncle Cloud's haggling abilities, while Uncle Cloud was impressed with Uncle Seaburn's ability to get everything in writing. They were well pleased with each other.

Uncle Don was given the price list for materials and commitment list for the labor. Now it was time for Uncle Don to get in touch with the owner of the little gray house on Maple Street. The little house had been unoccupied and neglected for quite some time. Uncle Don would use that information to his advantage when he was ready to strike a bargain.

Uncle Cloud was curious about Uncle Don's haggling abilities, especially all the way from California. He had forgotten about Aunt Effie's haggling skills. Aunt Effie could haggle better than anyone in the family. Uncle Seaburn called her the haggling queen.

Aunt Effie could sell ice to an Eskom and haggle over the purchase price for the same ice. She and Uncle Isaac owned a gas station and an ice cream truck. Aunt Effie took care of all the bookkeeping for both businesses; she could account for every penny. Uncle Don knew if his haggling was not effective, the haggling queen would be ready to step in and finish the haggling on his behalf. Uncle Isaac knew to get out of her way when she was haggling.

Uncle Don's haggling skills worked just fine; a purchase price had been agreed upon. Janice Blackshire Jones, attorney at law, would be used to close the deal on the little gray house on Maple Street. Uncle Don was required to give Mrs. Jones power of attorney for the purchase of the little house. The signed documents giving power of attorney to Mrs. Jones were received, and right away, a closing date was scheduled. The day of closing, Uncle Seaburn was given the keys to the little house on Maple Street. He was in charge of overseeing the repairs and the commitment from each of the siblings.

The first thing Uncle Seaburn and his sons did was to put a tarp over the hole in the roof. The tarp would keep any rain from doing more damages to the little house. The first weekend of sunny weather, Uncle Seaburn, William, Daniel, and James began the roof replacement. Harold, Kay, and Jerry were right there to remove roof rubbish from the yard. The grass was all grown up and out of control. Harold and Jerry walked to Uncle Seaburn's house; they came back with a push mower and a sling blade. Together, Harold, Kay, and Jerry chopped grass, mowed grass, pulled weeds, and raked the cut grass to the pile of roof rubbish. The little gray house was looking as if it was loved again.

Uncle Cloud and Aunt Lizzy came by to see all that was being done to the little house. Everyone was excited about doing their part to insure Grandma and Grandpa Ward didn't have to do anything, just start living in the little house on Maple Street. Uncle Cloud measured the windows; he was ready to get started building the new window frames and cutting the glass for those new frames. Aunt Lizzy walked through the little house with her decorating eye; she found the perfect place for the dresser and mirror. Aunt Lizzy had a knack for mixing, matching, and making everything look good together. Uncle Cloud said, "Lizzy, too bad you don't get paid to decorate...we'd be stinking rich."

The materials needed for the repairs were stored in the little smokehouse out back. The roofing materials were stacked close to the house for easy access. The smokehouse was padlocked and Uncle Seaburn had the only key. He would make sure everything was right on schedule. "Everyone will get their turn to honor Grandma and Grandpa," Uncle Seaburn said.

Just as Aunt Ruby promised, she brought a bucket of cold water to drink with the lunch she had prepared. Uncle Seaburn called to the kids, "Let's eat some lunch." Aunt Ruby brought a few leftovers: fried chicken, potatoes salad, and some of her homemade chocolate fried pies. Uncle Seaburn finished his lunch but was in no hurry to get back on the roof. He just sat back and took a nice little rest until all the kids finished their lunch. Before Aunt Ruby took the leftovers back to her house, Jerry asked if he could have one more of her chocolate fried pies for Mary Jane. Aunt Ruby wrapped up two of her fried pies: one for Mary Jane and one for Jerry. Aunt Ruby was that kind of nice.

It took Uncle Seaburn, William, Daniel, and James two days of hard work to finish the new roof. Down on the ground looking up at the new roof, it was well worth it. The rain couldn't hurt the little gray house ever again.

When Jerry got home with Aunt Ruby's chocolate fried pies, Mary Jane was past excited. Mama was a good cook, but she couldn't make fried pies like Aunt Ruby. Mary Jane and Jerry had to eat dinner before they could eat a chocolate fried pie. Mary Jane's idea was if you eat really fast, you can get to the dessert faster. Jerry couldn't eat fast because he was too busy telling Mama and the others about cleaning up the yard and cutting the grass at Grandma and Grandpa Skippy's new house. "Uncle Seaburn thought we did a fine job."

Mama would see for herself what a fine job Jerry, Harold, and Kay had done when she measured for new curtains. Ladies who enjoy sewing can never pass up a bargain on cloth and other sewing materials, Mama was no exception. She had a large assortment of cloth, but would there be enough of one cut to make curtains? Mary Jane wanted Mama to make pink curtains...that was her favorite color. "I don't think Grandpa Skippy would like pink curtains," Mama explained. "I sure like pink," Mary Jane softly said.

The big yellow school bus came to give the kids a ride to school. Mary Jane waved bye to all the kids on the school bus. "When I get big, I can go to school and ride the big school bus?" Mary Jane asked. Mama didn't really answer the question; she gave Mary Jane a soft pat on the back. A soft pat on the back from Mama was the same as her saying yes.

Mary Jane and Mama were off to the little gray house to measure for curtains. Mama let Mary Jane carry the little notepad she had used for the check-off list. It was a nice day for walking and only a sweater was needed. The bright sun was shining through the still broken windows of the little gray house. They could see what a fine job Jerry, Harold, and Kay had done on the yard. Mary Jane said, "The little house looks like it just had a haircut."

A mimosa tree was growing right at the edge of the front yard. Somehow, it had been spared from all the cutting that had taken place. Mama thought it might have purple blooms later. She also pointed out the little mimosa tree was not for climbing, just for looking.

When Mama and Mary Jane finished with the measuring, Mama suggested a nice visit with Aunt Ruby. Mary Jane thought it was a good idea; she could play with Diana while Mama visited with Aunt Ruby. Aunt Zuvie had come to visit Aunt Ruby too.

Aunt Zuvie was Aunt Ruby's sister. Mary Jane and Jerry called her Aunt Zuvie just like the other kids. Her husband was Sam Hinkle, but Mary Jane and Jerry called him Mr. Hinkle, not Uncle Sam.

Mr. Hinkle had dropped Aunt Zuvie off to visit with Aunt Ruby while he went to town on business. It was a rare treat for Aunt Zuvie to come for a visit. Usually Aunt Ruby and her little ones would walk to visit her. Aunt Zuvie was older than Aunt Ruby, and her health was not the best. Mary Jane enjoyed the visits to Aunt Zuvie. She had two granddaughters, Sheila and Twyla, who were lots of fun; they didn't mind sharing their toys with others.

Mama and Mary Jane followed a newly made trail from the little gray house to Uncle Seaburn's back door. Aunt Ruby and Aunt Zuvie sat drinking coffee at the kitchen table. The kitchen table was more like a large picnic table. It had long white benches on both sides and only one chair at the head of the table. Everyone knew that was Uncle Seaburn's chair, and it was off limits, just like his big overstuffed chair in the living room.

The big door to the kitchen was open, but the screen door was latched. Aunt Ruby could see Mama and Mary Jane walking the little trail right to her back door. Mama didn't even have to knock on the door; Aunt Ruby was right there to unlatch the screen.

Mama joined Aunt Ruby and Aunt Zuvie for a cup of coffee, and Mary Jane got to play with Diana. As usual, Mary Jane was having too much fun and didn't want to leave. On the walk home, Mama told Mary Jane, "You don't want to wear your welcome out." Mama was trying not to impose on Aunt Ruby's visit with her sister. Mama was considerate like that.

Chapter 10

The new windows and frames for the little gray house had been built, installed, and painted. Uncle Cloud was pleased with how the new frames looked; Uncle Seaburn agreed they looked like store-bought windows. With the exception of the new screens the outside repairs were completed. The gas cook stove and the little heaters were in working order, but Uncle Seaburn and Uncle Cloud wanted to double-check for any gas leaks.

Once the stove and little heaters were checked for leaks, the gas was turned off at the meter next to the house. The water meter was located at the edge of the front yard; it to would be turned off after checking for leaks. While the water was turned on Aunt Lizzy, Aunt Ruby, and Mama all took the opportunity to fill their buckets for cleaning.

The little house had been a safe haven for dirt daubers, cricket, spiders, wasps, and cobwebs; but the cleaning crew would be removing all signs of them. The sunshine gave enough light to do the cleaning, but the wall repairs and painting would require electricity.

Aunt Velma and Uncle LG had committed to screens for the windows and doors. Cochran Motors in Pine Bluff was owned and operated by Aunt Velma and Uncle LG. He was the salesman and she was the bookkeeper for all transactions. They had one child, Danny, who helped Uncle LG clean the cars inside and out. After putting pen to paper, Uncle LG figured it would be cheaper to hire someone to honor their commitment instead of closing their business for a day or so. Aunt Dolly and Uncle Sonny were hired to do the screens.

Aunt Dolly and Uncle Sonny both worked at the cotton mill located at the west end of town. Uncle Sonny brought the screen doors and the screen frames to his house to save time. He could work on the screens after work and weekends without all the driving back and forth. There were three screen doors to the little house—the front door, the back door, and the side door—located in the bedroom. The only porch to the little house was right off the bedroom. Uncle Sonny decided to give each of the screened doors a fresh coat of varnish before taking them back to the little gray house. He was proud of his work and was sure Grandma and Grandpa would be just as proud once the secret was revealed.

Grandma and Grandpa Skippy had no clue of the work being done to the little house. The children of Will and Parthina Ward could definitely keep a secret. Hitching a ride to town didn't include driving by the little gray house on Maple Street; Aunt Lizzy and Uncle Cloud made sure the secret was safe with them, letting the cat out of the bag…not from them.

Mary Jane had confused *convince* Grandpa Skippy to move to town with *trick* Grandpa Skippy to move to town. Mama tried to explain the difference between *convince* and *trick*: to persuade somebody to do something, *convince*; *trick*, a cunning action or plan that is intended to cheat or deceive. Mary Jane said she understood, but Mama was not sure.

To err on the side of caution was the best way Mama could control what Mary Jane might reveal. Grandpa Skippy was bull headed, as Grandma called him, and if he got a whiff of any kind of trickery, he would never agree to move to town.

If Aunt Lizzy wanted to visit some of the families on her go-to-town day, it would have to be someone other than Mama and the "Little Miss I Can't Keep a Secret" Mary Jane. It also included Uncle Seaburn's house since it was on the same street. Grandma and Grandpa Skippy would be able to see all the work that had been done to the little gray house.

Aunt Shorty and her family lived in Atkins, and that was too far to drive with groceries in the back seat of the car. Aunt Dolly's house would be the best to go for a visit. If Aunt Lizzy had any perishables she would put them in Aunt Dolly's refrigerator while they had a nice visit. Uncle Sonny had a workshop out back where he worked on his projects. None were allowed in the workshop without first being invited by Uncle Sonny. Grandma and Grandpa Skippy didn't give the workshop much thought when they came for a visit.

Aunt Dolly was always happy to see Grandma and Grandpa come for a visit and the person who brought them too. Aunt Dolly was always ready to feed her guest. Her kitchen was equipped with the newest and the best appliances money could buy; it would be no trouble to whip up a little something for them to eat. Grandma and Aunt Lizzy agreed that a glass of sweet tea would really hit the spot while Grandpa Skippy and Uncle Cloud would enjoy having a cup of her fine coffee. Coffee was always coffee, but sweet tea was always served in a glass with ice. If you asked for tea without saying what kind of tea, you would probably be served hot tea, and yes, it would be served in a proper teacup with a saucer.

The Smith children—Larry, Charles, and Donny—were out playing while Brenda was taking a nap. The boys looked like they had been playing in mud puddles. When asked what in the world they had been doing, Larry explained they had been throwing mud balls. Mud balls were like snowballs but with mud. The back door was as far as the boys were allowed with their muddy shoes. If there had been no company, Aunt Dolly would have made them strip down to their underwear right there at the back door.

The muddy shoes were left at the back door, and the boys softly walked to the kitchen table to give Grandma and Aunt Lizzy a kiss on the cheek and to say hi to Grandpa and Uncle Cloud. The only place that was not covered with mud was their lips. Walking softly kept the mud from falling off on to the floor.

The boys were now acquainted with the new neighbors at the very top of the hill. The Davis family had just moved from Clayton, North Carolina. They had four daughters. The Davis and the Smith children had all been throwing mud balls. Ms. Carol, as the neighborhood kids called her, was a second-grade schoolteacher. Ms. Carol was substituting until the new school term started in September. Mr. Davis was a quality control manager at the cotton mill.

His new position at the mill was the reason for their move to Morrilton. Alice was in the first grade, and Mrs. Jackson was her teacher, same class as Jerry. Mrs. Jackson's classroom had a small version of a real house. Alice was a nice polite little girl; her personality was more on the logical side. She liked to think things over before making decisions. Dixie Davis was in the third grade, Ms. Mary Sims was her teacher, and Lizzy Davis was in the fourth grade; Mrs. Long was her teacher. Alice, Dixie, and Lizzy were more like Ms. Carol, red hair and a temper to match. Lizzy hated wearing cute little dresses and having her long, red hair pulled back with hair ribbons; she was a tomboy. Dixie, on the other hand, loved dresses, bows, and ribbons in her long, red hair. Connie was only two; she had brown hair like her daddy.

Larry, Charles, and Donny changed their muddy clothes and washed up as best they could without taking a whole bath. Their muddy clothes were put into the washing machine right away, and Aunt Dolly checked their ears and behind their ears for any leftover mud balls.

The boys used all their energy from their breakfast and their lunch. Aunt Dolly teased the boys about having a hollow leg because they could eat anytime and lots of it. Graham crackers and a glass of milk were offered to the boys as a snack; of course they accepted. Aunt Dolly placed some of the graham crackers on a small plate and placed it in the middle of the kitchen table. Grandma Ward could never pass up an offer of graham crackers. Grandma switched drinking sweet tea to coffee. She liked to dip her graham cracker in her coffee.

Both Grandma and Grandpa Skippy had a sweet tooth. Grandpa Skippy had only one tooth left in the back, and he called it his sweet tooth. Grandma wore dentures, store-bought teeth, and Grandpa Skippy believed all those store-bought teeth were her sweet tooth.

Uncle Sonny didn't care one way or another about sweets, but Aunt Dolly had to have her sweets. Grandpa Skippy suggested Aunt Dolly had inherited her sweet tooth from Grandma. "All you kids inherited Grandma's sweet tooth, and the good looks and charm came from me," Grandpa proudly announced. They all had a good laugh, even Grandpa Skippy.

Right at three o'clock, all of Aunt Dolly's clocks began to ding, chime, and coo. Her collection of clocks was lovingly placed all through her house. Grandpa Ward had an old pocket watch he inherited from his father, Seaburn Ward. According to Grandpa Ward, his pocket watch kept perfect time. William Murphy Ward was the only son born to James Seaburn Ward and Mary Jane Cagle. Grandpa Ward had six sisters: Carrie (Hammer), Dora Ellen (Petty), Frankie (Goats), Nettie, Mollie, and Vallie (Thompson).

Grandpa checked his pocket watch to make sure Aunt Dolly's clocks was correct with his time. His pocket watch time was the only time Grandpa considered to be the correct time. He would argue till the cows came home; his pocket watch was always correct.

It seemed that all of Aunt Dolly's clocks were correct—pocket watch correct. "Since its three o'clock, don't you think we should be heading for Birdtown?" Grandpa asked. Aunt Lizzy and Uncle Cloud gave him a nod; they were ready to head home too. Uncle Sonny offered to put them up for the night and feed them supper.

As nice as his invitation was, none took him up on his offer. Aunt Lizzy and Uncle Cloud had three boys at home, and they were sure they were running wild. Gene was like Uncle Cloud, anything outdoors was all right with him. He even had the knack of working with wood and old furniture. Edward concentrated on his schoolwork, always reading. He planned to go to college by hook or by crook; he was going to college. Roy, the youngest, seemed to be leaning toward the outdoors and living off the land. He was too young to say for sure, but Roy was never too far behind Gene. Gene was teaching Roy how to track deer.

"According to Gene, if Roy was going to follow him, he might as well learn something useful." Uncle Cloud had bought Roy a rifle, but Gene taught him gun safety. Not until Gene was satisfied that Roy understood gun safety could he take his rifle to the woods. Roy was still able to go to the woods and learn from Gene; it didn't matter if he had his rifle or not.

The two hunters wearing camouflage and orange vest would go out looking for signs of deer. Gene had a deer stand all set up and waiting for deer season. Before daybreak, Gene and Roy would be sitting high above the ground waiting for the opportunity to bag a big buck. Gene promised Roy he could help dress out the buck when and if they got one.

Gene had given Roy special instructions on the need to be very still and quiet. While in the deer stand, they would be using some sort of sign language; no talking was allowed. Roy would use binoculars to spot any bucks coming their way. If a buck was spotted, Roy was to tap Gene on the shoulder and point to the area the buck was seen. Once a buck was spotted, all they could do was watch, wait, and hope he got close enough for a shot. If the buck was spooked and changed direction, they would have to patiently wait for another to come by.

Gun safety, tracking for signs of deer or other game, the sign language use by hunters, and learning to walk softly in the woods were beginning to be second nature for Roy; however, the patiently waiting was not so easy to learn. Some might say Roy didn't have the patients to be patient. Uncle Cloud once told Roy, "Nature could not be rushed. If you plan to be a good hunter, you must be ready to sit in wait for the animals to come to you."

That was pretty much the same thing Gene told him, just in a different style. You can't get in a big hurry when hunting and you must be willing to wait; otherwise you would be wasting your time and the time of anyone who might be hunting with you. Roy would take what Uncle Cloud told him and what Gene told him and combine the two ways of doing things to make it his way. By combining the two ways, he didn't hurt anyone's feelings.

Roy didn't find hunting to be as much fun as he thought it would be, although he did understand and appreciate the gun safety. All the rules when out in the woods seemed to suck all fun out of hunting. Fishing with Grandpa Ward seemed to be what Roy enjoyed. Grandpa could tell some of his whoppers from his covered-wagon days. If the fish weren't biting, they could always move to another area and keep on fishing. Digging worms for bait was fun. Grandpa liked to use the big and fat worms for his bait. He called dibs on the fat worms. If Roy and Grandpa caught a mess of fish, they would clean them, fillet them, and take them home to Grandma for a fish supper. Sometimes the filleted fish would be taken home to Aunt Lizzy and Uncle Cloud for a fish supper at their house. If the fish supper was to be at Aunt Lizzy and Uncle Cloud's house, Uncle Cloud would drive over to pick up Grandma and Grandpa. Grandpa Ward was physically able to walk over for a fish supper, but Grandma had arthritis and a walk like that would cause her great pain.

After a nice visit with Aunt Dolly and Uncle Sonny, Grandma and Grandpa Ward were driven right up to their front door. Aunt Lizzy and Uncle Cloud carried the two grocery bags into the house for them. Uncle Cloud looked around the house to make sure there was no boogieman lurking about. He never found a boogieman lurking about, but his looking for one made Grandma feel safe. Grandpa said, "I feel sorry for the boogieman that is stupid enough to mess with Grandma. He'll be leaving this house wearing a cast-iron skillet for a hat."

Grandpa knew firsthand about the cast-iron skillet hats, and he didn't recommend getting on Grandma's bad side. Grandma and Grandpa had an agreement; Grandpa would do his best not to get on her bad side, and Grandma would *not* give him a cast-iron hat, if he didn't get on her bad side. Uncle Cloud thought the whole agreement thing was funny; he would laugh out loud at them. Grandpa looked at Uncle Cloud and asked, "Have you ever worn a cast-iron skillet hat?" Uncle Cloud was happy to say he had never worn a skillet hat, but he did own up to having worn an egg hat. It was now Grandpa's turn to laugh—out loud. Grandpa wanted to know the cause of his egg hat. "I don't rightly know, but I hope I never do again."

Aunt Lizzy looked at Grandma and pointed out, "With the cast-iron skillet and the eggs, we could have made an omelet." Now they all had a good out loud laugh. Grandpa looked at

Uncle Cloud with a grin on his face; Uncle Cloud gave a grin right back to Grandpa.

"Did you see the egg coming at you?" Grandpa asked.

"No, sir, I was headed out the door when I got smacked in the back of the head with a brown double-yolk egg." Uncle Cloud went on to explain that he had to go collect more eggs before Lizzy could finish cooking breakfast. Grandpa Ward gave Uncle Cloud some free advice: "When fussing with the wife, never turn your back on her." Every time Uncle Cloud saw a brown double-yolk egg, he remembered getting smacked in the head with one. Aunt Lizzy wasn't about to let Uncle Cloud forget his run-in with a brown double-yolk egg. Uncle Cloud enjoyed his eggs over easy. At breakfast, Aunt Lizzy would ask him, "One yolk or two?" They started their day with a good laugh—at least she did; eventually he did too.

Aunt Lizzy looked at Uncle Cloud and asked, "Are you ready to get home, egg head?" When Uncle Cloud got a little embarrassed, his ears turned red, but when he got really embarrassed, his face and ears both turned red. Trying to keep a stern look on his red face caused an outburst of laughter; egg head was ready to get home. Grandpa Ward gave Uncle Cloud a little more of his free advice: "Having a good sense of humor is not required, but it sure does come in handy. I'm sure, at least I hope Parthina didn't clobber me with a cast-iron skillet when our children were around. Therefore, she must have given cast-iron skillet lessons,"

Grandma replied, "I did not, and yes, I did."

"Eggs, cast-iron skillet, and omelets make me want breakfast for supper," Grandpa announced. The room became quiet, and everyone stared at Grandpa; they were trying to figure out if he was still joking around or if he was serious. "Would breakfast for supper be too much trouble?" Grandpa asked. Grandpa always bragged about Grandma's homemade biscuits. Grandma added a cup of love to all her recipes. Her biscuits were always perfect.

Aunt Lizzy thought that breakfast for supper would be a nice change. Grandma extended an invitation to Aunt Lizzy and Uncle Cloud to stay for supper. Once again, Aunt Lizzy had to decline a supper invitation. She was anxious to get home and see what the boys had been doing; she was hopeful the house was still standing. "If our house is still standing, I think breakfast for supper will do nicely," agreed Uncle Cloud.

"If your house is not still standing, come on back and stay with us. We might be able to find a brown double-yolk egg," snickered Grandpa. Grandma and Grandpa watched from the front porch as Aunt Lizzy and Uncle Cloud drove away. "I believe those two are going to be just fine now that Cloud has found his sense of humor," said Grandpa. "Now let's hope he doesn't misplace it," Grandma said.

Grandma was frying some bacon, making her biscuits and then milk gravy. The bacon drippings were always used for her gravy and used as a seasoning for other meals. Grandpa was very particular about the pork he ate; if the pork didn't come from his own hogs or hogs from a family member, he would not eat it. Grandma understood his reasoning on pork.

The children of Will and Parthina Ward were instructed *never eat pork from a stranger*. Before their move to Birdtown, Grandpa and Grandma and their children were sharecroppers for the Cartwright family. The Cartwright family was of Cajun decent and talked with a French dialect. Understanding the dialect was hard for Grandpa and Grandma, but the children became familiar with their broken English. The local rumors were that Mr. Cartwright had inherited money and property from his grandfather. Unless the rumors put food on his table or took food off his table, Grandpa Ward didn't care about rumors.

Walter Cartwright traveled to and from Louisiana on a regular bases, leaving his wife and two teenage sons to take care of his business in Arkansas. His trips seemed to last longer than the one before. Grandma felt sorry for Betty Cartwright and her sons; on occasion, Grandma would invite Mrs. Cartwright to sit in the shade and have a glass of her sweet tea.

Mrs. Cartwright and Grandma became friendly. She had even agreed to let Grandpa and Grandma fix a hog pen to keep some hogs. Mrs. Cartwright didn't see any harm in allowing the sharecroppers to raise a few pigs to help feed their family. Mr. Cartwright was a horse's butt; he didn't want his sharecroppers to have anything that might make life easier. Grandma described Mr. Cartwright as having a dark soul. Grandpa called him rotten to the core. Mr. Cartwright enjoyed having others totally dependent on him. The more he traveled, the more independent Mrs. Cartwright and her boys became. Mr. Cartwright didn't like that at all.

Once Grandpa had finished building his hog pen, Mrs. Cartwright came by with her boys to inspect the pen. His hog pen was not as good as Grandpa would have liked it, but it would do for now. Mrs. Cartwright wanted to strike a bargain with Grandpa: to build her and the boys a hog pen down at their house. Mrs. Cartwright would pay for the lumber and pay for some hogs if Grandpa agreed. She also agreed to keep some of her hogs in Grandpa's pen.

Mrs. Cartwright thought the Ward family would have more slop to feed the hogs, since their family was much bigger. Grandpa and Mrs. Cartwright shook hands; a bargain was struck. Grandpa measured for the lumber that would be needed. Mrs. Cartwright called the lumber yard to have the lumber delivered. She bought more lumber than was needed; the new lumber went straight to Grandpa's hog pen. Grandpa was pleased as punch with new lumber.

Getting to the sale where hogs could be purchased was going to be a little difficult; Grandpa didn't drive even if he had a truck and Mrs. Cartwright could drive, but she didn't have a truck either. "Don't worry, missy, we'll get someone to take us to the sale and bring those little piggies home," Grandpa said with confidence.

The bargain with Mrs. Cartwright was more helpful than Grandpa ever imagined. When it was time to butcher a hog, Mrs. Cartwright would ask Grandpa to do the butchering. She offered to pay Grandpa with cash money or half of the meat from the hog. Grandpa made a counter offer to Mrs. Cartwright; he would butcher the hog for some cash money and some of the meat. Grandpa Ward was a wheeler and dealer, but he was not a greedy man. Mrs. Cartwright had been very kind to Grandma and Grandpa Ward. How much cash money and how much meat was left up to Mrs. Cartwright. Grandpa knew she would be fair.

Grandpa thought it would be a good idea to have Robert and Clanton, the Cartwright boys, watch and help with the butchering. They would someday need to know how to butcher a hog at least that was Grandpa Ward's opinion. While Grandpa was teaching the Cartwright boys how to butcher a hog, Grandma was getting ready to teach Mrs. Cartwright how to make cracklings and lard from the butchered hog. Mrs. Cartwright was finding out exactly how much she didn't know about hogs, crops, and the rustic everyday living.

Chapter 11

Grandma now called Mrs. Cartwright by her given name, Betty.

"Betty, how is it that you don't have much experience in…well, just about everything?"

"Until I married Walter, I had servants and housekeepers—well, my parents had the servants and housekeepers. I did however bring to the marriage a nice dowry and a monthly allowance. My parents did expect the dowry to keep me in the lifestyle I had become accustomed to, but as you can see, I have not done as well as my parents had hoped. This home and the property were to be part of my dowry after five years. Walter and I have only been married two years; he was a widower when we met. I'm ashamed for my parents to know how bad things are now."

"The deed to this property will never be signed over to Walter Cartwright if my father has anything to say about it. My father will expect to see a prospering son-in-law and a good husband to his only daughter. Not the black-hearted person we all know him to be."

After months of being away from his family, Mr. Cartwright was surprised to see them doing so well. Robert and Clanton were growing up to be hard-working and well-respected men; something they could not say about their own father. Mr. Cartwright no longer had complete control over his wife and kids; they had tasted the sweet taste of independence.

Mr. Cartwright tried driving a wedge between his family and the Ward family. He called Grandpa and Grandma Ward the do-gooders. He didn't think it was appropriate for his family to become too familiar with the hired help.

"How do you think we survived the past six months, or did you even care?" Betty had been around Grandma Ward just enough to learn how to spit fire when it was necessary. "You made sure at least you thought you made sure to leave us to sink or swim. For that, I thank you. While you were gone, the boys and I learned how to swim with the help of *the do-gooders*. The boys have learned to be respectful, and they have stopped the back talking."

The tongue lashing from Betty was very much out of character. Mr. Cartwright was caught off guard by her words and attitude. He didn't like it at all, but Betty enjoyed every minute. This was the first time Betty had ever seen Walter dumbfounded.

Robert and Clanton heard Betty giving their father the tongue lashing that was well overdue and well-deserved. The living room became quiet before the boys entered the room. Mr. Cartwright didn't have much to say to the boys except "Go get the box of dirty clothes from my truck. Robert and Clanton thought they would be glad to see their father, but they were sadly mistaken. The boys didn't realize how cruel and hateful their father could be until he returned home. Robert and Clanton had changed for the better; Mr. Cartwright had not.

"I expect those dirty clothes to be washed tomorrow," barked Mr. Cartwright. Betty didn't say one word, but the contempt was all over her face. "You boys need to stay away for those sharecroppers. If you can't find something to do, I will be happy to find some work for you."

The next morning, Robert and Clanton drew the water for the laundry. Betty spent most of the day scrubbing on an old washboard. Robert and Clanton offered to scrub some to give Betty a break, but Mr. Cartwright would not have his boys do woman's work. Mr. Cartwright called Robert to go to his truck and bring back what he found under the front seat. Robert brought back a bottle of whiskey; Clanton was then ordered to bring him a glass of cold water. The boys watched their father sitting in the shade drinking hard liquor while his wife was doing the laundry. Robert and Clanton were ashamed of their father.

Robert took Betty by the hand and walked her over to an empty chair in the shade; Clanton brought her a glass of cold water. She was instructed by the boys to rest. They would finish the laundry on her behalf. "What do you boys think you're doing? My sons will not be doing laundry if I have anything to say about it!" The Cartwright boys didn't hesitate at all. "Fine, we will not be your sons…Walter. We will be Betty's sons from this day forward, and if she will allow us, we will call her Mama. So, Walter, what do you think about that?" asked Clanton. "What do you think about us calling you Mama, Mama?"

Betty choked back the tears while her stretched arms welcomed her new sons. Walter sat in the shade with his drunken mouth open. "Damn woman! What have you done to my sons?" Robert and Clanton finished hugging their new Mama before addressing Walter.

"What part of 'no longer your sons' do you not understand, Walter?" asked Clanton. Betty was proud to see her boys turn into strong, caring men right before her eyes. They were no longer the mean, hateful, or sassy-mouth brats that Walter had deserted six month ago. Betty suspected that under those sassy mouths were hiding two good men. She was right!

"Your days of bulling this family are over, Walter," Robert announced. "If you can't play nice with others, you'll have to go play somewhere else," Clanton said. "Does that sound about right, Mama?" asked Robert. Betty agreed wholeheartedly with her new sons.

Partaking hard liquor didn't change Walter's personality; it just increased his already nasty dispersion. "Of all the different kinds of drunks, I had to get the mean and nasty drunk," said Betty. Walter was so drunk he was on his way to blackout drunk.

"Who are you talking to?" growled Walter.

Betty quickly replied, "Me, myself, and I, and don't interrupt us." Betty and the boys thought her answer to be very funny. Walter didn't have much of a sense of humor when he left, and upon his return, he had even less. Betty gave the boys some good advice. "Beware the evils of hard liquor." She then pointed to Walter who was rocking in a straight back chair with his eyes closed. When Walter rocked right out of his chair, Betty said, "I rest my case." She snickered again.

Robert and Clanton agreed to finish the laundry while Betty took care of Walter. Betty didn't say she would take *great care* of Walter—just take care of him. She brought an old tattered and torn quilt and an old pillow from the house. The quilt was spread out on the ground, and Walter was rolled over to sleep on the quilt, and the pillow was placed under his head.

The boys asked, "Are you going to let him sleep on the ground?"

"Yes, but I will fix the couch just in case he wakes up and can make his way to the house."

Robert looked at his brother with such a smile. "Why didn't we think of that?"

Betty gave both boys a big smile as she headed for the kitchen to cook supper. "A plate of food will be left on the kitchen table, just in case he finds his way to the kitchen. As you can tell, I don't have much sympathy for drunks," added Betty. "Sympathy for a drunk is a waste of sympathy."

Homemade vegetable soup and cornbread was on the menu for the Cartwright family…minus Walter. He was in one of his drunken stupors under the big shade tree. The soup was warming on the stove; the cornbread was baking in the oven. The glasses for drinking sweet tea were placed in the freezer, insuring the sweet tea would be at its coldest. Betty picked a few green onions from her vegetable garden to top off their fine supper.

Robert and Clanton finished the laundry just as they promised. The first two loads were ready to be taken down from the clothesline. The whites were always washed first…at least that was how Betty did laundry. "No more laundry for you today, missy," laughed Robert.

Betty rinsed and dried the washtubs as well as the scrub board. When not in use, the washtubs were hung on the wall just inside the back door. The scrub board was stored close to the tubes but on the floor. Clanton needed a pair of work gloves to keep his hands from getting all wrinkled from the water, at least that was the story he told Betty. She thought his request was a little odd, but she showed him where she stored the work gloves. Robert continued to take dry clothes down and hang wet clothes up; at least until he saw Clanton wearing a pair of ladies' multicolor gardening gloves. "I'm afraid to ask," laughed Robert.

Clanton waited for Robert to get his laughing done before revealing his plan. "Oh yea, I forgot, here's your multicolor girly gloves." Robert refused to wear the girly work gloves until Clanton gave more details of his harebrained idea. Clanton's harebrained ideas were never as good as this one. The Cartwright boys folded the dried laundry, including the sheet and pillow cases to make more room in the laundry baskets. Walters's clothes would be in a separate laundry basket. Betty would have no need to touch Walter's clothes.

The boys left the household laundry sitting beside the clothesline. Robert and Clanton were both armed with their girly work gloves. To the woods behind the house and past the hog pen they went to find a big mess of poison ivy or poison oak— either would do nicely. Poison ivy was found first, the three-leaf plant was climbing the trunk of an old tree.

There was plenty of poison ivy to go around; the boys didn't have to share. Walter's clean laundry was turned inside out and gently rubbed with poison ivy. Special attention was taken with his underwear, socks, and handkerchiefs. A few of his so-called work shirts were rubbed in the armpits area. Betty would not be expected to iron Walter's work clothes. They took extra care to insure Betty would not be affected by any of Walter's special laundry.

Walter's special laundry was folded and ready to be put away. Robert and Clanton returned to the clothesline to find that Betty had taken the folded household clothes into the house and put them away. Finding the laundry all folded was such a treat; she didn't even notice that Walter's laundry was not in the basket. As a matter of fact, she had forgotten that Walter was passed out under the shade tree. Out of sight, out of mind, that was Walter: a good way to remember Walter.

Betty was in the kitchen getting ready to set the table. Clanton took the opportunity to distract Betty so that Robert could sneak past and put Walter's special laundry away. "Look, Mama, my hands are no longer wrinkled like a prune," Clanton announced. His distraction had worked. Betty and Clanton examined his silky soft hands while Robert put the Walter laundry away. Walter had a pet peeve about his clothes; his clothes were *never* to be stored with anyone else's clothes. The modest little house only had two closets; one in the boy's bedroom, and one in Betty and Walter's room. Walter laid claim to the closet in his, as he called it, bedroom. Walter did need the closet; he had twice as many clothes than Betty.

Betty had taken an old broom handle and nailed it across a corner of the room. Her clothes were hung on the old broom handle as her closet then a sheet was draped over her clothes. The dresser in the bedroom had four drawers; Walter used three, and Betty used one. Before Walter's return, Betty had considered taking over his closet space. The dresser drawers had been fitted with new liners, but that was as far as she had gotten…then Walter came home.

Robert and Clanton put their girly work gloves in the trash to be burned at the end of the week. Before supper, the boys took extra care to wash anywhere they may have been touched by the poison ivy. It wasn't out of character for the boys to be quiet as a mouse during supper, but this time, their quietness was different. Betty could tell they were up to something.

Clanton was a little jumpy about keeping their secret, and Robert looked like the cat that ate the canary. "What are you boys up to, and do I need to be worried?" asked Betty. Clanton wanted to tell, but Robert insisted there was no need for her to be worried. "Did you boys slip off to visit the Ward girls?" asked Betty. Robert was surprised by her question. "You didn't think I knew about you being a little sweet on May Ward?"

Robert reluctantly answered, "No, Mama, I didn't know you knew."

"And she is sweet on Robert too," announced Clanton. Robert was a little embarrassed talking about May with his Mama.

"May Ward is a pretty young lady, a little on the shy side, and she comes from an honest hardworking family. There's not a slacker in the whole bunch," bragged Betty. "Robert, you couldn't find a sweeter young lady to be sweet on than Nettie May Ward. Clanton didn't hesitate to remind Betty and Robert of the harsh words Walter used to describe the Wards.

"Have we forgotten about today? Betty, you are now our mother, and Walter is…just a mean, hateful, spiteful drunk that you married. He no longer has any control over us. His opinion does not count in this family anymore. Walter can only hurt us if we allow him to hurt us." Robert's words were strong and he spoke from the heart.

Walter, the drunk, was mentally abusive, but sober Walter was physically abusive. The hung-over Walter could be tolerated, at least until the hangover was over. The mental and physical abuse was hurtful in their own way, but mental abuse hurts deep down and doesn't stop hurting when the words stop. Betty's heart had many scars from Walter's mental abuse; scars she didn't expect to ever heal. Walter returned to a family changed; a change they didn't realize until he returned. Betty, Robert, and Clanton all agreed: a change for the better.

Supper was over and the dishes done. "Since you didn't sneak over to see May…the Ward family, how about we stroll over for a short visit?" Betty said. Before supper, the boys washed up to get rid of any poison ivy; now they washed up to go see May and her family. Robert washed up, put on a clean shirt, and he even brushed his teeth. Clanton didn't understand why Robert was brushing his teeth; it wasn't bedtime. "You will understand when you get yourself a sweetheart," Betty explained. She also pointed out that girls like boys with fresh breath and sparkly teeth. "Fresh breath and sparkly teeth are for kissing, right?"

Clanton was teasing Robert about his fresh breath and sparkly teeth. It was good to see the boys laughing and teasing each other. Betty reminded them to be on their best behavior and that they couldn't stay too long. Betty had good manners and she wanted her boys to have them too. To drop by without an invitation should be a short visit.

Betty and the boys had timed their visit just right. The Ward family had just finished their supper and the dishes were all done. The older Ward girls were in charge of doing the dishes and in making sure the kitchen was clean as a whistle. Out of necessity, Ms. Parthina was always making or mending something, especially for the girls. She had even tried her hand at embroidering; May, Lizzy, and Effie all had their name embroider on a bib apron. Ms. Parthina had traded some of her homemade preserves for a bolt of cloth and treads. Curtains for the little sharecropper's house and aprons for the girls all came from the same cloth.

Mr. Will had built a large table with bench like seating for eating outside on days the hot kitchen could not be bared. The large oak tree provided shade for the front porch and the large eating table. The night breezes were quite enjoyable after a hard day's work. Mr. Will and Ms. Parthina sat quietly sipping a glass of lemonade. The family dog, Coley, was playing fetch the ball with

Mary Jane, Don, Shorty, and little Dolly. The older children were laughing about…no one really knew what they were laughing about. The nearest neighbor was the Cartwright family, and they lived a good mile away. So there was no need to worry about disturbing the neighbors; Ms. Parthina was pleased about that.

Mr. Will's keen sense of hearing detected someone walking toward the house. Before Betty and the boys were in sight, Mr. Will called, "Coley protect." Coley was ready to attack on Mr. Will's command. "It's just us, Mr. Will," shouted Betty. Mr. Will gave Coley the all-clear command. Coley greeted the visitors with a friendly sniff and a happy wagging of his tail. Just like Mr. Will , Coley was a good judge of character. Robert hardly spoke to Mr. and Mrs. Ward; he was scanning the faces of the girls to find May's pretty face. Ms. Parthina asked Lizzy and Effie to bring the pitcher of lemonade and more glasses from the kitchen. Everyone knew May and Robert was sweet on each other, except Mr. Ward. Ms. Parthina told Mr. Will, "You'd have to be deaf, dumb, and blind not to see the way those two look at each other."

Mr. Will cupped his hands behind his ears and yelled, "What'd you say?" Mr. Will gave everyone a good chuckle.

Ms. Parthina shook her head and rolled her eyes at him, like she usually did when he was being silly. The only advice Mr. Will had to offer the new sweethearts was "If you don't have a sense of humor, you best get one." Ms. Parthina suggested the front porch swing would be a good place for the couple to drink their lemonade. Then she shooed the other children away from the front porch. "Shoo, shoo…Mama said shoo," repeated May. "Bless their little hearts," Betty whispered. "Wonder which one is going to faint first," Mr. Will quietly laughed. "Will Ward how nervous were you when you first started calling on me?" asked Ms. Parthina.

"So nervous I puked like a buzzard every time I left your house."

By the time William Murphy Ward met Parthina Dudley, he had already been married, widowed, and had a small son, Alvie. Parthina never knew Will was the least little bit nervous when he came a calling. Parthina was smitten with him, and she never noticed him being a little green around the gills. "Love is blind, but the neighbors ain't," smirked Mr. Will. Betty watched and listened to Will and Parthina duke it out with their humor.

"Alvie, I thought your boys were Seaburn and Don?" Betty softly asked. "Alvie was two when Will and I married, and we lost him to tuberculosis of the lungs. He was twenty-five. We buried Alvie right next to his mother, Rhonda Bell (Petty) Ward, at the Walnut Grove Cemetery in Hector, Arkansas. Alvie had a great sense of humor, very entertaining. Alvie is in heaven taking care of baby Martha Jane…twin to Mary Jane. She was only three months when she passed. She is buried at the May Cemetery in Houston, Arkansas.

"Mary Catherine (Dudley) Lee, sister to Parthina, lives in Bigelow, Arkansas, as well as her brother David Clark Dudley and his family. Dave and Ellen (Reeder) added a small bedroom to their little house where Grandma Nancy lived surrounded by many of her grandchildren.

"When we get the chance to visit Perry County, we always go to May Cemetery and put a few wild flowers on baby Martha Jane's grave," Will somberly said. In her perky voice, Parthina told about having lunch on the ground at the cemetery, but only after the graves had been tidy up. She called it having lunch with baby Martha Jane.

Betty apologized for stirring up sad memories of their lost children. She was still trying to put names with faces. Of course, she knew May and her crooked little smile; Robert had pointed her out many times. Will and Parthina chose to remember the joy that Alvie and baby Martha Jane brought to their lives. "We are all just passing through; some of us get to stay longer while others do not. If we choose to dwell on the sadness, we will forever forget the love and happiness we received from our loved ones," said Parthina. Alvie only had a third-grade education, but he enjoyed reading. He read stories to the younger children; he even used funny voices to entertain them. His specialty was his practical jokes—so funny.

Will and Parthina took turns telling some of the shenanigans Alvie pulled on others. Most of the time, his shenanigans were meant for the children, but sometimes Parthina walked right in the middle of his jokes. "Like the time Alvie put a bucket of cold water above the back door, Parthina got her bath and it wasn't even Saturday," laughed Will. "Once Alvie even packed Will's pipe with dirt, he was trying to get Will to stop smoking," snickered Parthina. "I spent one whole day getting dirt balls out of my pipe," confessed Will.

Alvie had a partner in crime: Seaburn. Everyone knew Alvie loved playing jokes on his siblings, but they would have never suspected Seaburn would be involved in any way. Every prankster needed a good lookout person, and that was Seaburn. Most of the practical jokes were funny looking back on them now. The outhouse joke didn't turn out as funny as Alvie thought for Lizzy and Effie. The outside bathroom, called the toilet, could accommodate two people. After Lizzy and Effie entered the toilet, Alvie proceeded to turn the latch on the door; yes, he locked his sisters in the outdoor toilet. Locking the outside door would have been a lot funnier if Alvie had not been called away by Will. When Will called for the children, they didn't waste any time getting there. Needless to say, Alvie forgot about Lizzy and Effie locked in the toilet until they came looking to do bodily harm to him. Trying to be serious, Will asked Alvie if it was true. "Alvie explained it was just a joke…until you called, and then I forgot all about the girls."

Will wanted to know if the toilet was still standing, "If not, we'll have to build another." Lizzy and Effie were now laughing with the rest of the family. Effie did point out that the door could not be locked from the outside when not in use. Will and Parthina had to come up with a punishment for Alvie. Will instructed Alvie to get the hammer and some nails. "Go fix the outside lock on the toilet."

Parthina had a punishment she knew Alvie would absolutely hate. "Alvie will be helping you girls do the dishes and cleaning up the kitchen," Parthina said with a big smile on her face. "Effie and Lizzy will be in charge of Alvie, and the work he will be doing on their behalf." The younger children all found a nice place to sit and watch Alvie being bossed around by Effie, Lizzy, and May. Lizzy said Alvie should be wearing an apron; Effie said a hairnet or at least a scarf would be needed. "Out of hairnets…a head scarf would have to do," said Effie. Lizzy got a clean apron and tied it around Alvie. The head scarf was wrapped around his head with a big bow. May suggested Alvie should roll the legs up on his britches; girls didn't wear britches when working in the kitchen.

"He needs some of that lip rough," shouted Will. "Alvin pointed out, "The lip rough was for going to town, not for washing dishes." The girls never knew cleaning up the kitchen could be so much fun. Alvie was in charge of drying the dishes, and then he passed them on to May to be put in their proper places. "Do you suppose the people who pay to see a picture show have this much fun?" asked Shorty. The laugher was just about to die down, but Will had one more thing to say about Alvie. "Alvie, you are a good-looking young man, but as a girl, you have got to be the ugliest thing I've ever see."

Now with that comment, it's a wonder the whole Ward family didn't wet their pants. May wasn't a victim this time, so she took pity on Alvie. However, she did make him carry the bucket of slop. May tried to help her brother cope with his fear of hogs. "Alvie, just remember the food in the bucket is the same food we had for our supper." The hogs knew it was feeding time; they didn't have to be called to the feeding trough. Alvie was instructed to lean over the fence and start pouring the slop into the trough. "Try to spread it from one end of the trough to the other," May softly said. "And by all means, don't fall in the hog pen. They could eat you up before anyone could get you out." They can go through bone like butter, but you'll need at least sixteen pigs to finish the job in one sitting. They can go through a body that weighs two hundred pounds in about eight minutes. Alvie, you'd be a nice snack for the hungry pigs." May laughed.

"We have people-friendly pigs," whispered May. "People-friendly pigs," Alvie repeated. People friendly pigs are usually kept in a pigpen, feed a couple times a day, and they love to play in the mud…people-friendly pigs."

"Mama and Papa will never have any other kinds of pigs," assured May. "Unless you're planning to weigh two hundred pounds, have sixteen or more pigs. The people-friendly pigs will never harm you."

Once the pigs were feed, Alvie was allowed to go back to being a young man. Effie and Lizzy would never have to worry about being locked in the outhouse…at least not by Alvie. The telling of Alvie and his practical jokes were always a special treat for the other children. Mama and Papa Ward wanted to keep Alvie in the hearts and minds of their other children.

"We never get tired of the outhouse story," said Effie. Robert and May were still sitting in the porch swing while the other children were listening to the outhouse story. Betty stood up; that was her way of letting Robert and Clanton know it was time to go home. The boys remembered what Betty had told them about a "drop-by" visit. To stay any longer no matter how much fun they were having would be rude on their part. Robert was just seconds away from touching May's pinky finger with his pinky finger. *Maybe next time*, Robert thought.

Chapter 12

The Cartwright and the Ward family lived in Pope County, approximately two miles from the little town of Dover. Russellville, the big town, was about ten miles from Dover.

Mr. Bailey Floyd Ferguson and his wife Ida Augusta (Tutor) Ferguson owned and operated the general store right on the Main Street of Dover, Arkansas. Everyone called them Mr. Bailey and Ms. Ida. Mr. Bailey and Ms. Ida had five children: Olen, Mabel, Carlton, RD, and Myrl. Little Carlton went to heaven when he was only six years old. Mabel was studying to become a schoolteacher. RD was well on his way to becoming a river boat captain. Myrl also studied to be a schoolteacher; however, Myrl meet and married Winfield Tutor who was a pharmacist at the Brown's Corner Drugstore in Russellville. Olen fell in love with the sweetest young lady, Ruby McCord.

The day Olen and Ruby married; Mr. Bailey put Olen's name on the deed to the general store. Above the general store were two small living quarters. Olen and his new wife chose to live in one of the living quarters. Mr. Bailey and Ms. Ida were just like everyone else, trying to make a living, trying to keep the wolves away for their door, but never forgetting their Christian duties to all in need. Money was tight for everyone; sometimes bartering was the only way to get what was needed for your family—just like Ms. Parthina had done with her preserves to get a bolt of material and threads needed for her curtains. The general store was showing signs of aging, but not as bad as the church. Neither Mr. Bailey nor the Church had enough money for building materials and the cost of labor. Mr. Bailey met with Rev. Neville Vanderburg and the deacons of the Church to discuss the poor condition of the buildings. Mr. Bailey pointed out that buying in bulk was the best way to save money. If the congregation will donate their time to make the repairs for the church and the general store, it would be a win-win for all involved. Rev. Vanderburg called a special meeting to explain more ideas Mr. Bailey Ferguson had proposed. He also pointed out that the repairs on the church should be done first. Rev. Vanderburg was happy to report to Mr. Ferguson that the congregation had accepted his offer, and they would be pleased to help with the repairs on his general store. The little town of Dover was beginning to come alive again. The Dover Baptist Church was old, and half of her roof was missing. For the safety of the congregation, the little church was considered "not safe". All that could be salvaged from the church was stored around the county for safekeeping.

Rev. Vanderburg and family, wife Cathy, son Ben, and daughter Tiffney, had visited several churches until they found the Church and congregation that seemed to need them the most. A young clergy was sometimes looked upon as not having enough experience or enough living to be a good clergy. The Vanderburg family knew the Lord would show them where they were needed. Rev. Vanderburg had been invited to preach at the Dover Baptist Church; the reverend didn't know the building was in such poor condition. The building was no longer in use, but the faithful congregation still met every Sunday morning, comes rain or shine. On the rainy days, the congregation stood with their umbrellas and gave thanks for such a beautiful rainy day. Weather permitting, the Sunday morning sermon was followed by a picnic lunch right where they sat listening to the sermon.

The parson's house was a fine little house; the white picket fence with the flowers in bloom gave the illusion of gazing upon a beautiful oil painting. Reverend and Mrs. Vanderburg were happy to call Dover home and happy to raise their children there.

A few months back, Rev. Vanderburg and his family visited a rustic little Baptist Church in Hattieville, Arkansas. The Hattieville congregation was moving into their new church building when Rev. Vanderburg was moving on to his next church to visit, which was the Dover Baptist Church. Rev. James G. Martin from Hattieville had received word that Dover Baptist Church had asked Rev. Vanderburg to stay in Dover and be their new pastor. Rev. Martin was also pleased to hear the people of Dover had taken a liking to the Vanderburg family. Pope County was growing by leaps and bounds.

The rich soil was bringing new families to the county and the small towns in the area. With the growth came the need for a school. Once the little church was up and running again, it could also be used as a school. Some of the old-timers had doubts about getting the little church repaired or having a school in Dover. The planting and harvesting of crops had to take priority over going to school. The smaller children who were able to go the school would be expected to share their knowledge with the children that had to work in the fields.

The Ward children were all eager to learn to read and write. They had already seen how hard life could be without reading and writing. Ms. Parthina was determined to have each of her children learn to read, write, and maybe some arithmetic. Mr. Will was better with numbers; Ms. Parthina would leave the arithmetic to him, and she would teach the reading and writing. Mr. Will could figure numbers in his head, no paper required.

Saturday was always a good day to see what was going on in town. Robert and Clanton enjoyed their walk to Dover. Robert and May walked together; they seemed to be holding hands as they walked a few paces behind the others. It was now official; Robert and May liked each other well enough for the whole county to take notice. Robert made sure May walked on the correct side of the streets in town to make sure she wouldn't be splashed with mud, dirt, or anything else that might be flying from the streets. That was considered to be good manners. The little town was busy with Saturday business and Saturday errands.

There were a few automobiles in town, but mostly there were wagons. The people in town with a wagon were there to purchase supplies, whether it was building supplies or large bags of flour and corn meal and maybe sugar. Flour, sugar, and corn meal were bagged in ten-pound sacks; later the sacks were used to make dresses, sack dresses. Nothing went to waste. Most everything that would be needed to feed a family was home-grown.

The general store was now carrying something called soft drinks. The store also had a place in the back of the store…that you could sit and drink a soft drink. There were four tables with red-and-white checkered tablecloths. The soft drinks cost two cents, and Mr. Bailey would give you two straws so you could share your soft drink with you sweetheart.

Ms. Ida was always making some of her homemade fudge, cookies, cakes, and even pies to sell in their general store. Before putting her baked items on display in the store; she wanted the Ward and Cartwright children to have a taste. Ms. Ida had taken a shine to the Ward and Cartwright children, and this was her way of giving them a tasty treat. Her cakes and pies could be purchased by the slice or the whole thing could be purchased. Ms. Ida had the best baked goods in the whole county. If the children liked her baking, they would get the word out to others. Ms. Ida called giving the children a taste to be good advertising.

Before leaving the general store, Ms. Ida inquired if any of the children would like to take what was left of a German chocolate cake home with them. Most of the children raised their hand to say yes. Ms. Idea cut what was left of the cake into halves. Now both the Ward and the Cartwright families could have a taste of German chocolate cake for dessert.

Ms. Mabel Ferguson, eldest daughter of Mr. Bailey and Ms. Ida, had just graduated from Blue Mountain College, Blue Mountain, Mississippi. During school holidays, Mabel stayed with her grandparents, Mr. Bailey Franklin Ferguson and Mrs. Savannah Eldorado (Bagwell) Ferguson. The Ferguson family had deep roots in Pontotoc County, Mississippi. In his golden years, Mr. Frank was frequently confined to a wheelchair because of his arthritis. Ms. Savannah, too, suffered with bouts of arthritis, but nothing as bad as her husband. Her arthritis affected her hands and her fingers. There were things that Mr. Frank couldn't do, but Ms. Savannah could do for him. Mr. Frank and Ms. Savannah laughed about how they complimented each other: what he couldn't do she could, and what she couldn't do he could. Mabel was going to miss her grandparents, but she was so looking forward to seeing her parents again. A letter from home wasn't the same as a hug.

During holiday breaks, summer breaks, or spring breaks, Mabel always worked odd jobs to make sure she would be able to continue her education. Mabel's father had given her a small ledger to keep up with how her money was spent. The money Mabel earned from her odd jobs was offered to her grandparents for allowing her to stay with them while on school breaks. They never accepted her money; Grandpa Frank called it an investment and was proud to be able to contribute to Mabel's education. Grandma Savannah teased Mabel about having beauty and brains. Grandma Savannah was very proud of Mabel too.

Mabel had her teaching certificate and was ready to start teaching. The little town of Dover was in need of a teacher, and Ms. Ferguson was in need of a teaching position. The general store was being looked after by Lt. James Hugh Mauldin. Lt. Mauldin served in several cavalry units during the War Between the States.[2] Family history has it that he was at Shiloh and Corinth as a partisan, later joining the cavalry when it was formed under Solomon Street. He was a first lieutenant in Company A, Second Mississippi State Cavalry. The Second Cavalry was later placed under the command of General Nathan Bedford Forrest. He returned to Benton County following the war where he worked as a blacksmith and farmer.

Lt. Mauldin resided in Pope County, Arkansas, for a short time before moving back to Benton County, Mississippi. After the war, James H. Mauldin was always called Lt. Mauldin out of respect by all true Southerners.[3] He is buried at Little Hope Primitive Baptist Church Cemetery in Tippah County, Mississippi. His grave is lovingly maintained by his great-great-great granddaughter, Shannon Hamilton. With the changing of the seasons, Lt. Mauldin's grave receives flowers of the season, never to be forgotten.

Everyone in the Pope County knew Lt. Mauldin; they loved to hear some of his war stories. Mr. Bailey and Ms. Ida needed someone to look after the general store; Lt. Mauldin came to mind. He was an honest man, and he wouldn't let anyone walk off with their merchandise. Mabel was coming home by way of bus, and Mr. Bailey and Ms. Ida wanted to be there when she stepped off the bus. The closest bus depot was in Russellville. The arrival time of the bus was uncertain, but that didn't matter to Mr. Bailey and Ms. Ida. They would wait all day if necessary. Mabel left for college as a young girl and would be returning as a grown woman with her own ideas about life.

Mr. Bailey and Ms. Ida's excitement had spread through the whole town of Dover. Even the new people to the community were wondering about the excitement. Lt. Mauldin was using the big pickle barrel as a table for his game of checkers. Everyone knew the best place to get information or the latest news was at the general store. Lt. Mauldin was pleased to tell all that one of Dover's own young ladies, Ms. Mabel Ferguson, had graduated from college in Mississippi and was on her way home after four long years. She could now be a teacher.

Normally, the little town of Dover would be put to bed by five o'clock, but this day Dover was still buzzing; everyone want to get a look at what they hoped to be Dover's new schoolteacher. The arrival of the new teacher was good for business at the general store. The tables in the back had pie eaters and coffee drinkers. The coffeemaker behind the counter was mostly for Mr. Bailey's personal use; the old Confederate soldier knew for a fact: coffee made everything taste better. He made coffee and charged five cents a cup to go with the slices of pie or cake.

New to the area, Cecilia Bell brought her two sons, Adam and Noah, to the general store to try one of those new cola beverages. Mrs. Bell's parents, Mike and Donna Evans, had come to Pope County to check things out before making a decision to move to the area. Mr. Mike wanted to try his hand at farming; Ms. Donna was a nurse, and she would have no trouble finding a job in Russellville. Mr. Mike worked for the Pulaski County Sheriff's Office; after twenty years of blood and guts, Mr. Mike was ready to retire.

Mr. Bailey and Ms. Ida had no idea the general store would get so busy when they asked Lt. Maudlin to look out for things. However, just on the small chance the store did get busy, Mr. Olen and Ms. Ruby were to help out with what needed to be done. While Lt. Maudlin visited with customers at the pickle barrel, Mr. Olen and Ms. Ruby kept the shelves stocked and cleaned up after the customers. A very few of Mr. Bailey and Ms. Ida's customers had a small credit account where they could buy now and pay later. Mr. Bailey was very discreet with his credit accounts; he expected those customers to be discreet with the general store's business. At times, those credit accounts were paid with bartering.

The streets of Dover were lined with well wishers and those just wishing to get a peek at the new college graduate. A few of the old-timers waited in town to welcome Ms. Mabel home out of respect for Mr. Bailey and Ms. Ida—the same old-timers who had doubts of the church being repaired and having a schoolteacher. The repairs to the church were still an ongoing project. The little Baptist church in Hattieville and her congregation had pitched in with labor and a few of her leftover building materials for the not-so-new church.

The little Dover Baptist Church was about thirty days away from being finished; the new schoolteacher had arrived. The word had been put out; all stored items from the church were ready to be returned. The ladies of Pope County had cleaned and polished all the wood inside the church. The two vases on each side of the pulpit were filled with wild flowers. The Dover Baptist Church extended an invitation to Rev. Martin and his congregation to join in the celebration, the first sermon to be given inside the newly repaired Baptist Church.

Rev. Martin with ten people from his congregation showed up bright and early to help with any last-minute details. They were pleasantly surprised to find that the last-minute details were already completed. Mrs. Vanderburg requested the ladies with covered dishes to bring them by way of the back door to the room where lunch would be served.

Chapter 13

It had taken six months to complete the repairs on the little church. Rev. Vanderburg was so thankful for all the hard work and dedication; he became a little emotional while giving thanks. Mrs. Vanderburg said, "There wasn't a dry eye in the whole church."

Betty and her boys started attending church pretty regular since the church was repaired. Walter's plan was to stay about three weeks before going back to Louisiana. Pope County Arkansas was a dry county; meaning, it was against the law to buy or sale hard liquor or any other kind of spirits. The unpleasant incident with Walter and his laundry was never revealed to Betty. Robert and Clanton spoke to Walter as little as possible.

Walter had mosquito bites from sleeping on the ground under the big shade tree. Betty placed a bottle of calamine lotion in front of Walter and walked away. Walter barked for Betty to come put the calamine lotion on his bug bites. Calmly, Betty replied, "You're the one who got blind running drunk. Take care of your own bug bites." Walter smeared the pink lotion on all his mosquito bites. He drank a few cups of coffee then he headed off to the shower.

Dinner was missed by Walter due to his drunken behavior; breakfast was also missed. Betty and the boys sat down each morning to a good breakfast before starting their day. The breakfast plate for Walter was sitting on the kitchen stove. It was cold, but it was all his.

Walter thought himself to be a fine figure of a man; once, Betty thought so too. By the time Walter was ready to eat breakfast, Betty and the boys were almost to town. Robert saw May on their way to town; he promised to come by for a visit on the way back. Betty walked to town like a woman on a mission with no time to spare.

The post office was right next door to the Dover Bank and Trust, and two doors down was the general store. It was too late for breakfast and too early for lunch; Betty gave the boys a nickel to get one of those soft drinks. Betty said to the boys, "As soon as I finish my errands, I'll come to the store, and maybe I'll try one of those drinks." Betty's father, Thomas Baker, had advised her to close her bank account and open another without Walter on the account and put Robert and Clanton as authorized signers in case something was to happen to her. The money in the bank was what Betty brought to the marriage plus her monthly allowance.

Betty did exactly what her father had suggested. She took the signature cards to Robert and Clanton to be signed. They were enjoying their soft drinks and a good game of checkers with Mr. Bailey. Betty returned the signature cards to the bank before mailing a letter to her parents in Louisiana. The letter was more of a thank-you note to her father.

The walk back home was a much slower pace. "To mail a letter to my parents is where we have been," said Betty. Just as Robert had promised, he stopped by to see May for just a few minutes. He couldn't stay long. Walter was back, and as usual, he was in a bad mood. Betty and Clanton chose to keep walking to give Robert and May a little sweetheart privacy.

Walter had showered, shaved, and had on clean clothes. He didn't like his breakfast, but he did eat it. When Clanton saw Walter wearing his clean clothes, he so wanted to burst out laughing. He recognized the work shirt as being part of Walter's special laundry. Walter was walking up and down the rows in the garden. There was still a cool breeze whistling through the tall cornstalks.

Walter snapped at Clanton, "Where have you been so early in the morning?"

"We went to the post office to mail a letter. Mama didn't have any stamps."

"Mama? When did you start calling Betty mama?"

Clanton looked at Betty and then back to Walter.

"Yesterday, don't you remember?" Walter was a little fuzzy about the day before.

"Where's your brother?"

Clanton quickly replied, "He was walking too slow, and we didn't wait on him, but he's on his way home."

"I hope Robert ain't sniffing around one of them do-gooder girls." Walter could tell by Clanton's face he didn't know what "sniffing around" meant. Before Walter could explain in his own foul-mouthed manner, Betty called Clanton to come get a basket to pick some of the vegetables for supper. By the time Clanton got back to the garden, Walter had forgotten all about the do-gooders and their daughters.

Betty watched Walter watching Clanton as he gathered the vegetables. Walter found pleasure in pointing out others' shortcomings. Robert heard Walter in the garden with Clanton; he ever so lightly sneaked up to the back door, hoping Walter would not see or hear him. He took special care with the screen door not to let it slam behind him.

Robert was eager to hear anything he might have missed concerning Walter. "You were walking too slow, that is why Clanton and I got home before you. Our trip to town was to mail a letter to my father…nothing more and nothing less," explained Betty. Robert kind of understood, sort of understood, and not really understood; but if it kept Walter from cussing, fussing, and carrying on like a crazy man, that was good enough for him.

Betty had made a decision about Walter; she would never again lay with him as her husband. Walter was still in the garden with Clanton, still telling him how to gather vegetables. Betty was ready to do a little furniture moving while Walter was out of the way. Robert helped Betty carry one of the mattresses from what was once her bed to the boy's bedroom. Their bedroom was a small room, but not so small that Betty couldn't squeeze in her mattress. The twin beds were moved around to make more room for Betty.

Robert and Clanton were like most teenage boys: as long as they had food, a bed, and a roof over their heads, that was pretty much all that mattered. They weren't the best in making their beds, but at least they tried. Betty put fresh sheets on what was now Walter's bed and Robert helped. Robert wanted to know, "Why not put his butt on the couch instead of you giving up your room?"

"Right now I'd rather give up my room to keep the couch from becoming a flop bed." The couch was a hand-me-down from Betty's parents; it still looked brand-new. She wanted to keep it looking new.

"I guess that makes sense," said Robert.

'Now that we call you mama, can we call Mr. Thomas and Ms. Octavia grandma and grandpa?"

"I think they would be very pleased to be called grandma and grandpa," Betty softly said. "I will let them know in my next letter…they are now the grandparents of Robert and Clanton Cartwright. Grandpa Baker might just have to pass out a few cigars."

Betty moved into the bedroom with her boys without much being said by Walter. Other than adding a few more beans to the pot, Betty tried not to give Walter much thought. Robert and Clanton went about their daily chores. There were days Walter watched the boys as if he was their overseer. Walter taunted the boys with name-calling: sissies, mama's boys.

Trying to stay as far away from Walter was a chore in itself. After three days, Walter left early in the morning; he didn't return until almost dark. Betty thought his face to be a little flush from the whiskey he had been drinking. Walter had located a bootlegger.

When Robert and Clanton saw the red face on Walter, they knew it wasn't a flush from the whiskey. Walter's special laundry had finally started to work. Since Betty didn't know about the special laundry, she would have no reason to think it was anything but the whiskey. Seeing the rash that was no doubt beginning to show, Clanton felt a little remorseful until Walter the drunk barked to bring him a glass of cold water.

Playacting could have been Robert and Clanton's calling; they played deaf, dumb, and blind when the cause of Walter's rash became clear—it was poison ivy. He had the rash in all the right places. Walter was pretty sure he didn't have the rash when he returned from Louisiana. He didn't remember seeing any poison ivy around the house or the trees close to the house. The more Walter itched, the more he fussed and cussed. He always wanted to blame someone else for whatever happened to him, never taking any responsibility.

Walter had no problem stepping behind a tree or bush to urinate. Betty called it marking his territory like a dog. Between the fussing and cussing, Betty asked questions about where he found the bootlegger. "I bet you, your bootlegger was way back in the woods somewhere?" Walter didn't see what the location of the bootlegger had to do with his condition. "Drinking hard liquor is the reason for your condition," snapped Betty.

"You slept on the ground under the big shade tree: mosquito bites. You went traipsing through the woods to buy hard liquor from a bootlegger. Whiskey is not the only thing you got from your trip to the woods: poison ivy, chiggers, and ticks." Robert and Clanton never said a word; they just watched Walter squirm from his rash and bug bites. Betty suggested a hot bath and a change of clothes might make him feel a little better.

Betty handed Walter a paper sack for his infested clothes, a bottle of bleach to add a few drops to his bathwater, and the bottle of calamine lotion. His infested clothes were taken to the backyard where they would remain until they could be washed. Not knowing exactly what Walter had gotten into, she thought it best to wash Walter's clothes separately.

The thought of Walter putting on clean clothes from his special laundry brought smiles to Robert and Clanton's face. Walter barked orders for someone to wash his back; there wasn't anyone there to hear his orders. As usual, Walter had missed supper, and yes, Betty did leave a plate of food on the stove for him. Betty didn't mind leaving a plate of food for Walter, if it kept her from having to sit at the same table with him. She wasn't ready to share a meal.

The short time Walter had been home, Betty and the boys had been walking around on eggshells just to keep him from ranting and raving. Betty told the boys, "Misery loves company, and Walter didn't want to be alone." Robert thought her statement to be funny and sad at the same time. "To allow Walter to change the way we live and to keep us away from our friends and those we love *is to give him power over us again*," said Betty.

Betty and the boys headed down the road to visit Mr. Will and Ms. Parthina so that Robert and May could spend some time together. Betty had picked some Granny Smith apples from the trees in the backyard; she had baked an apple pie and a few fried pies to take to the Ward family. The trees had produced enough apples to have pies for both families.

Betty carried an apple pie, Robert carried a bushel basket filled with apples, and Clanton carried a plate piled high with fried apple pies. May had passed on an invitation from Ms. Parthina to come for a visit after supper. Since Robert and May were sweet on each other, there'd been lots of visits. Before Walter returned, the two families would take turns with their visits. Mr. Will suggested Betty and the boys should visit at their house, at least while Walter was home. Mr. Will knew Walter called them the hired help and the do-gooders.

Ms. Parthina thought being called the do-gooders was a fine compliment. There was nothing wrong with being the hire help, but the way Walter said it just left a sour taste in Mr. Will's mouth. Betty said, "The hired help, try being married to him."

"Oh no, no, thanks, Betty, that's your job," replied Mr. Will. Betty gave Mr. Will a smile.

While the do-gooders were visiting, Ms. Parthina asked May to go make a pot of coffee. "Take Robert with you…someday he may need to know how to make coffee." The small dessert plates and eating utensils were placed on the table. May served pie while Robert served coffee and milk for the little do-gooders. The kitchen was not too hot to have pie and coffee, but Mr. Will and Ms. Parthina gathered the children to eat outside on the big table under the shade tree. Robert and May ate pie and sipped on black coffee alone in the kitchen. May made a funny little face when she sipped the black coffee; she preferred her coffee with canned milk and sugar. The sweetness of the pie made the black coffee tolerable. May called strong black coffee manly coffee and milk and sugar coffee as girly coffee.

Effie and Lizzy brought the dishes to the kitchen and started the dishwater. They shooed the sweethearts out to the porch swing. Everyone knew Walter was back from Louisiana, but nothing much was said about him. May inquired if Robert and Clanton were happy to have their daddy home. Robert had to give her question some thought before giving an answer. "Well, I haven't seen him that much since he's been home," fibbed Robert.

To change the subject, Robert complimented May on her sweet honeysuckle perfume. "Honeysuckle, but not perfume…it's from a real honeysuckle bush. No matter where we live, Mama always has honeysuckle close to the house. When the wind blows, the sweet smell of honeysuckle fills the house. You don't have to have a green thumb to grow honeysuckles."

Wild flowers and honeysuckles together in a vase made for a pretty centerpiece, so pretty that no one even noticed the vase was a mason jar. Berry picking was a good time to bring home wild flowers. Some days wild flowers were the only thing to bring home; the berries weren't quite ready for picking. During the berry-picking season, Ms. Parthina tried to save enough sugar for making cobblers, jam, jelly, sugar, and canned milk berries and sweet berries over shortcake. What Ms. Parthina made depended on the amount of sugar and berries. If there was no sugar to go with the berries, the berries were washed and eaten plain.

Chapter 14

Betty and her boys returned home with an empty plate, an empty pie pan, and an empty bushel basket. Robert noticed everyone drank, as May called it, manly coffee. Betty noticed the same thing. Maybe they were out of sugar.

"Ms. Parthina usually offers cream and sugar when she is serving coffee. That makes me think she was out of sugar," said Betty.

Clanton suggested buying Ms. Parthina some sugar on their next trip to town; Robert agreed. "Boys, I know you want to do something special for Ms. Parthina, but I'm afraid she will think your act of kindness as a handout." The boys would have to come up with an idea to get Ms. Parthina to accept the sugar and maybe a couple cans of evaporated milk. "With sugar and canned milk, May could enjoy her coffee...girly coffee," Robert said.

"May likes girly coffee...then why not give a gift of sugar and canned milk to May?" suggested Betty. She will share her gift with the rest of her family and Ms. Parthina will have sugar to cook those apples—and have girly coffee too. Robert and Clanton were well pleased with Betty's idea. "Maybe we can go to town in the morning?" Robert asked.

It was finally morning—just barely morning—Robert was up and about before the old rooster crowed. Robert thought about making coffee for Mama and Clanton, but he only had one lesson in the art of making good coffee; he thought maybe he better wait. Mama was up and around, but Clanton was still sleeping.

"I know you're anxious about going to town, but you need a proper breakfast before we go," said Betty. Robert was a little disappointed, but he knew Betty was right, plus Clanton was still sleeping. He watched her pull a mason jar from the refrigerator with leftover coffee. The coffee was poured into a cooking pot to be reheated. Sleepy Clanton came to see what was going on so early.

"Why are we up before the chickens?" yawned Clanton.

"The chickens are up…and we're going to town. Go brush your teeth and brush that wild hair down," Robert said. The pitch in Robert's voice was high with excitement; if it got any higher, he would be able to sing soprano in the church choir.

Bless his little heart, Robert was so ready to get started. Betty drank her girly coffee and made scrambled egg sandwiches for them to eat on the way to town. Clanton had done just as Robert told him; that wild hair was all slicked down, hopefully he brushed his teeth, but Robert wasn't going to smell his breath. Betty did ask to see his teeth; they were clean.

Everyone knew a scrambled egg sandwich had to have mayonnaise. One slice of bread could have a lot of mayonnaise or both slices could have mayonnaise; either way, the mayonnaise added to the flavor and would keep the scrambled eggs from falling out of the sandwich. Clanton smashed his sandwich to make sure the mayonnaise would hold his eggs. That was a good idea; Betty and Robert both smashed their sandwich.

The coffee that was left in the cooking pot and enough scrambled eggs for Walter to have breakfast were left on the stove. As much as Betty disliked Walter and his rotten ways, she wasn't going to let him starve. However, her kitchen was not a café where people could order whatever they wanted from a menu. He could eat what she cooked or do without.

The cool breeze made for an enjoyable walk to town. Betty pointed out that there was no need to be in a big hurry; the general store didn't open until seven o'clock. Robert's walking speed was also his eating speed: the faster he walked, the faster his sandwich was gobbled. The Ward's dog, Coley, didn't alarm the family of strangers walking by; he just wagged his tail and allowed Betty and the boys to keep walking. Robert was happy that Coley didn't make a big fuss; he wanted his trip to town to be a big surprise for May and her family.

Betty, Robert, and Clanton sat dangling their feet from the porch of the general store. Mr. Bailey and Ms. Ida could be heard talking to each other as they prepared to open the store. Betty stood back and allowed Robert to place his order. "Ms. Ida do you have any wrapping paper or bows? This is a gift for May Ward and her family," asked Robert.

Ms. Ida was sorry to say that she had no bows and only had butcher paper. However, she did have something that might give his gift a little splash of color. Ms. Ida had taken different lengths of rope and dyed them and until right then she wasn't sure how she would use them. "The colored rope can be used to tie a package and give it some color, making for a beautiful gift," explained Ms. Ida.

Mr. Bailey was ready to tally the cost, but Betty wanted to add one more item to the bill.

"With your permission, Robert, I'd like to add two pounds of coffee to the bill." Robert thought adding coffee was a good idea; it would be a shame to have all this sugar and canned milk and not have any coffee. The sugar and coffee were each wrapped in butcher paper; the canned milk was put in a small paper bag. Ms. Ida filled the box and measured the red rope. The box wasn't heavy, just a little bulky; if it was heavy, Robert never noticed.

Ms. Parthina was starting a stew for supper. Lizzy and Effie had just started the laundry, and May was stripping the beds. Robert nervously knocked and asked to see May. Ms. Parthina called to May, "Robert is here to see you."

Robert stood like a statue just inside the front door, still holding the box. Ms. Parthina took the bundle of laundry from

May and help Robert the statue to the kitchen. "Robert, don't keep her too long. She has work to do."

Robert didn't know exactly how to present May with a gift; May didn't know exactly how to accept a gift from him. "I hope you don't think this gift to be too practical," said Robert. May's response was "I like practical."

"Now you can have girly coffee," whispered Robert.

Some might consider canned milk, sugar, and coffee to be a practical gift, but May thought it to be the sweetest practical gift she could ever receive.

Betty and Clanton didn't walk too far ahead of Robert; they wanted to hear what May thought about her gift. "Mama, I thought I was going to fall over with fright before I even saw May. Ms. Parthina joined the other girls out back doing laundry; I got to be alone with May in the kitchen. May hugged me and kissed me on my cheek…this cheek right here." Clanton wanted to know, "Did you like being hugged and kissed on the cheek?"

"I did, but my face turned red…I could feel it turning red." The rest of the walk home was all quiet.

Walter was drinking leftover coffee under the big shade tree; his face was covered with pink calamine lotion. Betty and the boys had to get their snickering over before they got too close; they didn't want Walter to hear them. The closer they got to Walter, the more they wanted to burst out laughing. It was easy to hold a snicker inside, but a bust-out loud laugh was very hard to hold. They tried not to stare, but it couldn't be helped. Walter snapped, "What are you gawking at?" The bust-out laughing could no longer be held inside.

Betty sent the boys on to the house before Walter could start his fussing and cussing. The more Walter talked the more Betty laughed. The boys were listening and laughing just inside the back door. Usually, Walter's fussing and cussing came with a red face, but not this time. His red face couldn't be seen for all the pink; from his forehead all the way down his neck and both ears were covered with pink lotion. Of course, Walter didn't see the humor at all.

"Don't you care that I'm sick?" Walter pouted.

"You did this to yourself, and not really," smirked Betty. The only thing Betty was willing to do for Walter was to keep him from starving. She hoped he would grow tired of being ignored and go back to Louisiana. Walter was such a big baby and a whiner when he was sick. "Poor little Walter."

The sun was high in the sky. Robert and Clanton were finished doing their chores. Walter the drunk took two shots of his bootleg whiskey and went back to bed. Robert and Clanton went fishing, maybe they could have fish for their supper. Betty was making bread: two loaves of regular bread and one loaf of cinnamon raisin bread.

Walter had finally come to the conclusion that no one was happy to see him. Between shots of whiskey to ease his rash and bug bites, Walter talked about leaving; he made it clear that he was waiting for laundry day. Having clean clothes was the only thing keeping Walter from leaving. Betty gathered Walter's clothes and put them in one of the big washtubs with detergent and cold water. The big black boiling pot was filled with water and a low fire underneath would be for rinsing. Betty didn't use the rubbed board; she wasn't going to touch his rash- and bug-infested clothes. His clothes were soaked in the wash water until the boiling pot was ready for rinsing. Walter's laundry was done with a lick and a promise.

Betty wasn't overly fond of doing laundry, but this time was different. Clean laundry was a small price to pay to get rid of Walter. Robert and Clanton were surprised to see Betty doing laundry; they knew it wasn't laundry day, and it was too late in the day to start laundry.

"Look, Mama, we got fish," shouted Clanton. Betty was wearing a pair of her girly work gloves, which made Robert and Clanton a little uneasy.

Robert volunteered to clean the fish; Clanton was volunteered by Robert to hang the laundry to dry.

"No need to worry, Clanton, the soap and hot water killed the rash and bug bites from Walter's clothes," Betty softly said. "I don't think you'll need to wear work gloves this time," Betty said with a wink. Clanton quickly agreed and headed to the clotheslines.

Did Betty know what the boys had done to Walter's laundry, or was she just fishing for information based on what she thought she knew? Robert and Clanton agreed to never admit what they had done. Once the poison ivy took over, Walter was too busy itching, scratching, and drinking whiskey to make their lives too miserable. To hear all it would take to get Walter to leave was clean clothes and a packed suitcase was music to the ears. Robert and Clanton now understood why Betty was doing laundry so late in the day.

Robert filleted the fish, Clanton hung Walter's laundry to dry, and Betty made coleslaw and hush puppies. Betty and the boys had managed to avoid sharing a meal with Walter since his return. Some meals at the Cartwright house were purposely planned to avoid him.

Morning came with the smell of coffee, but there was no smell of breakfast. Walter was surprised to find his clean laundry folded and packed in his suitcase. The suitcase laid open in the middle of the kitchen table waiting for the rest of his things to be packed. Betty had even packed Walter a sack lunch for his trip. Walter drank his coffee and stared at the suitcase.

Walter yelled for Robert and Clanton to come to the house; they didn't move an inch. The second call was the same; they didn't move an inch. There was no third call. Walter flung the screen door open and left a streak of cuss words from the house to the shade tree. "I know you heard me calling twice. Why didn't you come to the house?" yelled Walter. He was all red in the face waiting for an answer. "I told the boys they were old enough to decide whether they would come a running or not when you called them."

Walter flew into a fit of rage; he slapped Betty across the face, knocking her out of the chair where she sat. Robert jumped to her defense, giving Walter what he had given to Betty. Robert and Clanton rushed to see if Betty was all right; they tenderly help her back to her chair. Walter was wiping blood from his nose when he got to his feet.

Robert and Clanton stood as a shield to protect Betty. "Why are you boys taking up for her? I'm you daddy."

Robert quickly replied, "Betty has been more of a mama than you have ever been as a daddy!"

"Needing clean clothes was the only thing keeping you from leaving…now you have clean clothes, and it's time for you to leave," said Betty with a forceful voice.

"Come on, Walter, let's make sure you're all packed and ready to go," Robert said with a slight nudge. Robert's soft tone seemed to take the fire out of the situation. Betty and Clanton watched as Robert gently directed Walter to the house.

Robert helped Walter double-check for anything he might have forgotten to pack. Walter had carefully packed his bootleg whiskey in a box of clothes. Robert helped him load his belongings into the cab of the old truck. Never raising his voice, Robert told Walter there was no need for him to come back. "I took no pleasure in striking you, but if you ever slap or hurt my Mama again, I will do more than give you a bloody nose."

Robert felt a little sad as he watched Walter drive away. He thought maybe things could have been handled better, but when Robert saw Betty's face, his sadness went away. There was no doubt Betty was going to have a black eye. An ice pack was applied to hold down the swelling. Robert and Clanton thought getting rid of Walter would be much more enjoyable. They never meant for Betty to get a black eye because of them, and for that, they were sorry.

Betty apologized to the boys; she felt as if she had put them right in the middle of the Walter saga. "A man that abandons his family for any reason, is a poor excuse for a father, a husband, and a man," said Robert. "Starting tomorrow, we will start not missing Walter," Clanton said with a chuckle. It was agreed; tomorrow they would start *not* missing Walter.

Chapter 15

Tomorrow came, and it was a fine day to start not missing Walter. It didn't take long for Betty and the boys to get back to their regular routines. Before Betty moved back to her bedroom, she cleaned, scrubbed, and disinfected everything that Walter might have touched. The drawers from the chest were disinfected and set outside to dry. The mattress was disinfected and flipped. Anything Walter left in the closet or chest was put into the trash barrel to be burned later. Life was good; Betty and her sons were happy.

Robert and Clanton worked hard to get their chores done. Chores were to be done before any playtime; however, suppertime was quitting time. Most after-supper visits were at the Ward's house; Betty didn't have a big table under her shade tree. Robert and May called Saturday their date day. All the older children went to town on Saturday, but they waited until Robert and May had already left before they started their walk to town. Robert and May enjoyed walking with just each other. Later, they would all meet at the general store and walk home together. Robert liked date day; he got to hold May's hand most of the day.

On Sunday mornings, May would be sitting on the porch waiting for Robert to walk her to church. It was hard for the small Ward children to walk two miles to church, so Ms. Parthina had Sunday school at home.

"Papa doesn't go to church. Why do I have to go?" pleaded Seaburn.

"I'm not raising a pack of heathens, you're going to church. Papa believes in the Heavenly Father he just chooses to talk to him in private."

Mary Jane, Don, Shorty, and little Dolly were feed their breakfast before putting on their Sunday's best. Ms. Parthina made sure their clothes were clean and pressed for Sunday. Ms. Parthina had an old Sunday school book that she taught from along with her Bible. Mr. Will avoided the rush to get dressed for church by checking on the crops, whether the crops needed it or not. He always drank his first cup of coffee with Ms. Parthina before the clanging and banging started from the children. As Mr. Will walked up and down the rows of corn, he left little puffs of smoke from his pipe. Shorty and Don called the little puffs of smoke smoke signals; they liked to pretend they could read smoke signals.

After Sunday school, Mary Jane and Shorty helped Don and little Dolly change back into their everyday clothes; their Sunday clothes were put away for the next Sunday. Lunch usually consisted of leftover fried chicken, pinto beans, potato salad, sliced tomatoes, and a fresh pan of cornbread. Ms. Parthina tried to have enough leftovers from Saturday's supper to have for lunch on Sunday. Lunch was usually topped off with a slice of fresh coconut cake.

With the changing of the seasons came barn dances, harvest balls, and church socials. Although Seaburn wasn't much for dancing, he did serve as an escort for Effie and Lizzy. There were plenty of young men for dancing; Effie and Lizzy had no problem getting a dance partner. Of course, May and Robert danced with each other only; they were what you called "going steady." Seaburn was protector for his sisters until they arrived home.

Shortly before the last harvest ball of the season, Robert finely got around to asking Mr. Will for May's hand in marriage.

"Now let me get this straight...you only want to marry her hand," Mr. Will snickered. Robert was so nervous the little joke went right over his head. Mr. Will slapped Robert on his back and told him, "Breathe, Robert, breathe," Mr. Will asked a few questions that a future father-in-law should ask before turning his daughter over to anyone.

Robert pulled a pretty little ring from his pocket for Mr. Will to inspect.

"This ring once belonged to my grandmother…Octavia Watkins Baker, and then it was passed down to Mama…Betty Baker Cartwright. If May will have me, this ring will be passed down to her."

"When May says yes, we will be happy to call you family. It has taken you two years to ask for her hand, let's hope it doesn't take two years to get you too married."

Robert quickly replied, "No, sir, it will not take that long."

Betty and Clanton had been invited to have coffee with Ms. Parthina while the young folks attended the harvest ball. Betty and Ms. Parthina were pretty sure this would be the night Robert would propose to May, but the where they didn't know. This was not the first time Robert stood frozen at the front door. Mary Jane asked, "Are you going to faint, Robert? Your legs look a little wobbly."

Ms. Parthina shooed Mary Jane and Shorty off to the kitchen for cookies and milk. Effie and Lizzy strolled to the kitchen to show how pretty they looked for the harvest ball. Seaburn was sure Robert was going to faint, but with a little nudging, he got Robert to the couch. The kitchen was full of onlookers.

Robert met May in the center of the living room. He commented on her beauty with a kiss to her hand. The kiss to her hand was followed with a declaration of his love. He quickly dropped to one knee, revealing the engagement ring. May was taken by surprised; she looked to Mr. Will and Ms. Parthina, who, along with the rest of family, stood in the doorway from the kitchen. Mr. Will said, "Don't look at me. We've already had our little talk. Now it's up to you." As May said yes, Robert placed the engagement ring on her now shaky finger.

"Getting engaged should be shared with your friends. Go to the harvest ball and show off your new fiancé and that beautiful engagement ring," said Ms. Parthina. Betty agreed. Mr. Will left the kitchen and returned with an old violin case, which held a well preserved violin. "A little toe-tapping music would be nice about now," he said. Betty had no idea Mr. Will could play the violin; she found him to be quiet entertaining. Mary Jane, Shorty, and Don pretended to dance, and little Dolly bounced to the sound of the music.

Ms. Jennifer Byrd and Ms. René Saavedra were the first to see May's engagement ring. Ms. Jennifer was there to chaperone her girls, Devin and Megan. Ms. René was there to chaperone her daughter Kiaya and her son Zech. Mr. Joey Tutor, brother to Ms. Jennifer and Ms. René, had two daughters, Katie Beth and Leia, and two sons, Joseph and little Jake. Besides being there as a chaperone, Mr. Joey was on punch patrol. He was to make sure the punch wasn't spiked with hard liquor. Anyone caught with hard liquor was asked to leave.

It wasn't long until everyone at the harvest ball heard the news. The young ladies were flocking to see the engagement ring. Some of the young men looked as if they were being dragged to the gallows; some thought that if they got too close, they might catch something, and others were "squirming like a maggot in hot ashes."

Seaburn was able to pull Robert from a circle of squealing girls. "Look at May...she is beaming like a bright star," said Robert. Seaburn had never seen May look so happy; she wasn't her usual shy self. With great pride, May gave the details of how Robert had proposed; his proposal was "very romantic."

"Now all these girls will be expecting a romantic proposal," laughed Seaburn. Robert pointed out, "Speaking from the heart should be romantic." Seaburn reluctantly admitted he had no romantic bones in his body—much less those mushy words. Robert admitted that neither did he, until he met and fell in love with May.

Now for his last question, Seaburn wanted to know, "What took you so long to propose?" Robert snickered, "I had to make sure Mr. Will wouldn't kill me and feed me to the hogs. First, I talked to my mama who talked to your mama who talked to Mr. Will. Mr. Will told your mama, who told my mama, who told me that I was safe from the hogs as long as I didn't mistreat May. He had me running all over the place, trying to catch him alone." There was no doubt where Alvie and Seaburn got their love for practical jokes.

Robert and May managed to slip away for a cup of punch and then a dance. Everyone seemed to be having a good time. Seaburn was even seen out on the dance floor. Between dances, Effie and Lizzy would visit with May and Robert. Bales of hay were used as chairs; while Effie and Lizzy rested, Robert went for punch.

Seaburn was in charge of the time; it was his responsibly to make sure the girls got home by their curfew. Mr. Will's curfew meant inside the house with the door latched, not sitting on the porch smooching. Ms. Parthina set the curfew, but Mr. Will was the one to enforce it. Getting engaged was a special occasion; Ms. Parthina extended the curfew to eleven o'clock. The reputation of a young woman could be ruined by something as simple as staying out too late. Ms. Parthina made sure all the children understood the importance of a good reputation.

"Mama and Papa got married at the Pope County courthouse on October 16, 1905[4] by a justice of the peace, and we got engaged on their anniversary," said May. "Our knowledge of a wedding or planning a wedding is very limited," admitted Effie. "Mama will be happy to help, but only if she is properly asked by the bride or the bride's family."

"I would very much like Betty to help with the planning of our wedding," May softly said.

May admired her engagement ring all through breakfast. Her girly coffee even tasted a little sweeter when a touch of happiness was added. Ms. Parthina piddled around the living room as she anxiously watched for Betty and the surprise she promised to bring. She didn't know what the surprise was, but she was sure it would be special. Coley barked a couple of times just to let the family know there was company, friendly company. Betty was carrying a black garment bag, which at first glance wasn't noticed. May was given the garment bag with the assurance she was not obligated to wear the dress if she didn't like it.

The dress was the most beautiful dress May had ever seen; the silhouette was ball gown or duchess; it was white satin with a choker neck, long sleeves, and decorative hair pins to match the torso of the dress instead of a veil. May was in awe; she was almost speechless, and Ms. Parthina was speechless.

"You do like the dress?" asked Betty. May quickly said, "Yes, yes, yes, I love it!"

Ms. Parthina sent Effie for her sewing basket while Lizzy helped May try on the wedding dress. The length of the dress was just right, but the rest would need alterations; May was a little smaller than Betty. Until the dress was measured for the alterations, no one would have ever guessed May to have a cute little figure.

"This hen party is disturbing the worms out back," Mr. Will jokingly said. Wanting to see a hen party up close and personal caused Mr. Will to forget the can of worms in his hand. One look at May in her soon-to-be wedding dress took Mr. Will by surprise; all he could say was "Lordly, lordly."

Shorty spoke up. "Papa, you're not suppose to see the bride in her dress until the wedding day. Isn't that right, Mama?"

"It's the groom, Robert, but since Papa has seen May in her dress, I think he should be sworn to secrecy."

163

"Papa gets in trouble when he swears. Couldn't he just make a big promise, instead?" asked Shorty. Mr. Will made a big promise not to tell Robert how beautiful May looked in her new dress.

Mr. Will thought Don was old enough to go fishing with him and Seaburn. "Get some shoes on and don't forget you little straw hat."

"Can Robert and Clanton go fishing with us, Papa?" asked Don. "If it's all right with their mama, it's all right with me. Us boys need to stick together," laughed Mr. Will. Ms. Betty gave her all-right nod to Mr. Will. "Mama, can we eat the fish that I catch, and can Ms. Betty, Robert, and Clanton eat fish supper with us?" asked Don. Ms. Parthina thought Don's idea was a good idea, and she said yes.

Ms. Parthina shouted from the front porch, "Have fun and be careful." Mr. Will raised his arm high in the air with a slight wave to acknowledge he heard and understood. By the time Mr. Will and the boys got to the Cartwright house, Robert and Clanton had just finished digging worms for a day of fishing. "Look, Clanton, I get to go fishing, and I'm in charge of our big fat juicy worms. Big fat worms catch big fish. I'm going to catch a big fish to have for our supper, and Ms. Betty said y'all can eat fish supper with us tonight."

"Papa says fishing and loud talking don't go together. If we need to talk, it should be a whisper," Don proudly said. Mr. Will and Robert fished next to each other, and they talked in whispers. Don was sure the fish couldn't hear them because he couldn't hear them. Seaburn caught a fat fish, and Clanton caught a little fish and Don was still trying to catch a fish.

Seaburn added a bobber to Don's fishing line so he would be able to tell when he had a fish on the line. Don sat patiently watching the little cork bobber swirl around in the water. Finally the little bobber went under the water; Don jerked his little cane pole to secure the fish on his hook. He wanted to bring his first fish to the bank without help from anyone, and he did. The little fish was on the ground flipping and flopping; Don was jumping up and down. "I did it...I did it! I caught a fish all by myself."

Clanton removed the hooks from Don's fish, and Seaburn put Don's fish on the stringer. He didn't mind the help with the hooks and stringers; he could get back to his fishing faster. Don had already learned how to bait his hook with a big, fat, juicy worm; but he needed to practice on how to cast his line. Don never did catch that big fish for supper, but he did catch four little fishes; according to Mr. Will four little fishes is equal to one big fish.

"Catching fish makes me thirsty, Papa. Do we have any cavalry water?"

Mr. Will always carried an old canteen that once belonged to Ms. Parthina's Papa, David Dudley. Private David Dudley [5] served with Company G Twelfth Regiment, Alabama Cavalry, CSA (Confederate States of America). The children of Will and Parthina Ward referred to the water from the old canteen as cavalry water. Once upon a time, Ms. Parthina had an old tintype photograph of Private Dudley in his Confederate uniform, but with all the moving from pillar to post, it was lost. Also in her possession was a Bible that once belonged to her mama, Nancy Elizabeth Jinks Dudley. The oversized King James Version was in very poor condition; the cover was no longer to be found and the pages were becoming brittle. Ms. Parthina had gently tied the pages together with a small piece of ribbon; it was then placed in an oversized boot box, which was stored in the top of her closet.

Don drank from the old canteen, and then it was passed around so the others could have a drink. Their stringers were full, and their stomachs were empty; it was time to head to the house. Mr. Will allowed Don to carry the old canteen; the long strap made it easy to carry. He slipped the strap over his head and one shoulder, the same way Mr. Will carried it. Any leftover bait was given to the fish still in the pond. Don walked straight and proud; he caught four fishes, and now he was carrying the old canteen that held the cavalry water.

Betty met Mr. Will and the boys on her way home. Robert and Clanton were planning to help Mr. Will clean the fish after a little lunch. "Ms. Parthina said y'all should be home shortly for some lunch. After you help Mr. Will clean the fish…y'all should come home. You will have time to visit when we come back for supper. I'm going to make an apple cobbler for dessert, and Ms. Parthina is planning to have homemade vanilla ice cream to go with the cobbler."

Robert and May's engagement was truly an occasion to be celebrated.

Chapter 16

Most of the time, a fish supper would be considered casual, but this wasn't one of those times. Everyone was dressed in their Sunday's best; the table was set with a lace tablecloth and cloth napkins. The center of the table was adorned with freshly cut honeysuckle. There was plenty of happiness to go around; some might call the happiness contagious.

The ladies had put their heads together and came up with Valentine's Day for the wedding date. May sweetly looked to Robert for a sign of his agreement. Mr. Will congratulated Robert for his ability to see; he had no choice when that many women were in agreement. "These women are on a mission…it would be best to stay out of their way, otherwise they will run you down," advised Mr. Will.

Letters were written to family members to announce the engagement of Ms. Nettie May Ward to Mr. Robert Chesterfield Cartwright on Sunday, February 14, 1928, at Dover Baptist Church.

Mrs. Mary Jane (Cagle) Ward, mother of Mr. Will Ward, and his sister, Mrs. Frankie (Ward) Goates, answered the invitation right away; they were planning to attend. Mrs. Dora Ellen Petty and Mrs. Vallie Thompson, sisters to Mr. Will, could not give a definite yes or no; but they would try their best. Ms. Parthina was happy to hear from her sister, Mary Catherine (Dudley) Lee, and David Dudley, her brother; they would attend also.

Ms. Betty's parents, Thomas and Octavia Baker, seemed to be extra excited to hear the good news. Mr. and Mrs. Baker just recently became the happy grandparents of Robert and Clanton Cartwright. Grandma Octavia was very proud to hear that Robert had given May the engagement ring that had been passed down through her family, the Watkins.

Ms. Betty and Ms. Parthina called on Rev. Vanderburg who agreed to perform the wedding ceremony. The reverend's wife, Mary Catherine, served the ladies tea while they discussed details for the wedding. Their tea was served in a proper teacup with a saucer; Ms. Parthina didn't realize drinking tea from a proper teacup with a saucer was known by others.

Mary Catherine quietly listened while sipping her tea. Ms. Betty described the wedding dress with great details. Mary Catherine didn't want to step on the reverend's toes, but it was time for a woman's touch. "We should plan the wedding around that beautiful wedding dress," said Mary Catherine. "What about having the wedding right after the Sunday service? Many of your friends and family will already be in the church."

The church meeting area was perfect for the reception. Ms. Ida volunteered to make the wedding cake and the use of her heavy-duty coffeemaker. Mary Catherine would provide the punch. "Now for the decorations, Ms. Carol Taylor had set up shop in the back of the general store. She is trying to get her business establish. I'm sure she will be happy to haggle for her services," snickered Mary Catherine.

Ms. Carol's service included bows for the church pews, the bride's bouquet, and white carnations for the groom, father of the bride, and the best man. Ms. Betty and Ms. Parthina would wear red carnations. The bridesmaids would have to be both Effie and Lizzy; there was no way she could choose one over the other; they would wear red carnations.

Ms. Carol also offered to provide small paper plates, napkins, and plastic forks for two jars of Ms. Parthina's blackberry jelly and one jar of Ms. Betty's apple butter. A bargain was struck. Money and a few jars of jelly seemed like a good deal for all. Ms. Carol had two children, Toney and Jessica, and they sure loved Ms. Parthina's blackberry jelly. The apple butter was for Carol. If Toney and Jessica had their own jar of jelly, they wouldn't be fussing over the jelly. Ms. Carol was lucky; her kids didn't much like apple butter.

Rev. Vanderburg would perform the wedding ceremony, the refreshments were chosen, including the wedding cake, the flowers, and other decorations. May and Robert chose the colors for the wedding. They chose their wedding cake from a picture in one of Ms. Ida's cookbooks; it was to have three tiers.

Four months to plan and execute a wedding wasn't as easy as some might think. Ms. Parthina was sure happy that Ms. Betty had experience. Grandpa Tom, Betty's father, had sent money to help with the wedding cost. The ladies took a trip to Russellville to shop for material for dresses and maybe some shoes. Ms. Parthina was a practical spender; she wanted to style the dresses for Effie and Lizzy a little different from each other so they could be worn after the wedding; they would have a new Sunday dress.

A bargain was struck between Ms. Parthina and Ms. Betty; Ms. Betty would pay for the cloth and other sewing notions and new shoes for May, Effie, and Lizzy. In return, Ms. Parthina would make the bridesmaids dresses, a traveling dress for May, alter the wedding dress and a suit that once belonged to Walter.

The Ward sisters found a pattern with three different styles of the same dress. The material was a soft red with white dots— not polka dots but Swiss dots. Each of the sisters chose which style they wanted for their dress; May got to choose first. Ms. Parthina was surprised to see there was no fussing about the styles; everyone got the style they wanted.

The girls were so excited about getting new shoes. Their feet were measured to get the perfect fit. With the perfect fit, there was no need to stuff the toes of the shoes with paper. If the shoes were too tight, water was poured into the shoes and then worn until they dried. Another good way to stretch shoes is to fill the shoes with pinto beans and water then soak overnight; the shoes are stretched and the beans are soaked and ready to cook.

Ms. Carol finished her shopping and patiently waited for Ms. Parthina and the others to finish. Ms. Parthina and Ms. Betty rode up front in the truck with Ms. Carol. The sisters were huddled under a quilt in the back of the truck, holding the boxes that held their new shoes.

Ms. Parthina and Ms. Betty put their heads together and came up with the best Thanksgiving dinner either family ever had: baked ham, baked chicken, chicken and cornbread dressing, green bean casserole, sweet potato casserole, mashed potatoes with gravy, congealed salad (the green stuff), and Ms. Parthina's homemade biscuits that melted in your mouth. For dessert, there were chocolate pie, pumpkin pie, pecan pie, fudge pie, and banana pudding. "With that much food, you couldn't help but gobble like a hog, eat like a field hand," according to Ms. Parthina.

Planning the Thanksgiving menu gave Ms. Parthina and Ms. Betty a chance to think about something other than wedding plans. Both Effie and Lizzy were ready to help Ms. Parthina with her dressmaking; it was time to make their dresses. The alterations to the wedding dress were completed. The alterations to the suit for Robert were also completed. May's travel dress was ready for the final fitting; the bridesmaids' dresses were ready to cut out.

Ms. Betty wasn't one to sew, but she did know how to mend and hem. May, Effie, and Lizzy were called to the bedroom for one last fitting; they were allowed to try on their new shoes with their new dress. Just like May, Effie and Lizzy had been hiding a cute figure under those sack dressing they had been wearing. "Beautiful, all of you," said Ms. Parthina.

Mr. Will didn't allow sneaking around, whispering, hiding things from others...except at Christmastime. Mr. Will and Robert seemed to have their heads together a lot; was it a

Christmas surprise or a wedding surprise, no one knew for sure. On the third week of December, the children headed to the woods to find Christmas trees: one for the Ward house and one for the Cartwright house. Robert and Seaburn were in charge of the axes while the others search the woods for the perfect trees. The Cartwright's Christmas tree was decorated without any help from the Ward children. Ms. Parthina reminded everyone that this is the season to ask no questions. Who knows, maybe Santa Claus has already dropped off some gifts, and Ms. Betty is his helper. "I didn't know Santa Claus could come early," said Shorty.

Ms. Parthina invited the little ones to the kitchen for milk and a buttered biscuit with jelly while she told them about Santa Claus.

"Mr. and Mrs. Santa Claus live at the North Pole. Santa and the little elves work all year long making toys for the children. When a Christmas present is really big, Santa delivers it early with the help of mamas and papas. Some of Santa's presents are wrapped in pretty paper and some are just placed under the tree. Some mamas and papas tell their kids that they have to be good or Santa won't bring them a present. Santa and I had a good talk about that very thing. He told me that good or bad, every child should get a present. If Santa doesn't leave a present, it's because he ran out of toys."

Shorty's little face was all lit up with excitement. "Mama, does Santa have a jolly belly?" Maybe she meant a "jolly laugh" and a "round belly"—a jolly belly. "Mama, if I whisper to you what I want Santa to bring me, will you tell him for me? Will you tell him I have been a good girl, and I should get a good present?"

Don and little Dolly shouted, "Me too, me too, Mama." There was one more request from Shorty. "Can we save some jelly for Santa's buttered biscuit and milk?"

"Blackberry jelly is Santa's favorite. We will save some for his buttered biscuit," promised Ms. Parthina.

Ms. Parthina told the children, "I think we should write a letter to Santa Claus to make sure he doesn't forget your Christmas wishes." Shorty could write her name all by herself, but anything else, she would need help. Don and little Dolly watched as Shorty wrote her letter to Santa. Shorty wanted to keep her wish a secret; Mama helped Shorty write "jacks and jack ball."

"Don and Dolly can't read so they won't know what my wish is, ain't that right, Mama?" Mama agreed. Ms. Parthina wrote Don's letter to Santa; he wanted a ball used for playing catch. Little Dolly wanted a toy for her Christmas present; she didn't care what kind of toy—just a toy, she said. Ms. Parthina put the three letters in one envelope to be mailed to Santa Claus at the North Pole. Shorty got to write "Santa Claus" on the envelope.

Ms. Parthina had gotten a little carried away talking about Santa Claus. Now there were letters to Santa to be mailed. The next morning, Ms. Parthina and the little ones made a trip to town to mail their letters. Ms. Parthina spoke softly to Mr. Scoggins who worked the front window at the post office. Mr. Scoggins leaned over the counter to see Shorty holding a letter addressed to Santa Claus. Mr. Scoggins had a little talk with Mr. Rainey who worked in the back of the post office. Mr. Rainey brought a large container with a little note attached, "Letters to Santa Claus, The North Pole. No postage needed."

"Are we too late to mail our letters to Santa Claus?" asked Shorty.

Mr. Rainey assured the little ones that all letters to Santa Claus were delivered right away. *Mr. Dale Rainey is* Santa's special postman.

Mr. Rainey shook hands with Shorty, Don, and little Dolly. Before leaving the post office, Mr. Rainey gave Shorty a sheet of paper to give to Mr. Bailey at the general store. "You still have time to mail your letters to Santa Claus at the North Pole. No postage needed, signed by Santa's special postman."

Mr. Bailey carefully read the notice from Santa's special postman. "Oh my, I have been meaning to drop by the post office for this notice," said Ms. Ida. Mr. Bailey shook Shorty's little hand, which was the second time in one day that Shorty had her hand shook. "Helping Santa's special postman is a very important job. I think I have a few Christmas cookies that need tasting before I make more. Will you taste the cookies and let me know if they taste good?" asked Ms. Ida. Shorty thanked Ms. Ida for a chance to taste her Christmas cookies. For a proper taste test of her Christmas cookies, Ms. Ida provided a cup of milk to help with the taste.

"Sometimes I forget about Santa's special postman. Our children are all grown up, and it just slips my mind." Mr. Bailey talked about Santa Claus, the North Pole, the special postman, and polar bears as he pointed to the open door leading to the back of the store. Ms. Ida soon closed the door; she and the little ones could hear Mr. Bailey talking.

Ms. Idea kept the little ones occupied with cookies and milk while Ms. Parthina and Mr. Bailey talked business. As usual, Ms. Parthina didn't have much cash money, but she always had things to barter. Ms. Parthina planned to make pinafores for Shorty and Mary Jane and a new dress for little Dolly. Mr. Bailey had just the right amount of material Ms. Parthina needed, and Ms. Parthina had just the right amount of money Mr. Bailey needed.

The general store's glass display case held exactly what Shorty and Don wanted from Santa Claus. Ms. Parthina was wondering how they came to ask for those items for Christmas. Mr. Bailey brought the soft ball, the jacks set, and even the cutest Kewpie doll from the display case. Ms. Parthina hated asking how much, but this was what Santa Claus would bring her children. Mr. Bailey was ready to strike a bargain. "Are we talking cash money or barter?" he asked.

"Barter," replied Ms. Parthina. "Since the items are slightly used, and the little Kewpie doll has no clothes, how about two jars of your sweet pickles and one jar of your blackberry jelly?" Ms. Parthina agreed. Mr. Bailey wrapped three packages in brown butcher paper and tied each with a piece of red rope for decoration.

"You can bring the pickles and jelly the next time you come to town. I trust you, and besides that, I know where you live."

Ms. Parthina called to the children, "It's time to go home." Shorty thanked Ms. Ida for their Christmas cookies and milk. She proudly told Ms. Ida her Christmas cookies were very good, and it would be all right to make more. Mr. Bailey thanked Shorty for bringing the notice from Santa's special postman.

The whole way home, Shorty talked about meeting Santa's special postman and how she got to be his helper. Don and little Dolly met Santa's special postman too but they didn't get to be his helper. Don thought maybe the postman picked Shorty because she was taller; even so, he was excited for her. "Mama, did you know that Santa's special postman was Mr. Rainey?" Ms. Parthina could honestly say she did not know.

The little ones were so excited about their trip to town and all that happened, they never noticed Ms. Parthina was carrying a bag that looked to be full to the brim. Ms. Parthina reminded the little ones that it was too close to Christmas to be asking questions. Not knowing what was in the bag wasn't that important; they met Santa's special postman.

Ms. Parthina and her sewing machine were hidden away in the bedroom. Effie, Lizzy, and May took over Ms. Parthina's duties while she finished the Christmas sewing. By suppertime, Ms. Parthina was ready for a break. Ms. Betty brought a covered dish and dessert each night to have supper with the Ward family. Ms. Betty and May were both becoming good cooks. Mr. Will was no longer worried that Robert might starve from May's cooking.

Each evening Ms. Betty brought a present to put under the Christmas tree. She had been doing a little sewing of her own. The presents were wrapped, and they had name stickers. Occasionally the little ones were allowed to hold a presents with their name. The presents were shaken and sniffed; they even tried to sneak a peek if there was a gap in the taping.

Two days before Christmas, Ms. Parthina emerged from the bedroom to announce that her Christmas sewing was finished. She didn't tell that she was also finished with the wedding sewing. May, Effie, and Lizzy all agreed to wrap their new shoes and place them under the Christmas tree. Everyone would have a present to open on Christmas morning.

Ms. Betty and the Ward girls were double-checking the Christmas menu. Christmas plans, wedding plans—Ms. Parthina was in need of a soothing cup of tea. Effie put the pot on to boil. Lizzy set out the teacups with saucers with the matching creamer and sugar bowl. The matching teapot was filled with hot tea to be served by May. Effie called drinking tea from a teacup with a proper saucer sissy tea. Sissy tea wasn't Effie's favorite way to drink tea.

"Pickles and jelly," said Ms. Parthina. "Oh my goodness, I forgot to get Mr. Bailey his pickles and jelly."

"Mama, two jars of sweet pickles and one jar of blackberry jelly was taken to Mr. Bailey the same day you and the little ones meet Santa's special postman. Seaburn, Robert, and Clanton delivered the pickles and jelly. They were going to town anyway," said May. Ms. Parthina wasn't thinking when she asked why the boys went to town; Christmas secrets are allowed, remember?

Christmas Eve supper was breakfast: bacon, eggs, white gravy, and plenty of biscuits. Shorty was in charge of Santa's buttered biscuit with jelly. She added a little extra butter and a little extra jelly "because Santa works hard to bring stuff at Christmas." Mr. Will was put to bed with the rest of the children; he put up a fuss just like the rest. Ms. Parthina had herself a nice cup of tea as she waited for all to be fast asleep. Mr. Will was asleep, and he snored. If anyone was still awake, they were good at playing possum.

Santa's wrapped presents to the little ones were gently placed under the tree. Santa brought so many hanging clothes, Ms. Parthina made a clothesline to display them. Santa brought Mary Jane and Shorty new pinafores, little Dolly got a new dress, and Don got a new pair of long pants. Mr. Will and Seaburn got new shirts.

Ms. Betty made new hair ribbons for Mary Jane, Shorty, and little Dolly. She gave Don a little black bowtie. May, Effie, and Lizzy were given hair combs; each set of combs were different. Santa Claus had brought the exact things the little ones asked for in their letters. Shorty was ready to play jacks and Don was ready to play catch with his new ball. Little Dolly was very happy with her Kewpie doll. Ms. Parthina had even made a little diaper for the little doll. The presents from under the Christmas tree were all opened; all the hanging clothes had been claimed. Ms. Parthina came strolling into the living room with three new dresses... two bridesmaid dresses and one travel dress for the bride. The dresses were so pretty and well made they could have been store bought dresses.

Ms. Parthina and Ms. Betty started putting Christmas dinner together. May, Effie, and Lizzy were off admiring there new dresses with their new shoes. Ms. Parthina couldn't remember ever having a Christmas this wonderful; neither could Ms. Betty.

The Christmas dinner was piping hot and ready to be enjoyed. May, Effie and Lizzy were all wearing the new hair combs they got for Christmas. Mr. Will gave the blessing. The bowls, plates, and platters were passed around the table. "My plate has shrunk or we have more food than the law allows," said Mr. Will.

"Mama, are we going to jail for having all this food?" asked Don. Papa looked at Don. "By the time we get finished with our dinner, we'll be safe from the law," snickered Mr. Will. Don was relieved.

Mr. Will watched the ladies clear the table and stack the dirty dishes before giving them another Christmas surprise. There is another Christmas, the Cartwright Christmas. "My Christmas present to my darling wife and my beautiful daughters, I will try my hand at doing the dishes. Now y'all close your mouths before you start drawing flies, get bundled, and go have a nice long visit with the Cartwright family, but before you go, can someone show me how to wear Mama's apron?" The children laughed while Mama showed Papa how to properly wear her apron. Mama tied a big pretty bow in the back; she snickered and kissed Papa on his rosy cheek.

The walk to the Cartwright house didn't seem cold at all; one might say they were too happy to feel the cold. Robert held May's hand all the way to his house. Ms. Parthina and Ms. Betty talked softly to each other while the others laughed and talked. Just before getting to the Cartwright house, Robert had May close her eyes. He asked the others not to say out loud what they saw. May opened her eyes to see a big outside table, just like the one at the Ward house. "May this outside table is for you from Santa Claus," said Robert. "Now everyone will have a place to sit when your family comes to visit us," he continued.

Shorty took one look at the big outside table. No wonder Santa Claus needed help; that table wouldn't fit in his sledge. Robert gave Shorty a smile before announcing there was more presents. Ms. Betty and Ms. Parthina stayed back to allow Robert to show May her next present. Again, May had to close her eyes. The next present brought plenty of excitement, but the others didn't let her hear their excitement. Keeping her eyes closed, Robert gently helped May make her way to the kitchen. There before her was a brand-new table with eight chairs. "Now when your family comes for supper, we'll have plenty of room for them," Robert softly said. May was totally overwhelmed by all the wonderful presents. Robert pulled a chair from the new table and helped her sit and rest before one more present.

"May, when I say *we*, *we'll*, and *us*, I'm taking about you and me, Mr. and Mrs. Robert Chesterfield Cartwright." May was hearing what Robert was saying about the presents, but it had just now started to sink in; now she understood. "Oh my goodness!"

"Oh my goodness" was about all May could say, and then she sobbed into her hands.

Robert helped May from her chair; he tenderly wiped her tears away and promised her only one more present. Of course, Ms. Parthina and Ms. Betty had silent tears running down their faces. The mothers again held back to allow Robert to show May what was to be their bedroom. The bedroom was beautiful. The walls had been freshly painted white; the curtains were especially made for the windows, white with little splashes of pink and pink sheers. The bedspread had been dyed to a lovely shade of pink; at the foot of the bed was one of Ms. Parthina's handmade quilts. There was no sign that the room was once Betty's room.

May was happy with all her presents, but extra happy with the pink accessories in their soon-to-be bedroom. "To have a bedroom like this is the most wonderful thing I could have ever hoped for I love you, Robert." May hugged Robert and Robert kissed May.

The others had gone to the kitchen where Ms. Betty was serving hot cocoa, coffee, and pie. Once all had been served, Ms. Betty left the room, only to return with a pile of mittens. There was a pair of red mittens for everyone. "One size fits all. You won't be able to lose just one, they are connected." There was even a pair of red mittens for Mr. Will.

To see Mr. Will wearing a pair of red mittens was going to be a real sight. Of course Ms. Parthina never thought she would ever see him wear an apron with a big bow in the back and doing dishes. For sure, this was a Christmas that would be remembered by all: Santa's special postman, presents from Santa, aprons with big bows, papa doing dishes, pink bedroom, and red mittens for all.

Chapter 17

Saturday before the wedding, out-of-town guests started flocking in from all over. Mr. Will's four sisters and Mrs. Mary Jane Ward, his mother, arrived early afternoon. Aunt Frankie (Ward) Goates had learned to drive a car. "Now don't that just beat all, Frankie driving a car," said Mr. Will. Aunt Vallie (Ward) Thompson had come all the way from New Orleans; she rode in the car with Aunt Dora (Ward) Petty and her son Robert, who lived in Bigelow, Arkansas. Aunt Carrie Jane (Ward) Hemmer lived in Russellville; she rode in the car with Aunt Frankie and Grandma Ward who also lived in Russellville. Aunt Frankie told Papa, "Now that I have learned to drive a car, we can come for a visit more."

Next to arrive was Ms. Parthina's sister, Mary Catherine (Dudley) Lee, her brother David Dudley, and his wife Ellen (Reeder) Dudley, also Ms. Parthina's niece Annie Lee and nephew David Lee. They had driven in from Bigelow, Arkansas, and planned to spend the night with Ms. Parthina and her family. All the Ward children were very fond of their Aunt Mary; besides being a very sweet lady, she looked a lot like Ms. Parthina.

Aunt Mary brought four quart jars of her homemade vegetable soup to help out with supper. Aunt Mary made some of the best vegetable soup in Perry County; she had the blue ribbons to prove it. Mama would make a big batch of cornbread to go with the soup. Papa finally persuaded Aunt Frankie and the others to stay for supper.

May anxiously waited for Robert, Ms. Betty, and Clanton to arrive. She was a little nervous to meet Mr. and Mrs. Baker, Ms. Betty's parents. Robert proudly introduced May to his new grandparents. Mr. and Mrs. Baker welcomed May to the family with a big Southern hug. The Ward house was full of Southern huggers.

Mrs. Baker presented Ms. Parthina with cold cuts and loaves of light bread for sandwiches.

"What a treat! Thank you, Ms. Octavia. Mr. and Mrs. Ferguson, at the general store, are clearly fond of you and your children; for every cold cut I ordered he doubled it, the same with the loaves of light bread." "We love them too." My sister, Mary has brought some of her famous homemade vegetable soup; famous in Perry County...County Fair Winner...four years in a row." "I do enjoy a good soup with my sandwich."

Ms. Octavia was a little too prim and proper acting. Ms. Betty, in a soft whisper like tone suggested to her mother she might want to tone things down just a little. Mr. Thomas was glad Betty said something. If he had said the same thing as Betty, he would be in the doghouse until next spring. Ms. Octavia was embarrassed for acting so uppity. She went straight to Ms. Parthina to apologize for being rude and offered to help in the preparation of supper. Once Ms. Octavia stopped putting on airs, Ms. Parthina found her to be quite pleasant. The women that influenced Ms. Betty the most liked each other; that made Ms. Betty happy.

May and Robert sat quietly as they watched and listened. The love that filled the house was the kind of love that flowed into your chest, wrapped around you heart, and gave your heart the sweetest hurt. It was new love, seasoned love, love between a mother and child, a love that will always be there no matter what happens, or wherever you go, the love is there.

Grandma Ward and the aunts had thoroughly enjoyed meeting May's nice young man and his family. Grandma Ward was almost overcome with emotions when she said good-bye to

Mr. Will. The frail little woman hugged her son as tight as she could and kissed his cheek. Aunt Frankie still new at driving a car said, "She would feel better if she got home before dark. All were in agreement, getting home before dark was the safe way to travel.

It seemed wedding secrets were allowed, just like Christmas secrets. Ms. Parthina and Ms. Octavia were off in the kitchen doing a lot of whispering. All that whispering didn't seem to bother Robert or Ms. Betty, which meant they already knew the secret. Aunt Mary patted May on the leg. "You'll find out the secret in the morning and not one minute sooner. May likes a good secret, but only when she is the keeper of the secret," said Robert.

"The groom is not allowed to see the bride in her dress before the wedding. The groom is not allowed to see the bride the night before the wedding, which means, Robert, you must leave before dark."

Mr. Will gave Robert a smile before telling him to go home. Ms. Betty and the boys gathered their coats and their red mittens. Mr. and Mrs. Baker shook hands with everyone and promised a wonderful wedding tomorrow.

Ms. Betty and Ms. Octavia chattered the whole way home. Robert had not heard one word that was said. Grandpa Baker and Clanton brought wedding presents from the trunk of the car. The presents were from Grandma Ward and the Ward aunts, from Aunt Mary and her family, and Uncle Dave and his family. The presents were taken to Robert and May's room where Ms. Betty and Grandma Baker arranged them on their new pink bedspread.

No one had slept in Robert and May's room since it was decorated for them. Robert and Clanton gladly gave their room to Grandma and Grandpa Baker. Ms. Betty and the boys had pallets in the living room. Clanton suggested they be on a camping trip. He sat the table lamp in the floor to be their campfire. As the boys sat watching their campfire, Ms. Betty went to make hot coco. "You can't go camping without drinking hot coco…with marshmallows." Robert had an idea for making them a tent, two chairs with a sheet stretched over them. "Sleeping in a tent, watching the campfire flicker, drinking cocoa. This is the best camping trip I have ever had," said Ms. Betty."

"Me, too," said Robert.

"Me, too," said Clanton."

The next morning, Grandma and Grandpa Baker tiptoed through the campsite; they didn't want to disturb those sleeping in the tent. Ms. Betty smelled coffee. Just as she stuck her head from the tent, Grandma Baker handed the camper a cup of hot coffee. "The next time y'all go camping, let me know…that's my kind of camping," said Grandma Baker.

Ms. Octavia was like Ms. Parthina; she could slap a hot breakfast together before you could get your hair brushed. This morning, it was homemade biscuits, bacon, and chocolate gravy. All campers were required to eat breakfast before breaking down camp. Ms. Betty suggested the boys go down to the creek and splash some water on their faces. When camping, pretend or real, there was always a creek for freshwater and washing your face.

When the boys returned from the creek, Ms. Betty was ready to say the blessing. She felt so blessed she hardly knew where to start, but she did manage. There was so much excitement; Robert was getting married, the boys met their new grandparents, they had gone on a pretend camping trip, and the best of all, they were all going on a honeymoon.

Breakfast was over, and the campsite had been folded and put away. It was now time to get ready for a wedding and finish packing for their trip to New Orleans. Grandma and Grandpa Baker had a guesthouse where Robert and May would stay during their visit to New Orleans; Ms. Betty and Clanton would stay at the main house with her parents.

Ms. Carol had turned the kitchen area of the church into a beautiful reception area. The tablecloths were white with lace toppers. The wedding cake with its three tiers was the most beautiful cake May would ever see. Ms. Ida had out done herself. The wedding cake was the center of attention at the reception; the bride was the center of attention at the wedding.

༄

The Ward family arrived at the church in the family's covered wagon. Mr. Will guarded the cargo; the bride and her maids in the back of the wagon. Ms. Parthina and Seaburn found the groom and his family hovering around the back door of the church. Ms. Parthina and Ms. Betty were pleased to see the church decorated just as Ms. Carol had described.

Seaburn escorted Ms. Parthina to her seat at the front of the church; Clanton escorted Ms. Betty also to the front of the church. Mary Jane, Shorty, Don, and little Dolly sat in the pew behind Ms. Parthina. The little ones were dressed in the new garments they got for Christmas; it was a special day, and they were planning to be on their best behavior. Effie and Lizzy took their place on the bride's side; Seaburn, the best man, and Clanton the groomsman took their place on the groom's side. Robert and his wobbly knees watched for his bride.

Mr. Will tenderly helped May from the covered wagon, at which time he got a close up look at her pretty face. "Daughter, I always knew you would grow up to be a pretty young woman, but today, I have to admit I was wrong. You have grown up to be a beautiful woman." Ms. Parthina had insisted Mr. Will carry a freshly laundered handkerchief, and now he understood why. His handkerchief came in handy for catching the bride's tears before they had a chance to smudge her face powder. The father of the bride had a few teas of his own, but that would be their little secret.

"Papa, you look very handsome today."

"Well, that's your mama's fault. She made me wear these fancy pants and a starched shirt. To top it off, I had to choose between my suspenders and my belt, she said I couldn't wear both. She said I would look extra handsome with my suspenders. *Looking extra handsome* is how she persuaded me to get a haircut. I suppose I'm a sucker for your mama's flattery."

Jared and Anna-Kate Hamilton, great grandchildren to Old Mr. Mauldin, were in charge of the church doors. The doors were carefully opened to showcase the bride. Mr. Will gave May a moment to feel the excitement that filled the church. Walking down the aisle should be at a slow pace, giving everyone a chance to see and admire the bride according to Ms. Betty. Mr. Will agreed with her; with anything other than a slow pace, one might think it was a shotgun wedding. Mr. Will got in trouble from Ms. Parthina for that remark.

Mr. Will and May had practiced walking down the aisle; it was now time to see if the practice worked. Everyone was standing to see the bride walk to meet her groom at the front of the church. Mr. Will walked tall and proud; he even stopped squirming in his starched shirt. Ms. Parthina and her sister Mary were both sobbing into their dainty handkerchiefs.

Once Mr. Will had given his daughter, he was allowed to join Ms. Parthina on the front row of the pews. Part of what Rev. Vanderburg said did not register with Mr. Will. His thoughts went from when his children were born to who they are today. Mr. Will was extremely proud of Ms. Parthina; without her, their children might have been raised like a bunch of heathens. Mr. Will held Ms. Parthina's hand all through the wedding with an occasional pat for reassurance. "You may kiss the bride..." Mr. Will gave Ms. Parthina a kiss.

Rev. Vanderburg introduced Mr. and Mrs. Robert Cartwright to their friends and family. The Hamilton children held the church doors open for Mr. and Mrs. Cartwright and the bridal party. Once the bride and groom left the church, the doors were propped open.

Before the reception, Robert shared the secret that most already knew. They were going to New Orleans for their honeymoon; they would be staying in the guesthouse of Grandma and Grandpa Baker. The guesthouse was just for them; no one would be staying there but them. New Orleans is within walking distance of the house. Mama and Clanton will be staying at the big house with Grandma and Grandpa. We'll have a whole week there.

The wedding cake was not to be overlooked; it was the first thing you would see when you walked into the room. Before the cake was cut, Grandpa Baker took a few snapshots of the bride and groom with their beautiful wedding cake. Ms. Ida stood ready to serve the guest a slice of cake while Ms. Carol was serving punch, nuts, and mints at the next table. The table that held the guest book was manned by Anna-Kate Hamilton; she was to ask the guest to sign the bride's guest book. Jared, her brother, liked opening the doors for the bride, but he didn't want any part of the wedding book; he thought it was too girly for him.

It was time for the bride to change into her traveling clothes. Mrs. Vanderburg showed the ladies to the reverend's office. Ms. Parthina and Ms. Betty offered to help, but May needed a few minutes alone. May was as pretty as a picture in her new dress, but she was on the verge of tears. May had never felt so many emotions—at least not at the same time. "We were wondering when all those emotions were going to catch up with you," said Ms. Parthina.

May needed a hug from her Mama, and Mama needed a hug from her. With one little hug, the floodgates were opened. Mrs. Vanderburg came to check on the ladies only to find them having a good old-fashioned cry. She knew the tears were happy tears, and Mrs. Vanderburg would never interrupt such a happy moment.

The top layer of the wedding cake was wrapped for the freezer to be eaten on May and Robert's first anniversary. Ms. Ida prepared a box with the wedding cake for the couple to have on their honeymoon, and Ms. Carol fixed a big jug of wedding punch for the couple. Robert and May were surprised that Grandpa Baker allowed "Just Married" to be written on the back window of his car, although he did put his foot down to the tin cans dragging from the back of his car. May snuggled close to Robert before slipping off into a blissful sleep. Robert watched her sleep until he too fell asleep. Clanton didn't understand why Robert and May were sleeping; it wasn't even dark. "Maybe he stayed up late while ya'll were camping. It sure looked like it was fun," said Grandma Baker. Her explanation made sense; they did stay up a little late, and they did have fun on their pretend camping trip. "Did May go on a pretend camping trip at her house?" asked Clanton. Grandma Baker explained, "Sometimes being excited and happy at the same time makes you tired, and you need a nap."

Grandpa Baker drove like a man on a mission; he stopped for gasoline and bathroom breaks only when necessary. If you didn't need a bathroom break when he got gasoline, you would be expected to wait until the next stop. However, if he started feeling a little sleepy, he would make an extra stop for to-go coffee. This trip was May's first long trip in a car and her first taste of to-go coffee, which also came in girly coffee.

It was a little past five in the morning when Grandpa Baker drove through the city of New Orleans. The merchants were getting ready for a day of business. Some merchants had small tables with umbrellas; the tables with umbrellas, according to Robert, were for coffee drinkers to sit and enjoy the weather. "One day we'll come to town to drink coffee."

Grandma and Grandpa Baker's house was a large two-story house with tall columns. The walkway from the house to the road was shaded by large trees on both sides. The driveway to the house that was once for wagons was now used for the family's automobile. The view of the driveway was concealed by tall hedges, only to be seen from the second floor balcony and windows. The exterior was a pale yellow with white trim; there were chimneys on both ends of the house. Other than a few well-placed gas heaters, electricity, and a slightly updated kitchen, the house remained untouched by time.

<h1>Chapter 18</h1>

Grandma Baker suggested getting settled and maybe take a nap. "We'll have brunch about ten o'clock…if that is all right with everyone?"

"Mama, I'm going to help Robert carry their luggage to the guesthouse," shouted Clanton. Clanton had already been given instructions; he was not allowed to hang out with Robert and May at the guesthouse. Robert stopped at the front door of the guesthouse to carry his new bride across the threshold. "What happened? Did May twist her ankle?" asked Clanton. Robert snickered; he explained that carrying the bride across the threshold was a wedding tradition.

While May was getting the tour of the main house, someone had brought a pitcher of mimosas, cold whipped cream biscuits, and a small dish of orange marmalade. The guesthouse was more modern than the main house. The living area was furnished with a comfortable couch, coffee table, bookshelves stocked with plenty of books, and a floor-type radio for enjoying music. The kitchen area was concealed by a three-paneled floor screen. The cupboards and the refrigerator were well stocked. Just off from the kitchen was a patio.

The bedroom and bath were located at the back of the house. The bedding matched the drapery. The comforter made May think of a big fat marshmallow—all fluffy. The closet was almost as big as the bathroom. There were double doors with screens leading to another patio; the view overlooked a well-maintained flower garden with bird houses and bird baths. The screens made it possible to have the doors open without the worry of mosquitoes or any other flying insects; the aroma of the flowers could flow all through the house.

Robert and May enjoyed their mimosas on the patio overlooking the flower garden. They finally had a nibble of a biscuits with marmalade. Music from the radio could be heard from the patio. "I'm no expert on honeymoons, but I bet this is the best honeymoon anyone could ever have," said May. Robert agreed wholeheartedly with his bride. May was right about the comforter; it was as soft and fluffy as a big fat marshmallow. The young couple fell asleep in each others' arms and drifted off to marshmallow heaven.

Shortly after ten o'clock, there was a knock the front door. A breakfast tray was left at the door for the honeymooners. May peeked around the corner to see if they had guest; she was happy to see *no guest* and equally happy to see the breakfast tray. "Today we shall have our breakfast in bed," said Robert. "Now scoot yourself back into the bed, and I will serve you." There were flapjacks with butter and warm maple syrup, bacon, scrambled eggs, orange slices, and a pot of piping hot coffee, with canned milk and sugar for making girly coffee.

Instructions came with the breakfast tray: when finished with breakfast, place tray and dishes outside your door. There was a note addressed to Mr. and Mrs. Cartwright: "Room service will bring your dinner at six o'clock. You are cordially invited to join your family for breakfast at eight o'clock; a trip to town is planned afterward. Comfortable shoes required."

Robert and May decided to take a walk through the beautiful flower garden they viewed from their patio. There were pinks, purples, and splashes of yellow all through the garden. There were magnolia flowers, which is the state flower of Louisiana, magnolia trees, and even Japanese magnolia trees which had pink blossoms. May was able to recognize the hibiscus, iris, and the crape myrtle. Aunt Mary Lee had those same flowers in her yard.

After their walk through the flower garden, Robert and May took a stroll up to the main house. The back door was open but Robert knocked anyway. Grandma Baker scolded him for knocking. She said knocking is for strangers and salesmen.

Robert smiled and said, "Yes…um." The small room before entering the kitchen was called the mud room; that's where you leave your muddy boots before you even thought about coming into the house. Grandma Baker, Betty, and Clanton were hovering around an old butcher's block. They were drinking fruit-flavored iced tea and nibbling on freshly baked tea cakes.

Clanton was happy to see Robert and May; this was the first time he wasn't allowed to hang around with them. "Tomorrow we are going to town to show you off to New Orleans," said Clanton. "Grandma says we all have to wear comfortable shoes."

Robert and May accepted Grandma Baker's breakfast invitation. They, too, were looking forward to going to town. "I'll be happy to help with breakfast," offered May. "Clara, the cook, would cut your fingers off and put them in the stew pot. She is not one for sharing her kitchen," said Grandma Baker. May withdrew her offer with a chuckle.

Breakfast was served in the dining room with its white tablecloth and linen napkins. Platters of food were passed around, while Clara poured coffee and offered water. Before leaving the dining room…Clara announced the stew pot was empty, and baked chicken was on the menu for dinner. "I forgot to mention Clara has a good sense of humor, but to be on the safe side…we don't eat her stew." Everyone laughed.

The walk to town was so much fun. Everyone laughed, talked, and acted silly, even Grandma Baker. "Back in my mother's day, once a young lady was married, her days of fun and frolic were over. It was not proper for a married woman to display any emotions in public. Even the old photographs from back then, the wives were not allowed to smile."

"Now we know why the ladies back then looked like they smelled dirty socks all the time," laughed Clanton. Grandma Baker, Betty, and May joined hands and skipped down the dusty road to New Orleans, laughing all the way.

"All right, ladies, we have arrived. It's time to put on our dirty-sock faces," whispered Grandma. There was not a dirty sock face among them; the more they tried, the more they laughed. The three women could not control their laughing. The more they laughed, the more Grandma Baker passed gas, the more Betty snorted like a pig, and the more tears Mary had rolling down her face. Robert and Clanton had no idea what was so funny. The first step into town, the ladies stopped laughing as sudden as they started. Robert was afraid he was going to be embarrassed for life. Clanton was still confused about what was so funny, but he sure didn't want them to start laughing again in the middle of New Orleans.

Even though Robert and Clanton were born in Louisiana, they had not seen much of New Orleans. "The magazines say this is one of the most beautiful cities in Louisiana," said Grandma. Robert had Clanton change places with May; he wanted to walk with her. He wanted to hold her hand and see the city thorough her eyes. He wanted her memories of New Orleans to be his memories of New Orleans. He never wanted to forget this day.

Just at the edge of the French quarters were a few shops for buying souvenirs. Inside the French quarters was as if you stepped back in time. The wrought-iron balconies, the hanging baskets of blooming flowers, the French Creole–speaking shop owners, and the horse-drawn carriages. One building started at Royal Street and ended at St. Peter Street, two blocks long and three stories tall. The cities streetcars were both necessary and entertaining. The early morning commuters were able to get to their jobs clear across town, while the visitors could take a leisurely tour of the city from early morning until late at night.

Robert and May took a carriage ride with a "Just Married" sign displayed on the back of carriage. The driver wore a black top hat and black bowtie; the white horse also wore a black bowtie. The people waved and shouted "congratulations" from the streets. The driver's black top hat signified a newly married couple was on a carriage ride.

Robert and May took a tour of the city with the family by way of a streetcar. Grandma Baker had seen the sights so much; she was like their personal tour guide. Somewhere along the way, Grandma Baker, Betty, and even Clanton had done a little shopping; they all had shopping bags. Robert inquired about the contents of the bags, but Grandma Baker said, "It's like Christmas. You're not allowed to ask questions." May was surprised to hear "You're not allowed to ask questions"; Mama and Papa Ward told their children that very thing at Christmastime. Keeping secrets at Christmastime were allowed at the Ward house.

"The Garden District is a neighborhood of Southern Mansions. Each home has its own unique structural design. The homes that can be seen from the streetcar are just a taste of the beautiful homes that can be seen from a Garden District tour," according to Grandma Baker.

Before leaving town, Robert wanted to find one of those little sidewalk coffee shops. He had promised May they would have coffee, sitting at a table with an umbrella. The coffee shop May chose had red umbrellas. The tables had menus of all the different ways to drink coffee: with sugar bowls, creamers, and flavored creamers were in the middle of each table. May only knew of two ways to drink coffee: manly coffee and girly coffee. May and Robert sat at their own table while Grandma Baker, Betty, and Clanton sat one table over. Of all the attractions New Orleans had to offer, Grandma Baker had never had coffee at a sidewalk coffee shop. May and Robert decided to try one of the coffee shops specialty drinks; Clanton wanted to try one of the specialty drinks too. Grandma Baker and Betty order girly coffee.

The coffee cups were enormous compared to the coffee cups at home. The coffee was topped with a mountain of whipped cream; the whipped cream was sprinkled with a mixture of sugar and cocoa. May and Robert had fun drinking their coffee, wiping whipped cream from their nose. As much as May liked her girly coffee, she liked this coffee much better.

The walk home was jovial, but there was no skipping; the walking pace was much slower. Clanton never knew having so much fun could make you tired until now. Grandma Baker pointed out to Clanton that he was too young to be tired from having fun.

Clanton tried to give Grandma Baker a compliment, but it didn't come out right. "Grandma, you're old. How come you ain't tired?" Clanton was walking just a few steps in front of Grandma Baker; she took the opportunity to swat him on his behind.

"Don't you know that old people are not allowed to get tired, having fun or not?"

Clanton wondered if that was true as he looked at his mama.

"Don't ask me, Clanton. I'm not that old yet." Grandma Baker tried to swat Betty on her behind, but Betty was too quick. Robert didn't laugh out loud, but he did snicker.

"Now that everyone knows I'm old, how about this old woman fix us a snack when we get home?"

"Maybe some finger sandwiches?" Poor little May, she couldn't help but give Grandma Baker a bug-eyed look. That was a look Robert had never seen from May. "A bug-eyed look is not very becoming," said Robert. For his comment, Robert got his very own bug-eyed look. By this time, everyone was laughing totally out of control including Robert and May; once again Betty started to snort like a pig.

The lively group entered the house by way of the mud room. The screen door was allowed to slam; they all stomped their feet to knock the dust from their shoes. For a moment, Clara thought the house was being invaded by a pack of teenaged kids. She was surprised to see Grandma Baker as their leader. Clara asked the group if they would like something to eat or drink. "No finger food." Grandma Baker asked Clara to put the kettle on for some tea. "I promised this rowdy bunch I'd fix them a snack." Grandma Baker fixed a tray of sliced apples, orange slices, cheese, sweet pickles, and crackers while Clara made the tea ready for serving. Robert and Clanton drank iced tea. They thought drinking tea from a fancy cup and saucer was too girly for them to drink. Before serving tea, Grandma Baker went to the cupboard for another cup and saucer; the cup and saucer was for Clara. Grandma Baker invited Clara to sit and have tea with her and her family. Betty was just as surprised as Clara.

"Today has been such a wonderful day. I have laughed so much today, I know my muscles will ache in the morning. Today I spent time with my grandsons and my new granddaughter. Today I remembered I still have a silly side, and so does Betty. Just one more thing about today, Betty still snorts like a pig when she laughs a lot."

The laughter from the kitchen brought Grandpa Baker to see what was so funny. The ladies enjoyed their tea and snacks. Robert and Clanton talked about the day in New Orleans. Grandpa Baker poured his self a glass of tea and pulled up a chair; he then instructed the boys to start from the beginning. "Everyone enjoyed the sights of New Orleans, but the walking to and from town was by far the most fun. Mama snorts like a pig, Grandma passes little puffs of gas, and tears roll down May's face— all when their laughing is out of control. They even held hands and skipped down the road on the way to town."

Grandpa Baker was happy to hear about all the fun; he wished he had been there to see it firsthand. "The people from the insane asylum must be looking for ya'll right now." Clanton was happy to report that they tried to put on their dirty sock faces before entering town. Grandpa didn't know what a dirty sock face was, and he was afraid to ask.

Chapter 19

Robert and May decided to make a special trip to New Orleans to pick up a few souvenirs for May's family. Clanton was invited to join them; Clanton wasn't going to turn down a chance to spend time with May and Robert. Their walk to town was quite peaceful until Clanton revealed what he overheard before breakfast. "I heard Grandpa talking to Mama about moving back to Louisiana. Grandma said Mama and I can live in the main house and y'all can live in the guesthouse to have your privacy, and Robert you will be the overseer for this whole place." Robert and May stopped in their tracks.

The color left May's face, and she began to cry without warning. Her shaky legs could barely hold her up. Robert was there to catch her when she fainted; he tenderly cradled her limp body as she slid to the ground. Robert tried to wake her, but she would not wake. "Clanton get Mama. She won't wake up!" Clanton ran back to the house as fast as he could; when he got close enough to be heard he yelled for Mama and Grandma.

Grandpa drove as fast as he could to get to Robert and May; to get May back to the guesthouse. He drove the car right up to the front door of the guesthouse where Grandma and Clara anxiously awaited. Robert's own legs were beginning to grow weak, but he would allow no others to help carry *his* May. Grandpa pulled the overstuffed chair from the living room; the chair was pushed right up against the back of Robert's knees, making him fall into the chair. Grandpa got right in Robert's face and gave him strict orders. Robert was to stay in that chair and out of the way, or he would have to leave the room.

The smelling salts had done its job, and May was awake. Robert had no regard for the person standing between him and May. He pushed his way to May's bedside where his weak knees and his raw emotions took over. The thought of losing May had allowed fear to enter every part of his body. Robert never knew fear could be so powerful until now. May comforted Robert by stroking his hair. She didn't know what to say because she didn't remember exactly what had happened. "Walking to town with Robert and Clanton, Robert was holding my hand, then I felt lightheaded, and now I'm here," May softly explained.

Grandpa and Clanton stood at the foot of the bed, happy to see May awake. "You sure gave us a fright, Mrs. Cartwright." May seemed to have a blank look on her face. "Oh, please tell us you remember getting married," pleaded Grandpa. "Mrs. Cartwright has such a nice ring to it, doesn't it?" asked May. May remembered everything except what made her faint. She found it hard to believe she fainted; she wasn't a fainting kind of girl."

Dr. Grandma prescribed rest and chicken soup with plenty of pampering. Robert understood the rest with plenty of pampering but not the chicken soup. According to Dr. Grandma, "Chicken soup is good for what ails you, and it's better to be safe than sorry. Eat chicken soup." Clara left right away to make chicken soup. Grandpa and Clanton were shooed back to the main house. May was instructed by Grandma to change into her nightgown and get ready to rest. "Robert, you may need to help her if she gets dizzy."

Mama returned with cheese and crackers, sliced fruit, and a teapot with freshly brewed tea. Normally a tray would have been left at the door, but this time, Mama wanted to make sure Robert and May were following Dr. Grandma's orders. May still looked a little frail, but Robert seemed to be taking good care of her. Clanton had even sent the couple a puzzle in a box, just in case they needed something to do while May was on bed rest.

"I believe you are suffering from exhaustion, and with a little extra rest, you'll be right as rain," said Mama. Her reassuring voice seemed to put Robert and May at ease. She didn't wait for the young couple to ask before giving her thoughts on May's condition. "Your body is tired and that's why you fainted. You're not sick…just tired." Clanton thought he had been the cause of May fainting. He didn't hear the entire conversation between Mama and Grandpa, but he repeated what he heard, and for that, he felt guilty.

Mama and Grandpa could see the guilt on Clanton's face. "This is not your fault, Clanton; May would have fainted if she saw a blue cow. She was just too tired to do anything but faint," said Mama. "I might have fainted, too, if I saw a blue cow," laughed Grandpa. According to Grandpa Baker, anything heard by eavesdropping should be confirmed before repeating. "However, if you had eavesdropped a little longer, you would have heard your Mama turn down my invitation. Therefore, there was no need to repeat what you heard."

Clanton was pleased May had no memory of what he had done, but he was sure Robert remembered every word. Grandma Baker suggested flowers for May would be a sign of goodwill, maybe even a show of remorse for his poor judgment. The thought of Robert never forgiving him was unimaginable.

Grandpa Baker showed Clanton how too gently cut flowers, which flowers had a sweet aroma, and which ones would add beauty to any bouquet. Clanton wanted to arrange the flowers without any help. "May will love the flowers, but don't expect Robert to be quite so forgiving," Mama sadly said. Clanton knew Mama was right.

Clanton walked to the guesthouse like a man walking to the gallows. His heart was broken from what he had done to May and Robert. Clanton softly knocked on the door. Robert was happy to see his brother; he wanted to let Clanton know he didn't blame him for anything that was said. May too was happy to see

Clanton, and the flowers brought a big smile to her face. May and Robert had started working on the puzzle Clanton sent over.

Robert and May spent the next few days enjoying their privacy. Clanton had even made them a cute little sign to hang on the doorknob, "Do not disturb." Each day, Clanton watched for the sign to be gone so that he might visit with Robert and May.

The carefree days in New Orleans were very different from the days at home. Being a lady of leisure was something to be acquired. Grandma Baker's routine consisted of overseeing the housekeepers, menu planning with Clara, needlepoint, and occasionally hosting an afternoon tea. Grandma Baker always looked her best.

The planting and harvesting of the cotton was supervised by Allen Wade, the overseer. Wade and Rebecca had two grown sons, Carl and Lester Wade. Rebecca drove the truck and her boys put out buckets of water at the end of some of the rows. Once the water buckets were in place, Carl and Lester went to work in the fields. Carl and Lester were paid the same as any other hired hands. After lunch, Carl and Lester helped put out more water.

Grandpa was eager to show off his horses, Chocolate, Cookie, Butterscotch, and Candy. Grandpa laughed when he introduced his grandsons to his horses. "Can you tell we like sweets?" he laughed. Grandpa and the boys took Cookie, Butterscotch, and Candy for a ride. Hunting and fishing were also on Grandpa's list of things he enjoyed.

May spent the afternoon with Grandma and Betty learning the fine art of needlepoint. Grandma had a gift to give May and Robert, but she just could not wait. She had crocheted "Cartwright" in the middle of an oversized doily; it was displayed in a beautiful old frame and ready to be hung on the wall at home. "I just finished it two days ago," said Grandma with relief. May absolutely loved the gift, and that pleased Grandma.

After hearing how much fun Robert and Clanton had riding Grandpa's horses, May wanted to go riding too. Shortly after breakfast, Robert and May came to asked if they could go riding. May was wearing a pair of long britches with an old pair of work gloves hanging from her back pocket. Grandpa commented on how snappy May looked in her long britches. Betty and Clanton were invited to go riding with the young couple. Betty brought her own long britches just in case she got the opportunity to go horseback riding.

According to Grandma Baker, Grandpa was to help with the saddling. All the horses were gentle, but Chocolate was by far the most gentle; Grandma wanted May to ride Chocolate. The boys were to unsaddle the horses when they finished their ride. Betty was to show the others how to care for the horses after the ride. The main instructions Grandma gave were "have fun and don't let May get too tired again."

Chocolate and Cookie slowly followed Butterscotch and Candy. The horses seemed to know where they were going. Grandma was right, Chocolate was a gentle horse. May didn't have much experience with horses, but she had ridden a few mules before.

"Before putt'n down hard roots, Papa wanted to see Ola Arkansas in Yell County, where Aunt Dora and her family lived. Aunt Dora and Uncle John (Petty) had two mules, Old Blue and Baby Kate. Old Blue got his name because his gums were sort of blue; Baby Kate got her name from Cousin Leah; she thought Baby Kate was a nice name for a mule—of course, we were kids. If the mules hadn't been worked hard during the day, Uncle John would let us ride the mules after our supper. Leah always rode Baby Kate. She wouldn't even let her brother Robert ride Baby Kate." May was happy to admit she enjoyed riding a horse named Chocolate over a mule named Old Blue.

Chocolate had given May the grand tour of Grandpa's cotton fields; he then made a turn and headed back to the stables. The others followed right behind Chocolate. "I guess we're tired," laughed May. Back at the stables, Chocolate, Cookie, Butterscotch, and Candy were treated like royalty. Fresh water, grain, and hay followed a good brush down for all. Grandpa Baker learned from his Grandpa, "You always take care of your horses before anything else. To be in the wilderness without a horse, you will surely die."

May, Robert, and Clanton were finally able to get back to town for a few souvenirs; however, Grandpa Baker insisted on driving them. Grandpa was worried that May might not be able to walk all that way. "Dr. Grandma has given May a clean bill of health," said Clanton. If Grandma said May was fine, that was good enough for Grandpa.

Looking for gifts to take home to May's family was harder than they thought. May was torn between practical or frivolous. Clanton was happy to say that he and Mama had already bought surprises to take home to the Ward family. Clanton didn't want to tell what he and Mama had bought, but he didn't want May and Robert to buy the same thing.

"Mr. Will is getting a clear jar filled with pipe tobacco. Ms. Parthina is getting a recipe box where she can write and keep her recipes, Little Dolly is getting ABC blocks, Don is getting a small tackle box made for young fishermen, Mary Jane is getting a book by Mark Twain, *The Adventures of Tom Sawyer*, Effie and Lizzy both are getting a box of perfumed dusting powder, Seaburn is getting a necktie, Mama said he looked very handsome in a necktie. Those are fine gifts…the family will think its Christmas," said May.

"We slipped off to town while May was catching up on her rest. Some gifts were bought when we went to town with Grandma. Y'all didn't even miss us when we snuck off to buy gifts," said Clanton. "Which time," laughed Robert. May and Robert carefully selected gifts they hoped the family would enjoy. Some gifts were selected to compliment or match the gifts from Mama and Clanton; some were not. With each purchase, May looked to Robert as if to ask, "Can we afford this?" May was not use to shopping for herself or anyone else; therefore, she never had to worry about the cost of gifts. "Papa says people who spend their last dollar on foolishness end up in the poor house," May said reluctantly.

Robert assured his timid bride that they were not going to end up in the poor house. Clanton snickered about the poor house. "Is the poor house big enough for me and Mama to come too?" Clanton never let an opportunity to use his quick wit pass him by. Clanton had a flare for shenanigans and harebrained ideas. At times, Clanton reminded May of her brother Alvie; he too had a flare for shenanigans. Both could make May smile.

Buying gifts to take back home meant their visit with Grandma and Grandpa Baker was almost over. May and Robert decided to have their dinner alone at the guesthouse after their day of shopping. The next day would be their last day before going back to Dover. May and Robert had breakfast with the family before taking one more ride on Grandpa's horses. Snacking on fruit, cheese, and hard biscuits was considered lunch. Snacking in the kitchen was a fun time for all. Clara enjoyed snacking in the kitchen with the family.

Dinner was the formal meal of the day. Everyone was expected to be dressed in what some might call their Sunday's best. The atmosphere was of grace and charm, which had been passed down from generation to generation. There was very little talking during dinner; only light conversation would be acceptable. Grandpa Baker might comment on what good weather they were enjoying. Grandma Baker might say, "Yes, the weather has been good."

Before going to bed Robert and May wrapped the gifts for the family. The wrapped gifts were put back into the colorful shopping bags. All were excited about taking a train back home to Pope County. Their luggage would be checked for their trip home; the shopping bags would be considered their carry-on luggage. Mama and Clanton were doing the same; they didn't want to take a chance their gifts might get broken or lost.

Catching the train home required getting up before the rooster could crow. New Orleans's Union Station suggested all travelers arrive one hour before departure time. Grandma and Grandpa Baker had already purchased the tickets; they sneaked to town again. Grandpa sadly passed out train tickets with a heavy heart. Grandma already had her dainty handkerchief wiping away her tears. Grandma watched with Robert and May as Grandpa and Betty said their good-byes. Clanton was sitting like a statue, but he was sound asleep.

Grandma was truly thankful for the joy and happiness her new grandchildren brought to her life. She would never forget how much fun they had walking to town and how much fun it was to come down from her high horse, as Betty called it. Grandma Baker could see how much Robert and Clanton loved and respected their new mama and how much she loved them. It had been a wonderful visit, but now it was time to say good-bye.

Everyone exchanged hugs and kiss before boarding the train. Grandma had been crying since they arrived at the Union Station; Grandpa was on the verge of crying, but he wouldn't allow his tears to flow. Clara packed a few buttered biscuits with jelly for their breakfast, peanut butter and jelly–sandwiches for lunch, and several magazines to help pass the time. Betty's heart ached as she said good-bye to her parents.

Grandma and Grandpa watched the train pull away from the station before leaving for home. Betty still had tears that needed to be cried out. May cried because Betty was sad, and nothing could be done to ease her pain. Robert held May and tried to comfort her; he looked like he was about to cry. "Am I supposed to be crying too?" asked Clanton. The tone of his voice was in a high pitch, which made his question even funnier. He stopped his Mama's tears and caused them all to have a good laugh. Hopefully there would be no more crying.

Grandma and Grandpa Baker were generous when they purchased the train tickets. Traveling from New Orleans to Memphis included an evening meal and breakfast in the dining car, which was a special treat. Breakfast was a good time to enjoy the scenery as it quickly passed while sipping your girly coffee. The smoking car was just past the dining car; each time the door opened, a slight smell of pipe tobacco could be detected. The smell of pipe tobacco caused May to become homesick; she was ready to see her Mama and Papa.

There was a short layover in Memphis before changing trains. The trip from Memphis to Little Rock was nonstop. However, from Little Rock to Russellville, the train stopped at every town that had a train or bus depot. May knew all the little towns on the railroad stops; she had lived or worked in the areas one time or another before her Papa put down hard roots.

Robert and May waited for their luggage to be unloaded while Ms. Betty and Clanton went to see if Marvin Young and his taxicab were available. Most of the time, Marvin and his taxicab could be found near the train and bus depot. Keeping up with the trains and bus schedules was necessary in the taxi business. Marvin was happy to see Ms. Betty and her family back from their trip to New Orleans. Being a taxi driver, Marvin heard all the news from those leaving and from those coming back. "I reckon the whole county has heard about that fancy wedding, and now they'll be expecting some stories about ya'll going all the way to New Orleans for a honeymoon," said Marvin.

The taxicab was loaded and ready to take the weary travelers home. May was happy to be home; she was ready to see her family. As the taxi drove past the Ward house, there didn't seem to be anyone stirring about. It was early…even for Mama and Papa, thought May. Marvin, the taxi driver, turned into the driveway leading to the back of the house; the lights were on and there stood Mama and Papa Ward smiling from ear to ear.

May barely waited for the taxi to come to a complete stop before running to hug her Mama. Ms. Parthina was more of a hugger than Mr. Will. Ms. Parthina's hugs were heartfelt and lasted longer than most hugs; Mr. Will's hugs were never closer than his bent elbows, but they did come with a soft pat on the back. Mr. Will called his hugs short but sweet.

Before the hugs were finished, the Ward children came running to welcome May and Robert home from their honeymoon. Of course, Seaburn was glad to see his sister, but he had missed his friends, Robert and Clanton. Seaburn, Robert, and Clanton all grabbed a suitcase and headed to the house. Lizzy and Effie snatched up the shopping bags and pointed May to the house. The girls were so happy to see May; they didn't even notice the shopping bags were filled with wrapped gifts. For that reason alone, May knew her sisters missed her.

Mr. Will took the last of the luggage into the house while Ms. Betty and Ms. Parthina made sure all of their belongings were gathered from the taxi. "Ms. Betty, your taxi ride has been paid in full, and again, welcome home," said Marvin. "Mr. Thomas Baker wired money for your taxi ride from Russellville and to deliver a telegram to the Ward family to let them know when you would be home," he continued. The taxi driver tip his hat and drove away.

Ms. Parthina was very pleased to hear the loud talking and laughing going on in Ms. Betty's kitchen. There must have been four or five different conversations going on at the same time; Mr. Will sat smoking his pip right in the middle of them. "Looks like Mr. Will missed the loud talking and laughing too," said Ms. Betty. "He did," replied Ms. Parthina. Ms. Parthina and Ms. Betty took a seat at the dining room table and, just like Mr. Will, listened to all the different conversations. Ms. Betty gave a sigh of relief; she was happy to be home.

Ms. Parthina offered to let Effie and Lizzy help make breakfast for May and her new family. Ms. Betty offered to help with breakfast; she wanted May to spend time with her sisters. May never said anything about missing her sisters, but Ms. Better knew she did. "Guess Papa got his fill of loud talking and laughing, he went outside," said May. While Ms. Betty and Ms. Parthina prepared breakfast, the loud talking and laughing moved to the living room. Ms. Betty and Ms. Parthina agreed: too much loud talking and laughing can be hard on the eardrums—especially old eardrums. They also agreed that they had old eardrums.

May called for Papa to come eat breakfast. Before the food was passed around the table, Ms. Parthina wanted to say the blessing. Hands were placed in the praying position with eyes closed. Ms. Parthina started thanking the Lord for all her blessings—one by one—until Mr. Will interrupted her with a loud "amen." Mr. Will was a man of few words; even when saying the blessing, Mr. Will was a "get in, get out, get it done" before the food gets cold.

Clanton had to admit he had missed Mr. Will and Ms. Parthina's way of conversing with each other; he found it to be very entertaining. Ms. Betty and Robert agreed with Clanton. Mr. Will took a sip of his coffee, cleared his throat, and said, "We do what we can. Ain't that right, Mama?" Mama and Papa Ward smiled at each other and busted out laughing.

Chapter 20

Being home in Dover made their time in New Orleans feel like a dream. Whether a dream or real, May and Robert would always treasure those memories. Some evenings the family talked about their time in New Orleans; they still laughed about the day they walked to town and all their fun. Since being back home, May learned to cook a tasty stew; she called it finger stew. According to Grandma Baker, Clara was very pleased to hear about the finger stew. May mostly cooked like her mama, but her finger stew was her own recipe.

Clanton loved to tease May about her cooking; mostly he wanted to know what body parts were for supper. In the beginning May looked to Ms. Betty for permission to do things around the house or the cooking. Ms. Betty explained that her days of being the lady of the house were over; May was now the lady of the house. She was in charge of her own home. Ms. Betty would be there to help; she would only give advice when asked. Well, on the advice part, Ms. Betty would try not to give advice unless asked.

Ms. Parthina waited a few days before inviting the Cartwright family for supper. Mr. Will had butchered a hog shortly before the newlyweds got home; Ms. Parthina was just itching to fix a pork roast. May and Robert accepted the invitation on behalf of the family. May offered to bring a peach cobbler for dessert. May and Robert agreed supper with the family would be a good time to give the gifts from New Orleans.

Clanton carried the peach cobbler; Ms. Betty carried the shopping bags with all the gifts. Robert and May walked hand in hand; sometimes Robert put his arm around May's small waist. While in New Orleans, Grandma Baker showed May how to gussy up her dresses by wearing a belt. Before leaving, Grandma Baker gave May a gift of three belts: a black belt, a brown belt, and a red belt. Even May's sack dresses were much improved by a belt.

Usually Ms. Parthina served homemade biscuits or cornbread with her meals, but this time, she was serving homemade yeast rolls. She had volunteered the family to be her taste testers. Ms. Parthina wanted to make sure the rolls were good before moving on to loaves of bread and cinnamon rolls. The rolls were served piping hot to ensure the best flavor. Little Dolly took one taste of a buttered roll, and that was all she wanted for her supper.

After supper but before dessert, May and Robert passed out gifts. Little Dolly thought Santa Claus had come because there were gifts. Everyone liked their gifts, but some were more excited than others. When Lizzy opened the package containing a lady's hat, she let out a loud squeal then headed for the mirror. Papa didn't squeal, but he was pretty pleased with his jar of tobacco; when he opened the wooden pipe stand with a place for his jar of tobacco, he was extremely pleased. Now he wouldn't have to ask, "Has anyone seen my pipe?" Seaburn was very happy with his new necktie. Seaburn did look handsome in a necktie.

During dessert, Lizzy and Effie started teasing Seaburn about being sweet on a girl from church. "Her name is Ruby Pruitt, if you must know. Her mama's name is Sarah Jane, her papa's name is Lee, and she has a brother and sister, and that's all I know right now," said Seaburn. Lizzy and Effie knew if they got Seaburn all riled up, he would tell everything he knew about Ruby Pruitt, and he did just that. Mama snickered as she told the girls to behave.

Mama and the little ones planned a trip to town, now that she knew her yeast rolls were good; she invited Ms. Betty to join them. The day after their trip to town would be a good day to start making bread and maybe even some cinnamon rolls. Ms. Betty invited Clanton to town with her and Ms. Parthina. She knew he would have to be convinced or he would want to stay home with Robert and May. "Besides giving Robert and May some privacy, me and Ms. Parthina may need your muscles to help carry our shopping bags back home."

Just as Ms. Parthina and Ms. Betty planned; they were going to bake bread. It was a little easier to do things at Ms. Parthina's house because of the little ones—mostly little Dolly. Don was old enough to tag along with Mr. Will and Seaburn. If Little Dolly was home, she didn't put up a big fuss when it was nap time, but not at home, a nap was not going to happen.

The day of baking bread, May and Ms. Betty showed up bright and early. Lizzy was to help Mama with the baking while Effie tidied up around the house and looked after the younger children. Mary Jane and Shorty together were able to make a bed; Don was good at keeping little Dolly still long enough for all the beds to be made. The floors were swept and a damp mob was used to finish the cleaning. After the tidying up, it was playtime.

While the dough was rising, Ms. Parthina heated some leftover coffee for her and Ms. Betty. She locked the back door to keep the men from stomping through the kitchen and killing her yeast bread. Coming from the front yard were sounds of happy children. Ms. Parthina and Ms. Betty went to the front porch to watch the children play. Effie was playing blind man's bluff with Mary Jane, Shorty, and Don; that's where most of the squealing was coming from. Lizzy was playing hopscotch with little Dolly; May helped little Dolly when it was her turn to hop on one foot. Little Dolly thought she was big stuff, playing hopscotch.

Mr. Will, Seaburn, Robert, and Clanton came stomping from the back of the house; just like Ms. Parthina thought, they would try to enter the house by way of the back door. "Wife, did you mean to lock us out of the house?" smirked Mr. Will. "Yes, husband, I did." Ms. Parthina explained the yeast bread was rising in the kitchen; it was not to be disturbed. She also explained the floors had been mopped, and he could not enter through the front.

Mr. Will gave Ms. Parthina one of his "please and thank-you" looks, hoping she would change her mind and let him go into the house. Ms. Parthina was not budging, no matter how sweet Mr. Will looked; she still said no. When Mr. Will's "please and thank you" look failed, he tried his pouty face—that face too was told no.

Lizzy continued playing hopscotch with little Dolly while May joined Robert on the porch. It didn't take long for the floors to dry, which made Mr. Will happy; he was ready for a cup of hot coffee, and of course, he wanted to smoke his pipe. He could smoke his pipe, but his hot coffee would have to wait; Ms. Parthina and Ms. Betty had finished off the coffee.

Fresh coffee was perking while the first batch of rolls and cinnamon rolls were baking. Ms. Parthina's powdered sugar icing was ready and waiting for the hot cinnamon rolls. Just as expected, the first batch of cinnamon rolls was gone in a flash. Mr. Will called them lip-smacking good, and the children agreed—lip-smacking good. The kitchen emptied as fast as it had filled once the cinnamon rolls were eaten.

Mr. Will and Robert took their coffee to the family table out front. In the kitchen, Ms. Betty was telling Effie and Lizzy about the fashions that were being worn in New Orleans. "When the women start talking fashion, you best leave the room—fast," said Mr. Will. If you get sucked into their conversation, you'll end up in the doghouse.

Robert was about to get his first advice about women and their butts. At some point in your married life, you're going to be asked, "Does my butt look big in this? Does this make me look fat? Do you think I'm getting fat?" As a husband, it's your responsibility, when asked, to convince your wife she is not fat, that her butt is not too big, she is perfect in every way, and I don't suggest waiting to be asked before commenting on her beauty.

Baking bread for two families was a little tiring for May. She was happy to be going home where she might take a few minutes to rest. The baked goods were put away before Ms. Betty and May would rest. Ms. Betty took her shoes off right there in the kitchen; she was too tired to care where she left them. She encouraged May to do the same. While May flung her shoes past the kitchen into the living room, Ms. Betty put the teakettle on for some soothing tea. There they sat, feet propped up with their toes wiggling.

Calling the Cartwright place home still felt a little odd to May, but after the flinging of the shoes, she felt right at home. Ms. Parthina didn't allow flinging shoes at her house; maybe that's what made May feel this was her home—she could fling shoes if she wanted too. Sipping a soothing tea from a proper teacup with saucer, their feet propped up, and their toes free to wiggle were just the things to ease their fatigue.

May's pretty face showed fatigue long before she would ever admit to being tired. For May, taking a few minutes to rest might be sitting down while mixing cornbread for supper; according to Ms. Betty that was not resting. For the Ward family, leisure time came at the end of the day; their rest came at night while they slept. "To keep you from feeling guilty, just come get me and we can rest at the same time," said Ms. Betty. May agreed.

The fields were being made ready for planting cotton. Ms. Betty and May put out buckets of water with easy access for the workers. The workers ate their lunch under any tree that put out some shade. The family table under the big shade tree was where Ms. Betty and Clanton had their lunch. May laid an old quilt under the shade tree for her and Robert to have a picnic lunch. Seeing the old quilt under the shade tree brought back memories of Walter and his last visit. Clanton shouted out, "Robert, don't get into any poison ivy." Robert assured May there was no poison ivy near the tree, and Clanton was just teasing them.

The farmers in the Pope County area were all hoping the weather would continue to warm, which would allow their cotton to be planted by mid April. Mild days and cool nights would not be enough to warm the soil; planting the cotton would have to wait until after the last frost. The family vegetable garden would be ready for planting about the same time. May wanted to add cucumbers to the family's vegetable garden; she wanted to make pickles using Ms. Parthina's sweet pickle recipe. *Bread and butter pickles might be nice too*, she thought.

Getting the pigs to market came soon after the cotton was planted. Ms. Betty and May finished their vegetable garden while Mr. Will and Robert made arrangements to get the pigs sold. Mr. Will and Robert agreed to expand their pigpens before buying new piglets. Mr. Will was pleased with the small portion from the sale of his pigs. However, according to Ms. Betty and Robert, *all* the pigs in Mr. Will's pigpen belong to Mr. Will. The generosity from the sale of the pigs was much appreciated by all, even Mr. Will.

When the pigpens were ready, Mr. Will and Robert traveled to Morrilton to buy piglets at the auction barn located on the west end of town on Highway 64. The Ward's family wagon was fitted with high sideboards to safely haul the piglets back to Dover. The wagon bed was also lined with straw to soften the ride for the little pigs. The trip to Morrilton by wagon and to be early at the auction barn required Mr. Will and Robert to be gone overnight.

Ms. Betty and Clanton took it upon themselves to keep May entertained while Robert was away. While Ms. Betty and May fixed hamburger for supper, Clanton fixed a large tent in the living room. The high-back chairs from the kitchen made for a large and tall tent. Just like before, a lamp was put inside the tent for the feel of a campfire. Robert had told May about how he, his mama, and Clanton slept in a makeshift tent in the living room the night before their wedding. Even though Robert was away, May knew she was going to enjoy sleeping in a tent with Ms. Betty and Clanton. It wasn't that May had never slept in a tent; she had never slept in a tent, just for fun. "When I was little, and before Papa decided to put down hard roots, we slept under the wagon in poorly crafted tents or a lean-to on the side of the wagon; this was all out of necessity and fun had nothing to do with it," said May.

The hamburgers and potato salad were served on old metal plates just like the pioneers might have used; their iced tea was served in a metal cups. "Mama, how did they wash dishes back in the old timey days?" snickered Clanton. "I don't know, Clanton… that was before my time," laughed Ms. Betty. All got a good laugh from Clanton's question. May admitted that was before her time, too, but she heard they washed the dishes just like they washed their children, in the cold water down at the creek. All laughed, and Clanton said, "Never mind."

Ms. Betty washed the pioneer dishes while May fixed a plate of sugar cookies to take back to the tent. Everyone was having fun and everything was going just fine until May got a whiff of the hamburger drippings in the cast-iron skillet; to the bathroom she ran where she lost her supper. She had noticed her sense of smell was somewhat off, but she had never felt this sick from just a smell before now. May brushed her teeth and returned to the tent as if nothing had happened. She blamed her upset stomach on eating too fast.

Ms. Betty wanted to ask questions about May's upset stomach, but since Clanton was there, she would let it go until later. May, Ms. Betty, and Clanton ate sugar cookies and laughed the night away before going to sleep on their own little pallet. The next morning, Ms. Betty and Clanton slipped out of the tent without disturbing May. They enjoyed coffee and buttered biscuits for breakfast on the family table out back.

May sleep until ten o'clock, which was not like her. She thought maybe she was coming down with a bug, maybe that's why she got sick, maybe that's why she sleep so late, maybe that's why she still felt tired. She fixed herself a cup of girly coffee and joined Ms. Betty at the family table. Ms. Betty had already done two loads of laundry; May felt bad that she was not there to help with the laundry. "We all get sick one time or another. You needed to sleep to help your body get well," Ms. Betty said gently. "Clanton helped me with the laundry."

If May was feeling well enough, Ms. Betty wanted to go visit with Ms. Parthina. The laundry was hanging out to dry, Ms. Betty assured May the laundry would be there when they returned home. May hurriedly brushed her teeth, combed her hair, and pinched her high cheekbones to add a little color to her seemly pale face. Ms. Betty gave May a cold biscuit to eat on the way to visit her Mama. May was happy to be going for a visit. She felt the need to see her Mama; she felt the need to hug her Mama.

Ms. Parthina was sitting on the front porch snapping bean for supper; the younger children were playing with Coley the family dog. Ms. Parthina said Effie and Lizzy were inside. "Find a mirror and you'll find them." May found them just where Mama said they would be; they were taking turns admiring themselves in Mama's full-length mirror. May watched and listened a bit before her sisters even noticed she was there. The two jumped with fright before they realized it was only May. Laughter filled the room. "You thought I was Papa standing in the doorway, didn't you?" asked May. "Papa says we're already pretty and looking in the mirror is not going to make us prettier. He would never let us hear the end of it if he saw us all prissy in front of Mama's mirror," laughed Lizzy.

Mama called for the prissy daughters to come to the front porch. "Ms. Betty has business in town today, and I need ya'll to look after the younger children. May will be going to town with us," instructed Ms. Parthina. "We might be gone a while so ya'll may need to start supper when it's time." May had no idea Ms. Betty had business to do in town. On their walk to town, Ms.

Parthina asked May a few questions about her being sickly. "Ms. Betty told me about your fainting spell while you were in New Orleans and about you getting sick after you smelled grease in the skillet. Ms. Betty thinks. "We think you're pregnant." May was in disbelief; she just got married, she couldn't be pregnant. Ms. Betty and Ms. Parthina chuckled as they explained where they were going. "They were going to Russellville to see old Dr. Hickey. They were hoping to catch the taxi driver, Marvin Young, on his way back to Russellville. Ms. Parthina figured if the taxi was going back to Russellville anyway, he might not charge them for a ride. After they saw Dr. Hickey they could ride the taxi back to Dover." Just as Ms. Parthina hoped, the young taxi driver didn't charge them for their ride.

Old Dr. Hickey confirmed what Ms. Betty and Ms. Parthina already suspected; May was expecting a baby, most likely the end of November according to Dr. Hickey. The taxi ride back to Dover was quiet; May and the two grandmas-to-be were all thinking babies. On their walk home, each grandma-to-be let out a really big shout. They were tickled pink with the idea of becoming a grandma. May had all kinds of emotions running through her body.

"Papa and Robert won't be home until late. We can't wait that long before telling the others the good news," said Ms. Parthina. May agreed telling the others would be fine as long as no one said anything to Robert. May wanted to tell Robert about their baby in private. Ms. Parthina, Ms. Betty, and even May had smirks on their face as they entered the house. "Ya'll look like the cat that ate the canary. What did ya'll do?" asked Effie. Ms. Parthina couldn't help herself.

"We went to Russellville to see old Dr. Hickey."

"Who's sick?" asked Lizzy?" Ms. Betty assured the girls no one was sick. "Who went to see the doctor?" snapped Effie. The whole time May never said a word; she just smiled.

Ms. Parthina, followed by Ms. Betty, went strolling to the kitchen where she filled the teakettle with water. May, Effie, and Lizzy watched from the kitchen doorway; Ms. Parthina pulled teacups and saucers from the cupboard. "Why is Mama making tea for all of us?" asked Effie. Ms. Parthina put her good tablecloth on the table; a serving dish with cookies was placed in the middle of the table. The matching sugar and creamer were filled and place on the table. Ms. Parthina gave the younger children cookies and milk. Ms. Betty served the tea as Ms. Parthina got the young ones settled with their cookies and milk.

The ladies sipped their tea; still they had no idea what was going on. "Would you like more tea, Grandma Cartwright?"

"Yes, thank you, Grandma Ward." Effie and Lizzy placed their cups on their saucers. "What did you say? Did you say, Grandma Cartwright, Grandma Ward?" asked both Lizzy and Effie. "Yes, we did, Aunt Effie, Aunt Lizzy. The squeals could have been heard in the next county. What a wonderful day…everyone was happy about May and Robert's baby. Effie and Lizzy now understood the tablecloth, the fine china, and the tea.

Ms. Parthina suggested vegetable soup and grilled cheese sandwiches for supper. She said the snap beans could wait till tomorrow. Soup with a grilled cheese sandwich was always one of May's favorite things to eat, and Mama aimed to please. Ms. Parthina left the tablecloth on the table; they were still celebrating. "Papa will think I put the tablecloth on for him."

Finally, Seaburn and Clanton came strolling in from the fishing pond. Ms. Parthina wouldn't let them near her tablecloth until they washed up good. They enjoyed their soup and a few sandwiches. Mary Jane and Shorty had been hanging around the kitchen hoping to hear more exciting news. Shorty just had to share the news. "May is going to have a baby, and it's a secret. Robert doesn't know yet." Secrets never did last long around Shorty.

Chapter 21

Mr. Will and Robert finally got home with their little piglets. Mr. Will had lanterns hanging above each mule; lighting their last five miles home. Robert had never seen a covered wagon with lights before. Mr. Will point out...they could look silly and get home tonight; or they could be like most and wait to get home tomorrow. Silly it would be.

Ms. Betty and May had gone home to wait for Robert and the little piglets while Clanton stayed behind to help unload Mr. Will's pigs. Mary Jane and Shorty were not allowed to see the cute little pigs until morning; Shorty might blab about the baby, and Ms. Parthina was taking no chances. Effie and Lizzy made sure the piglets were feed and watered while Mr. Will delivered the rest of the pigs in his covered wagon with headlights.

It was good that Clanton and Seaburn were there to help unload the piglets to make sure they had food and water. Robert never gave those pigs another thought once he saw May standing in the doorway. Mr. Will had to stop the wagon; Robert might have broken his fool neck jumping from a moving wagon. "Oh, to be young and in love, ain't nothing like it," said Mr. Will. "Ain't we going to wait for Robert to come help unload these pigs?" asked Clanton. "We should be able to handle this little group of piglets."

Clanton and Seaburn helped Mr. Will unload the piglets; they made sure they had food and water. Clanton wanted to tell Mr. Will the big news, but he knew it wasn't his news to tell. Mr. Will could always tell when Seaburn was keeping a secret; he would get all twitchy. Mr. Will knew if he waited long enough, Seaburn would spit that secret right out.

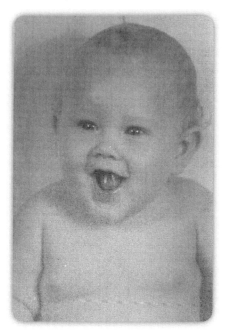

On the way home, Seaburn told the big news. Mr. Will stopped the wagon, stood up, and let out the biggest whoop he could.

"Does everyone know?"

"May will be telling Robert tonight...then we will all know," said Seaburn. "From what I understand, May has been a little sickly, so Mama and Ms. Betty took her to see old Dr. Hickey in Russellville this morning. That's all the information I know," continued Seaburn.

Mr. Will laughed out loud when he told Seaburn. "I'm almost too young to be a Grandpa."

Back at the Cartwright house, May and Robert were left alone in the kitchen. May was warming some supper for Robert; she was waiting for the perfect time to tell Robert about their baby. When the time came, May's words left Robert in disbelief, just as Dr. Hickey's words left her in disbelief. From the bedroom, Ms. Betty and Clanton came charging in with big hugs and many congratulations. No doubt this was a great day for both families.

The house was filled with such excitement. Ms. Betty was sure no one would be getting much sleep this night. She was eager to write her parents, letting them know about the baby. Clanton had already decided he was going to like being an uncle—"Uncle Clanton." Clanton insisted everyone try on their new names: Ms. Betty said "Grandma," May said, "Mama," Robert said, "Daddy." Robert thought "Papa" was a little old-fashioned and he liked the idea of being called Daddy. It was agreed…everyone had their new names.

The reason for May's fatigue made sense once her condition was revealed. Dr. Hickey sent May home with bottles of vitamins and a list of instructions to be followed *exactly* for the next few weeks. The vitamins were to make sure the baby was getting enough nutrients and extra iron for May. Dr. Hickey thought May was a little too thin; he instructed her to have a healthy snack twice a day at least until she started gaining some weight.

The vitamins helped with May's fatigue and the snacks helped with her weight gain. May and Ms. Betty spent their evenings making baby clothes, diapers, booties, and anything else that the baby might need. Ms. Parthina was making the baby a quilt. Lizzy was trying her hand at knitting booties and winter hats. Effie was making receiving blankets and bigger baby blankets. The ladies were in charge of the baby's wardrobe while the men were in charge of the new room that was being added to the house. Weather permitting the construction of the baby's room started early in the morning and stopped around three o'clock. Three o'clock was rest time for May; she usually took a short nap.

Mr. Will and Robert were working together to make the baby a bed; Seaburn and Clanton were making a rocking horse for the baby. Ms. Parthina wanted to make curtains for the baby's room. The baby's room would be painted a pale yellow since they didn't know the sex of the baby. Effie and Lizzy made May some maternity clothes. All were working hard.

Every day May was asked about names for the baby. May and Robert agreed: Robert Murphy Cartwright or Nancy Louise Cartwright. Murphy came from Mr. Will, his middle name was Murphy; Nancy came from Ms. Parthina's mama; Louise came from Ms. Betty.

The excitement about May's baby had overshadowed the fact that Ms. Parthina was having a baby of her own. Her baby would be coming in January. Ms. Parthina never went to see a doctor when having her children; that was just the way things were back then. With each visit to see Dr. Hickey May came back with a bottle of vitamins. Ms. Parthina's babies were all born healthy, and she had never taken prenatal vitamins.

Ms. Parthina's babies were all born at home with the help of Aunt Julia, the midwife. Mr. Will managed to get Ms. Parthina and the children out of the covered and into a house just before each baby was born. After the birth of little Dolly, Ms. Parthina insisted Mr. Will find his family a place to live and put down some hard roots. She wasn't going to be traveling the countryside like a bunch of traveling white trash. Putting down hard roots meant staying in one place more than two months, no longer living out of the back of a covered wagon.

Ms. Parthina wrote Aunt Julia a letter, letting her know the good news about the new babies that were coming. Aunt Julia quickly answered Ms. Parthina's letter; she would arrive by mid-October. Ms. Betty was happy to hear Aunt Julia would be there to help May with the birth of her baby. May and Robert were also relieved to know Aunt Julia was coming.

Mr. Will and Robert finished the new room for the baby and the new baby bed. Ms. Parthina's curtains finished the look of the room. Mr. Will had repaired an old chest of drawers he picked up at a trash dumping sight. He planned to wait until the baby was born to paint it: blue or pink. Baby clothes and diapers were finished. Ms. Betty and May also made a few baby clothes for May's little brother or sister. Ms. Parthina had saved her old baby clothes, but May wanted that new baby to have a few new things, not just hand-me-downs.

While taking her afternoon rest, May read a story to her baby. Grandma Baker gave the storybook to Ms. Betty just before they left New Orleans. The storybook belonged to Ms. Betty when she was a little girl, and now it was being passed down to Ms. Betty's grandchild. Grandma and Grandpa Baker were planning a visit sometime after the baby was born.

Having a baby didn't mean the day-to-day chores went away. May found working in her vegetable garden relaxing. She was well pleased with the bounty each plant produced, especially her cucumbers. Ms. Betty and May made sweet pickles, bread and butter pickles, and a few jars of dill pickles. Other than the dill pickles, May enjoyed a small bowl of pickles with the juice and crackers; she dunked her crackers in the pickles juice.

Canning vegetables from the garden insured the family to have food during the winter months. Ms. Betty and May just like Ms. Parthina made homemade vegetable soup to be canned. "New babies take up a lot of your time. You're going to need something easy to fix for supper," according to Ms. Parthina. "Robert could even fix that for supper," she snickered.

Berry picking with her mama and sisters was such a treat. Ms. Parthina thought picking berries should be fun; she brought big hunks of cheese and homemade bread and a big jug of water. The berry patches were not so far from home that bringing a lunch was needed. When May and the older children were small, Ms. Parthina made picking berries fun; they were pirates looking for gold. The little pirates were allowed to eat some of the gold as long as there was enough to put in their buckets. Little Seaburn always had gold smeared around his mouth. Alvie could be seen pouring some of his gold into Seaburn's bucket. Ms. Parthina always brought a jug of water and a little something to eat after a day of berry picking.

May brought home two large water buckets filled with berries. Making a clobber was first on May's list of things to do with the berries. While May waited for her cobbler to bake, she sat with her feet propped up. She had learned to listen to her body when she got tired. In the evenings, Robert would rub May's feet and ankles to help with the swelling. May and Ms. Betty made jelly and canned berries for days from that one trip to the berry patches.

Ms. Parthina had a talk with May about breast-feeding her baby. "Ms. Parthina encouraged May to have plenty of canned evaporated milk and bottles on hand, "Just in case you don't make enough milk to satisfy the baby. If you don't need the canned milk for the baby, you can use it for cooking. You will need bottles for giving the baby water and maybe juice."

After the berry patches were picked clean, it was time to move on to the apple trees. May wasn't allowed to pick apples unless they were on a low-hanging branch. Ms. Parthina and May sat on a quilt in the shade with little Dolly. Don was just the right size to start helping with the apple picking; he enjoyed helping, it made him feel as big as the others. Before taking the apples home, everyone sat on the ground and ate a freshly picked apple, still warm from the sun. These were memories the Ward children would share with their children.

Ms. Parthina was going to teach May and Ms. Betty how to make applesauce. Seaburn, Robert, and Clanton walked to town for more jars and sugar. Small jelly jars would be used for applesauce. "This applesauce will be just the thing to feed your baby when it's old enough to eat soft food," said Ms. Parthina. May and Ms. Betty still had much to learn.

The cotton was ready to be picked. Robert and Clanton placed water buckets out for the workers. Robert didn't want May to carry anything that weighed more than a basket of eggs. Ms.

Parthina and Ms. Betty watched how Robert doted on May. Robert was a good man; he made his Mama proud. Clanton was on his way to becoming a good man too.

Mid-October arrived and so did Aunt Julia. Ms. Parthina sent Mary Jane and Shorty to let the Cartwright family know they were invited to supper and to see Aunt Julia. "When you see Aunt Julia, you'll be able to tell they are related, Mama favors her," said May. May decided to make an applesauce cake to take for supper. She was excited to have her husband and new family meet Aunt Julia. Aunt Julia and Aunt Mary were May's favorite aunts.

After supper, Aunt Julia wanted to take a closer look at May and the baby. She would be able to tell if her baby was in the right position, or getting ready to move into the right position. She could also get an idea of how big the baby would be when born. According to Aunt Julia...May and her baby was right where they should be; her baby was going to be big. Ms. Parthina was next to be examined by Aunt Julia. Ms. Parthina and her baby were healthy and they were right on schedule. Both families received good news about their babies.

Aunt Julia was pleased to see that Mr. Will had settled down and got his family out of that covered wagon. Ms. Parthina now had a taste of real stability, and she was never living out of that covered wagon again; neither were her children. Ms. Parthina admitted she was happy that Mr. Will took a liking to stability; she would sure hate to lose him after all the years they had been married. Aunt Julia knew Ms. Parthina wasn't kidding.

The Cartwright family was hosting Thanksgiving dinner mostly because May knew if she walked to Mama and Papa's house, she would have her baby in the middle of the road. Since no one wanted May to have her baby in the middle of the road, the Ward family graciously accepted the Cartwright's invitation to Thanksgiving dinner.

Mr. Will hitched the wagon while Ms. Parthina and Aunt Julia got the little ones ready for a ride in the wagon. The children were all snuggled in the wagon; Seaburn, Effie, and Lizzy each held a dish of food or a dessert to share with the Cartwright family. The house was toasty warm and smelled of Thanksgiving dinner. Robert helped May take everyone's coat; they laid them across their bed. Robert didn't get too far away from May these days.

Since Robert was the man of the house, he was in charge of carving the turkey. The kitchen counters were filled with dishes of food. A small table had been setup for the desserts. Another table was set for the younger children. Aunt Julia and Ms. Parthina helped Don and little Dolly with their plates. Mary Jane and Shorty agreed to watch after the little ones so Ms. Parthina could eat at the big table with the others.

Everyone watched as May tried to figure out how to eat her dinner; her belly kept her from getting close enough to the table. "I need longer arm." At first she placed her napkin over her belly, but she still needed longer arms. "Let that baby hold your plate," suggested Mr. Will. "That's a good idea, Papa." May gave it a try. She lightly allowed her dinner plate to rest on her belly. "Normally I eat standing up, otherwise I might starve," laughed May.

"I see that you've been standing a lot," laughed Seaburn.

There was so much food; Mr. Will said he needed to rest before he got started on dessert. That was true for most of the adults… but not the little ones. They were ready for some chocolate pie and some coconut pie. Ms. Parthina gave Don and little Dolly a small slice of each. The dinner plates were cleared from the tables and made ready for washing.

Lizzy and Effie volunteered to help Ms. Betty tidy the kitchen and wash the dishes. May was so proud of the baby's room she had to show it off. Grandma and Grandpa Baker had sent a rocking chair for the baby's room. Ms. Betty made a yellow cushion that matched the curtains. The wood color of the rocking chair closely matched the wood color of the baby's bed. Mr. Will said, "I can stain the little chest to match the other furniture in the baby's room, if you'd like. I think I would like that Papa, if it ain't too much trouble."

After their tour of the baby's room, everyone returned to the kitchen. The dishes were done; the coffeepot was perking up some fresh coffee. Ms. Betty and May had something to give to Ms. Parthina; they wanted to do it before everyone started eating again. Ms. Parthina was given two bundles, each wrapped in a cloth diaper and tied with slivers of yellow cloth. The first bundle was flannel baby gowns with drawstrings; under the gowns was a flannel bed jacket for Ms. Parthina. The second bundle was cloth diapers and two pairs of booties.

The little gowns were passed around for all to see. Ms. Parthina loved her bed jacket and the baby clothes, she was about to start bawling. Mr. Will shouted, "Parthina and that baby are going to look beautiful in their new duds." When Mr. Will shouted, he scared the bawling right out of Ms. Parthina. Everyone, including Ms. Parthina laughed.

Aunt Julia gave May a quick examination before leaving. "Your baby is beginning to move into position to be born. Walking is good at this point in your pregnancy, but not long walks and not alone. Babies are usually born when they want to be born." Aunt Julia gave May a few more tidbits: "Eat when you want, sleep when sleepy, other than walking, rest as much as you can. You don't want to be too tired to help this baby come into the world." May was very thankful to have Aunt Julie as her midwife, thankful to have her as an aunt.

The most wonderful smell caught May's senses as she entered the kitchen. The smell of smoke from Mr. Will's pipe seemed to satisfy a craving. Aunt Julia helped the little ones get bundled for the wagon ride home while Ms. Parthina gathered enough leftovers to last a few days. Mr. Will left plenty of pipe smoke for May. For this day, all were thankful.

The cold November days seemed long. May went to bed early, slept late, and still she needed two naps a day. Just when she thought she couldn't get any bigger, she did. May was convinced that if she fell down, she would roll for days. Robert was good about helping her out of the bathtub, so when he needed help getting her out of the bathtub, it was time to switch to showers. May was looking forward to the day she could see her own feet.

The end of November had passed and so did May's need for sleep. Out of the blues, May woke early with energy to spare. She wanted the kitchen cabinets and draws to have new linings. The drawers were easy and didn't take much time. The cabinets would require standing on a chair to remove the dishes. While the coffee perked, May removed dishes from the cabinets. Ms. Betty was quiet surprised to see May still in her nightgown—no shoes and standing on a chair. Ms. Betty shooed her down from the chair before Robert could see her. "I have always heard that just before a baby is born, the mother gets big burst of energy,"

said Ms. Betty. "Looks like the old wives' tale might be true," she continued.

Ms. Betty offered to help May with her project, but only after they had breakfast. May agreed; together they would finish lining the shelves. Ms. Betty stated breakfast. May went for her housecoat and socks for her cold feet. Her housecoat no longer covered her front; her socks belonged to Robert. Her feet and ankles were big like the rest of her. Robert didn't mind sharing his socks; he didn't mind putting them on May's feet. "I feel like staying in my flannel gown, my housecoat, and your warm socks all day long. I will brush my teeth.

May ate a hearty breakfast and was ready to finish the kitchen shelves. Once the shelves were lined, May was ready for another project. Flipping the mattress on the bed was her next project. May invited Ms. Betty to help with flipping the mattress; pregnant or not, it was a two-person job. All day long, May went from one project to another. Ms. Betty was sure they would be having a baby very soon. May had a snack, a nap, and still no baby.

May ran out of things to scrub, wash, polish, and move before she was ready to have her baby. Finally the day came. The bellyache that woke her, that didn't go away, that started hurting more, May knew it was time to wake Robert and Ms. Betty. Ms. Betty and Clanton were calm; Robert was not calm at all. Clanton ran to get Aunt Julia and Ms. Parthina. Mr. Will had the wagon on standby for some time now. "Hot doggie, we're having a baby," shouted Mr. Will. Lizzy put the coffeepot on; it was going to be a long wait.

Ms. Betty, Aunt Julia, and Ms. Parthina took charge of May and her baby. Everything had been made ready for this day. Robert was told to boil water, Clanton was told to make coffee; Mr. Will was to keep them clam. During the first hour, Ms. Parthina asked Clanton to bring three cups of coffee and one glass of ice to the bedroom. He put everything on a tray, including cream and sugar. After another hour, Robert was asked to bring a pan of hot water to the bedroom. Shortly after the hot water, they needed more coffee.

Robert kept a watchful eye on the hot water; Clanton never let the coffeepot be empty too long; Mr. Will paced the floors. When Ms. Parthina came from the bedroom, Mr. Will knew it was time to take Robert and Clanton out of the house, as far out as he could. It wouldn't be long until May's baby would be born. Robert didn't want to leave the house. Mr. Will and Clanton did manage to get Robert to the big family table in the backyard. The sounds from the house were painful for Robert to hear, but once a baby's cry was heard, Robert began to sob. Ms. Betty came to the back porch and shouted, "It's a boy!"

December 5, 1928, Robert Murphy Cartwright was born. He weighed eight-pounds and 12 ounces.; Mama and baby were doing just fine. Mr. Will and Clanton got to see May and the baby for just a few minutes before being run off so that May and Robert could be alone with their son. Aunt Julia turned the boiling water off before pouring herself a cup of fresh coffee.

Ms. Parthina sat beside Mr. Will; together they had a sigh of relief. Ms. Betty took Clanton to the kitchen where she splashed water on his face; he seemed to be in shock. Once Clanton was back to being Clanton, he offered to go tell the other children that May was all right and little Robert was all right too. "You know they will want to come see the baby…what do I tell them?" asked Clanton. "Aunt Julia says no visitors until tomorrow."

Aunt Julia and Ms. Parthina were spending the night to help May with the baby. Guess who went off and left their change of clothes sitting right by the front door? Mr. Will had Clanton wait and ride back with him. Clanton would bring back the change of clothes for Aunt Julia and Ms. Parthina. Mr. Will and Clanton took one more peak at May and the baby before leaving. "You can stay and eat some supper with us. I know you got to be hungry."

Mr. Will had seen his share of newborn babies, but none as big as his new grandson. He was very proud that his middle name was the baby's middle name. Mr. Will talked about Robert Murphy the whole way home; he thought Robert Murphy had a nice ring to it. Clanton helped Mr. Will feed, water, and put the mules to bed in the barn. The Ward children were standing just inside the door waiting for someone to tell the news of May and her baby.

Mr. Will stepped through the door and shouted, "Robert Murphy is here! May is doing real good. Aunt Julia says May should be up for a visit tomorrow." Mr. Will gave as many details as he could remember. When Mr. Will stopped talking, he realized he was tired and very hungry. Supper was ready to be put on the table; Mr. Will and Clanton were ready for supper. Mr. Will ate his supper quietly; the events of the day were spinning in his head.

The Ward children were bundled and ready to go visit May and her new baby. The weather had turned bitterly cold; Mr. Will thought it might snow. May was awake, but Robert Murphy was sleeping like a baby. Of course everyone thought he was a beautiful baby. Lizzy noted that he had the kind of little cheeks everyone would want to pinch. Little Dolly thought he was a pretty doll, and she wanted to hold him.

Before the visit was over, Grandpa Ward was allowed to hold little Robert Murphy. Aunt Julia wouldn't let anyone enter the room with May and the baby until they had washed their hands with alcohol to kill germs. Robert couldn't even get past Aunt Julia without using alcohol on his hands. May visited as long as she could before falling asleep. Ms. Parthina shooed everyone out so that May could get some rest.

Aunt Julia wanted to stay one more night before leaving May and Ms. Betty on their own with a new baby. Ms. Parthina was tired and ready to be home with her children, ready to sleep in her own bed. She planned to take a nice long nap when she got home. It was time for Ms. Parthina to get plenty of her own rest; her baby would be coming soon.

May and Ms. Betty were quick to catch on to the care of baby Robert Murphy; Robert even helped with the diaper changing. Uncle Clanton enjoyed holding his new nephew but wanted no part of the dirty diapers. Aunt Julia required May to stay in bed the first week after Robert Murphy was born. She required bed rest for all her patients, especially the new mothers. May wasn't ready for Robert Murphy to be in his room; she had his new bed moved to hers. May tried sleeping while the baby slept, but sometimes she just watched him sleep.

Ms. Betty washed a load of baby clothes and diapers every day. The washing was done on the back porch, and the drying was done in the kitchen. Each afternoon, Ms. Betty fixed a pot of tea for herself and May. Together they watched Robert Murphy sleep as they drank tea from their proper teacup with a saucer. They each thought him to be a beautiful baby.

Aunt Julia, Ms. Parthina, and the children came for a visit once May was off bed rest. Ms. Betty and May served their guest small wedges of a tuna salad sandwich; in New Orleans they're called finger sandwiches—nothing like May's finger stew. The family took turns holding Robert Murphy; even little Dolly had a turn at holding the baby.

Christmas was not far off and needed to be discussed. Ms. Parthina wanted to host Christmas dinner at her house. "Papa has already found a good place to cut Christmas trees," said Ms. Parthina. The Ward family had decided that Santa Claus should come see the little ones. "We took a vote and all agreed," said Lizzy. "We are truly blessed, and being with our family at Christmas is all we need," added Ms. Parthina.

The next few days, Christmas trees were cut and brought home. May and Robert made a few more decorations for the Cartwright tree. The weather was cold—too cold to walk to town. Aunt Julia drove the wagon to town for a little Christmas shopping. Mr. Will and Seaburn stayed home with little Dolly and Don. Ms. Betty, Robert, and Clanton joined the Wards for a day of Christmas shopping. May was not ready to be away from Robert Murphy, but she did send her secret Christmas list with Robert. With the help of Clanton, Robert could get everything on May's list without being caught. Clanton enjoyed being sneaky at Christmas.

During the Christmas season, Mr. Bailey and Ms. Ida always stocked extra supplies and items that could be bought for Christmas gifts. The Ward girls had saved their money from picking cotton to use for Christmas. Santa Claus would bring gifts to the little ones. The families agreed they would be happy just spending the holiday with the family. That was true. However, everyone knew Christmas secrets were allowed.

Clanton didn't have to distract anyone *much*, they were secretly buying their own gifts to give at Christmas. While Ms. Parthina was doing her secret shopping, Aunt Julia took their supply list to be filled. Clanton almost forgot his own secret shopping. Mr. Bailey helped load the supplies into the wagon while everyone clutched the bags holding their secret gifts. Ms. Ida always sent a little something extra home for the Ward kids to enjoy. This time, she sent a bag of oranges and a few day-old donuts. Ms. Ida made good donuts, day old or not.

Seaburn helped unload the wagon, but he was not allowed to carry any of the secret shopping bags. "So much for Santa Claus bringing gifts for the little ones and no one else," said Seaburn. "Santa Claus will be bringing gifts for the little ones. The other gifts will be coming from each other, unless you still believe in Santa Claus," said Ms. Parthina.

For Christmas, Mr. Will and Seaburn were making a wagon for Robert Murphy. The sides of the wagon had been stenciled "Commando." For Christmas, little Dolly was getting a brand new baby doll; Mr. Will and Seaburn were making that new baby doll a rocking cradle. Ms. Parthina was making a soft mattress for the rocking cradle. For Christmas, Don was getting a windup locomotive and enough tracks to make a big circle. All other Christmas gifts were wrapped and placed under the tree—Christmas secrets.

Robert Murphy must have known it was Christmas morning; he woke everyone in the house. A few gifts were exchanged before breakfast. Robert Murphy got diapers from Grandma Betty, Santa brought him a rattler, and Mama and Daddy got him a music box to help lull him to sleep when he got a little older. Uncle Clanton gave him a baby's scrapbook.

Clanton was pleased with his new pocketknife from Mama, Robert, and May. Robert Murphy gave Grandma Betty a "Queen for a Day" certificate. The certificate included: breakfast in bed, manicure, pedicure, and a day of lounging around the house. Robert gave May a box of chocolate-covered cherries; May gave Robert a bottle of good-smelling aftershave.

Grandpa Will and Uncle Seaburn came in the covered wagon to pick up the Cartwright family. The wagon was loaded with Christmas gifts, Christmas food, and family. Clanton rode up front with Mr. Will and Seaburn, while the rest rode in the back where they would be shielded from the cold wind. This was Robert Murphy's first outing; he seemed to like it.

Grandpa Will was sure happy to have little Robert Murphy come for a visit. Grandma Parthina made a soft little place on the couch for the baby to sleep. Everyone would be able to look at him without any trouble. Gifts were exchanged before dinner. Everyone liked what they got for Christmas, but the gifts made by Grandpa Will and Seaburn were by far the best.

Robert Murphy was fed, changed, and was put right back to sleep shortly before dinner was ready. Most everyone knew Robert Murphy was not big enough to roll off the couch. Grandpa Will didn't want to take any chances; he insisted something be put in front of him just on wild change he might roll. May snickered a little, but she did as her Papa asked.

Chapter 22

Everyone enjoyed watching Robert Murphy grow and change almost overnight. Now it was late January and time for Ms. Parthina's baby to come. According to Aunt Julia, babies seem to come faster after you've had a baby. As soon as Aunt Julia said Ms. Parthina was in labor, Seaburn gathered the children and headed to May's house. The children would stay at the Cartwright's until their papa came for them. Ms. Betty and Robert returned to the Ward house to help anyway that was needed. Seaburn, Robert, and Mr. Will would pace the floors together. Since Ms. Betty was there to help Aunt Julia, Lizzy and Effie asked to be excused.

Just like with Robert, Mr. Will was told to get out of the house. Mr. Will walked down the road until he could no longer hear anything from the house, then he turned around and walked back to a place he could hear if he was called. Everywhere Mr. Will went, Robert and Seaburn were right behind him. Once the baby's cry was heard, Mr. Will with his wobbly legs waited on the front porch for Aunt Julia to call him back inside.

January 30, 1929, Velma Parthina Ward was born; she weighed six pounds and two ounces. "Mama, I believe this little baby is going to be the prettiest of the whole bunch," said Mr. Will. Of course Mr. Will said that same thing about all their babies. When Mr. Will was run out of the house, Lizzy and Effie went running out the back and past the hog pen. They wouldn't return to the house until they heard nothing coming from the house. To be sure it was all over, the girls snuck a peek through the bedroom window. Mama was holding the baby.

Aunt Julia gave Ms. Parthina the same instructions: one week of bed rest. Effie gathered night clothes and next-day clothes for the children at May's house. Aunt Julia ordered chicken soup or broth with crackers brought to Ms. Parthina; she was feeling weak. Aunt Julia feed Ms. Parthina the chicken soup; her arms were too weak to feed herself. Mr. Will worriedly watched as Ms. Parthina was tended by Aunt Julia. When the time came for Velma to be fed, Ms. Parthina was still too weak to hold her in the nursing position. Aunt Julia propped Ms. Parthina up with pillows; Velma was laid on a pillow in the nursing position. Mr. Will did not leave Ms. Parthina side for two days; it took two days to gain the strength back in her arms. Ms. Parthina followed Aunt Julia's medical advice, and each day she felt a little better. Little Dolly missed her mama; she didn't understand what was going on. When Ms. Parthina began to feel better, she let little Dolly and her new baby doll come for a visit and sometimes they even took naps together. Since Mama's baby doll was named Velma, little Dolly named her baby doll Patsy. Velma and Patsy were good friends.

Weather permitting, May, Robert Murphy, and Grandma Betty would take a wagon ride up the road to see Grandma and Grandpa Ward; well, Robert Murphy was the one riding in the wagon—the wagon he got for Christmas. He started riding in his little wagon before he could even sit up. On most afternoons, the squeaky wheels on Robert Murphy's wagon could be heard on the road going to see Grandma and Grandpa Ward.

May and Ms. Betty had a standing invitation to have tea with Ms. Parthina anytime after two o'clock. While the ladies drank tea, the babies rolled around on one of Ms. Parthina's handmade quilts. Mr. Will didn't drink fancy tea, but he did show up every day to play with the babies. Watching Mr. Will play with the babies reminded Ms. Parthina of how much time he had missed with the older children while trying to scratch out a living.

Sometimes Velma rode in the wagon with Robert Murphy; sometimes baby doll Patsy went for a wagon ride too. On windy days, Robert Murphy wore a little navy blue hat with flaps that kept the wind out of his ears. Velma wore a white bonnet that protected her ears from the wind. Don and little Dolly enjoyed going to town with a wagon full of babies. Dolly walked on one side of the wagon; Don walked on the other side of the wagon. The babies enjoyed the ride to town. Mr. Bailey and Ms. Ida at the general store always made a big fuss over the babies. When the babies were old enough to eat cookies, Ms. Ida never missed the opportunity to give them one of her homemade sugar cookies.

May and Ms. Betty were constantly making clothes for Robert Murphy. He was growing so fast they could hardly keep up with him. May believed Robert Murphy would grow to be a tall man like his daddy. His curly hair came from his daddy; May's hair was very straight. Mr. Will was sure he was going to be a handsome man, just like his Grandpa Ward.

The visits during the week were short compared to the Sunday visits. Most Sundays started with May and her family walking to Sunday school with Ms. Parthina and her children. Velma and Robert Murphy were both well-behaved babies, but even well-behaved babies got tired and fussy. Until Velma and Robert Murphy got older, staying for church would have to wait. The babies were put down for a long nap while Sunday dinner was put together. Velma and Robert Murphy were changed out of their Sunday clothes, just like the other children changed their clothes. Mashed potatoes, cooked carrots, and applesauce were on Sunday's dinner menu; for the babies, neither was a picky eater.

Grandma and Grandpa Baker came for a visit in early June. Grandpa Baker admitted he had been sick, but he never said from what. This trip they traveled by train; they found the train to be faster and less stressful. They took a taxi from Russellville just like May and Robert had done; Marvin Young was the same taxi driver. Robert Murphy was dressed in his Sunday's best when Grandma and Grandpa Baker arrived. He could have been dressed in a burlap bag and they would have never noticed; it was love at first sight.

Robert Murphy was showered with hugs and kisses; in return, Grandma and Grandpa Baker were given wet slobbery kisses. Grandma Baker thought his kisses to be the sweetest slobbery kisses she had ever had; Grandpa Baker agreed. Ms. Betty and Robert Murphy showed off his new bedroom while May and Robert drank coffee in the kitchen. Robert and May would be giving their room to Grandma and Grandpa Baker while they were visiting.

The first night a makeshift tent was made in the living room. This time May, Robert, and Robert Murphy were going to enjoy camping out in the living room. As usual Grandma and Grandpa Baker went to bed early. The tent was made large enough for the entire family. Robert and Clanton kept Robert Murphy entertained while Ms. Betty and May went for graham crackers and milk. Robert Murphy liked graham crackers, but now he had his first taste of graham crackers dunked in milk and May couldn't dunk them fast enough for him.

Early the following morning, Grandma and Grandpa Baker took a peek inside the family tent; Robert Murphy was fast asleep with his mama and daddy. Grandpa started making coffee while Grandma started making breakfast; they knew the sounds and aromas from the kitchen would wake the others. Grandma and Grandpa were right; the sounds and the aromas did wake the family. Robert Murphy woke with a smile in his little voice.

May and Robert quickly got dress; and Robert Murphy got a fresh diaper, his curly blond hair was combed, and his face and hands were washed to remove any leftover graham crackers and milk. Robert Murphy was wearing a pair of pajamas with matching socks. Grandma was making scrambled eggs just for Robert Murphy; "All babies like scrambled eggs," she said.

Ms. Betty greeted her parents with morning kisses on the cheek. Clanton and Robert took the family tent down and returned the chairs to the kitchen. Clanton greeted Grandma and Grandpa Baker with a hug for both. He wanted them to know he was happy to see them and that he was happy to have them as his grandma and grandpa. Clanton's show of affection gave Grandma and Grandpa Baker the most wonderful feeling of being loved by their grandson. Scrambled eggs, buttered biscuits with jelly, and white gravy were served for breakfast. Grandma Baker insisted Robert Murphy sit on her lap while she fed him breakfast; he thoroughly enjoyed his scrambled eggs and blackberry jelly. By the time the baby finished his breakfast, he and Grandma Baker would both require a bath.

After Robert Murphy was bathed and dressed for the day, he was ready for his bottle of milk and a short nap. His short nap was just enough time to get the kitchen all cleaned up. May and Ms. Betty were caught up on the housework and the laundry; picking vegetables from the garden was all that was left to be done. Sitting in the shade sipping lemonade was the only activity planned for the day, until it was time for Robert Murphy's wagon ride.

Ms. Betty admitted to her Mama that they didn't have Robert Murphy on a schedule; he had them on a schedule. May called him very smart because he could already tell time; he knew that when it was two o'clock, it's time to go for a ride in his wagon. Robert Murphy would have lunch, a bottle, and a long nap before his wagon ride. While the baby would sleep, May would pick fresh vegetables to have for supper. A few extra tomatoes and snapped beans were gathered to take to her mama and papa.

May was eager to show her new baby sister Velma off to Grandma and Grandpa Baker. Robert Murphy was ready to go bye-bye in his wagon. His hat would protect his face from the sun; some shading along the road would also help. His little arms were bouncing up and down; he was ready to go. Ms. Parthina and Velma were sitting under the big shade tree waiting for Robert Murphy to come for a visit. Ms. Parthina called to the other children as soon as May and the baby arrived. Everyone wanted a chance to hold him.

Just like clockwork, Mr. Will arrived just in time to play with Velma and Robert Murphy. Ms. Parthina served her guest iced tea; the babies got a graham cracker and a bottle filled with ice cold apple juice to wash it down. Both babies were happy—smiley babies.

Grandpa Baker, Mr. Will, Seaburn, Robert, Clanton, and Don had a fun-filled day of fishing. They fished from the banks and in the shade when they could. Clanton and Don fished together; Don still needed a little help getting his fish to the bank. They caught enough fish to feed the entire county, at least that's what Mr. Will said. Mr. Will enjoyed cooking the fish and hushpuppies. Ms. Parthina and the girls fixed coleslaw, sliced onions, and iced tea.

Grandma and Grandpa Baker stayed ten days before going back to New Orleans. During their visit, the families saw each other almost every day. Ms. Betty and Grandma Baker didn't always go with Robert Murphy on his wagon ride. Sometimes they walked the opposite direction; they needed to be mother and daughter and nothing more. Grandma Baker casually mentioned seeing Walter; he was having brunch with some foozle. Grandma and Grandpa Baker didn't speak to Walter, but they did give him a few hateful glances.

One August morning, Mr. Will and Robert hitched a ride to Russellville; they came home in a new pickup truck with a very loud horn. Robert pulled up in front of Mr. Will's house and honked the horn as loud and as long as he could. Before any of the Ward children could get to the front door, Ms. Parthina had them get away from that front door. Maybe she thought it was some young man honking for one of her girls; her girls were not to be honked for.

Robert offered to teach Mr. Will how to drive, but Mr. Will declined his offer. Mr. Will was quite content to travel by wagon. The long summer days provided plenty of daylight for driving lessons. Lizzy didn't enjoy driving as much as the others; driving made her nervous. She agreed to drive if there was an emergency, but only if there was no one else to drive. Lizzy and Effie could handle the mules and wagon as good as anyone else, but Effie enjoyed driving an automobile best. After learning to drive an automobile, it was now time for Ms. Betty and Clanton to learn to drive Mr. Will's wagon; Lizzy volunteered to teach them. Everyone who could drive an automobile could also handle a team and wagon.

On occasion, May, Ms. Betty, and Robert Murphy stopped by in the pickup to gather Ms. Parthina and the children for a trip to town. Everyone enjoyed going to town on Saturdays. Seaburn was able to see Ruby Pruitt in town on Saturdays. Ruby was accompanied by her brother Lee and her sister Zuvie. Effie and Lizzy enjoyed window shopping and talking about the latest in women's fashions. Clanton enjoyed visiting the blacksmith's shop.

Clanton casually waited by the general store for Seaburn, Effie, and Lizzy; they were to walk home together. A man in a pickup truck called out to Clanton; it was Walter. At first glance; Clanton didn't recognize Walter, his father. Walter parked his truck and crossed the street to talk to Clanton. Walter talked as if it had only been a few days since he had seen Clanton. Walter talked, and Clanton said nothing; Walter asked questions and Clanton said nothing. Walter was drunk, just like the last time Clanton saw him.

Mr. Bailey stood watching through the window as Walter tried to bully Clanton into talking to him. It didn't take long for Walter to lose his temper; still Clanton had nothing to say to Walter. Just as Clanton expected…Walter grabbed him in a fit of rage. Clanton patiently waited for Walter to strike the first blow, and he did. A fist at full force landed on the side of Clanton's face; he saw a few stars but he didn't fall down or lose consciousness. Everything happened fast. Before Mr. Bailey could grab his fighting stick and get out the door Clanton had already delivered two hard blows, and Walter was on the ground.

Clanton and Mr. Bailey stood looking down at Walter the drunk. Clanton's eye and cheekbone was showing signs of swelling. Seaburn and the girls came running as fast as they could run when they saw Walter punch Clanton in the face. Ms. Ida brought an ice pack for Clanton's face. Walter didn't seem quite as drunk when he opened his eyes, but he was still drunk. Clanton and Seaburn helped Walter up from the ground. He was in disbelief that Clanton had raised his hand to him. Once again, Walter was told there was nothing or no one in Dover, Arkansas for him; he need not ever come back.

Clanton and the others watched as Walter drove away from town and away from the Cartwright house. Ms. Ida sent Clanton home with an ice pack; Mr. Bailey sent him home with a fighting stick. All the way home, Clanton and the others keep a lookout for Walter. They thought he was just drunk enough to do something stupid, like come after them to start another fight. Clanton was anxious to get home to let Robert know Walter was in the area and what had happened. It was time to protect the family.

As soon as Mr. Will heard what had happened in town, he gathered his family to let them know about Walter and what to do if he came around any of them. Normally Ms. Parthina didn't allow a loaded rifle to be in the house with the children, but under the circumstances, she thought it would be a good thing to have handy. Mr. Will, Seaburn, and Coley the family dog headed down the road to the Cartwright place; Mr. Will was carrying a loaded rifle.

Before walking up to the house, Mr. Will yelled "Hello" in the house. Robert answered the call with a show of his loaded raffle. Mr. Will and Seaburn brought Coley to stay and guard the Cartwright family for a few days. "Coley knows Walter to be a black hearted coward. He will let you know if Walter comes anywhere near your family," said Mr. Will.

Ms. Parthina felt relieved knowing Coley was watching over the Cartwright family. Coley stayed with the Cartwright's for almost a month and not a peep was heard from Walter. Each day, Coley followed Robert Murphy on his wagon ride. Grandma Baker sent word that Walter had been seen back in Louisiana. The Walter scare was over; everyone gave a sigh of relief.

Robert Murphy and Coley had become good friends during the Walter scare. Coley was living back home with the Ward family, but each afternoon, he could be found sitting at the backdoor of the Cartwright home. Robert Murphy squealed with delight each time he saw his four-legged friend. Robert Murphy extended his hand to pet Coley; in return, Coley gave the little boy doggy kisses on his cubby little cheek. Once Coley was petted and Robert Murphy was given doggy kisses they were ready for a wagon ride.

It was a treat to see Robert Murphy and Velma playing together; of course, Mr. Will was right there playing too. Mr. Will asked Robert Murphy for some sugar; Robert Murphy wanted to give his grandpa a doggy kiss. A doggy kiss wasn't exactly what Mr. Will was expecting, but he took it anyway. "Robert Murphy might be spending too much time with Coley," snickered Mr. Will. Velma gave her Papa a regular baby kiss, which made him happy.

Ms. Parthina had a box fan blowing down on the pallet where the babies played. They were both cubby, and it didn't take long for them to get fussy because they were hot. When the babies started getting fussy, Mr. Will needed to be somewhere else. Ms. Parthina and May cooled the babies by wiping them down with a wet washcloth; ice cubes were added to their bottles of juice. When they were all cooled off, they would take a nap together.

Before Robert Murphy was born, May never understood how her Mama could fall asleep sitting straight up; now she understood. A glass of Ms. Parthina's iced tea, your feet propped up, and watch the babies sleep—life was good.

Robert Murphy knew that when his nap time was over, he was going for another ride in his wagon. Before leaving for home, May and Ms. Betty were hugged by Ms. Parthina; Robert Murphy was hugged and kissed by the whole family. When visiting the Ward family, you were hugged when you arrived; the same way that you were hugged when leaving. As a reward for walking the family home, Coley was given a snack and a bowl of cool water. Robert Murphy waved bye-bye to Coley as he started back home. Coley would be back tomorrow to visit his little buddy.

The cotton had been harvested; the hustle and bustle around the house was gone. The winter crops, mustard greens, cabbage, carrots, turnips, and potatoes were planted. It was time to butcher a hog if they planned to have meat through the winter according to Mr. Will. Mr. Will made a deal with Mr. Bailey at the general store: Mr. Bailey bought a hog from Mr. Will; Mr. Will would butcher the hog for a fee, of course. Mr. Bailey was very particular as to how he wanted his pork; he requested pork roast, bacon, and sausage to be wrapped and delivered. In return, Mr. Bailey would pay cash money upon delivery.

Mr. Will delivered Mr. Bailey's pork and received his payment. On his return home, Mr. Will gave one-half cash money to Robert and his family. According to Mr. Will, he always sleeps better with his cash money stuffed in his mattress. Of course if his mattress was too comfortable, part of their money was put in Ms. Parthina's secret money pouch. Ms. Parthina had a small drawstring pouch sewed to the inside of her dress.

After the families were stocked with plenty of pork for the winter, it was time to separate the hogs from the piglets. Russellville Meat Packing Company always bought a few of their hogs from the farmers in Dover and surrounding communities. There would be a better chance of selling the hogs if they were all in one place. Robert had the hogs and Mr. Will had the piglets. Now they were ready for the meat packing company to come buy their hogs.

Chapter 23

The weather was still warm in the middle of November, but the trees had changed to their beautiful fall colors. It was still warm enough for Robert Murphy to ride in his wagon. The meat packing company got the word out to those with hogs to sell; they would be in the Dover area the first week in December. Robert and Mr. Will were happy to hear the news.

Nothing much had changed about Robert Murphy's wagon rides; Coley was still coming to the house to be with Robert Murphy on his ride to see Grandma and Grandpa Ward. Coley soon found he had to walk on the other side of the road to keep Robert Murphy from reaching for him and falling out of his wagon. That little boy sure did love his Coley.

May and Robert Murphy started down the road to see Grandma and Grandpa Ward, but Ms. Betty had to run back to get the babies favorite napping blanket. This was the first time anything for the baby had been forgotten. May was pulling the little wagon just fast enough that Robert Murphy didn't get upset. Just as Ms. Betty let the screen door slam shut; she heard all kinds of sounds coming from down the road—one sounded like a gun shot.

Ms. Betty paused for only a moment before running to the road to see what was going on, but the dirt from the road was still thick in the air. The first thing Ms. Betty was able to see was Walter's old truck that had been run into the ditch. She began to call for May and Robert Murphy; when there was no answer, she began to call for Coley. When she got to Walter's truck, she saw Coley dead on the ground; the door to the truck was open, and there was blood—a lot of blood. Ms. Betty called and screamed for help; she screamed for May and she screamed for little Robert Murphy. Robert and Clanton were close by when they heard the screams. Robert didn't know exactly what had happened, but he sent Clanton to get Mr. Will and he was to bring his rifle.

Ms. Betty was in shock. She couldn't get the words out to say what she thought had happened. Robert stepped over Coley to get to the horn of the truck; he had Ms. Betty, who still couldn't speak, honk the horn until help arrived. Mr. Will and Seaburn came running down the road to help. Robert was trying to talk and Ms. Betty was still honking the horn. Robert couldn't find his family; he couldn't find his May and his baby Robert Murphy.

Mr. Will saw Coley on the ground, and Ms. Betty looked to be bleeding. Clanton helped his mama sit down on the ground; he was happy to report that blood was not her blood. "Go get your mama. Have her bring the medicine bag. Get the wagon and hurry," yelled Mr. Will. "Bring the rifle too." Clanton and Seaburn ran as fast as they could. Ms. Parthina was standing by the road trying to see when Seaburn shouted, "Papa needs you and your medicine bag." Ms. Parthina didn't even ask what was wrong; she grabbed her bag and down the road she went. She was not a runner, but she could walk pretty fast, especially in an emergency.

Seeing Walter's old truck, Ms. Parthina thought she had been called to bandage drunken Walter. But when she got there, Robert and Mr. Will were combing the bushes for May and Robert Murphy. Ms. Parthina fell to her knees in disbelief, and there she stayed until Robert yelled he had found them. When Mr. Will and Ms. Parthina reached May and the baby they knew Robert Murphy was dead. May had managed to drag herself to where Robert Murphy had been thrown; there she cradled him in her arms. He looked like he was taking a nap.

Finally Seaburn and Clanton returned with the wagon; Mr. Will stepped from the bushes a long way from the old truck. Mr. Will used the old horse blanket from the wagon to move May and Robert Murphy to the wagon. May was not going to let anyone wake the baby from his nap; she would hold him for a little while longer. It took all of them to lift the blanket into the wagon. Ms. Parthina rode in the back with them; Ms. Betty was also put in the wagon.

May was put to bed so that Ms. Parthina could see to treat her injuries. May's legs were broken, and the bones were sticking out; she had blood coming from her nose and her ears. May agreed to take some of Ms. Parthina's pain medicine and let her set her legs, but only if they promised not to wake the baby from his nap. May let Robert hold Robert Murphy while she got her legs set, but she wanted him right back. May was given a big swig of laudanum before Ms. Parthina started to work on her. Mr. Will and Seaburn helped hold her, but she passed out from the pain. Robert Murphy's favorite blanket was put in his little hands while he was rocked to sleep by his daddy.

Mr. Will sent Seaburn and Clanton to bring the children down to see May in case the Lord called her home. When the screen door slammed shut, Ms. Betty regained her senses. She went to the bedroom where May laid all broken and Ms. Parthina kneeled by her bed praying. Ms. Betty heard the rocking chair in Robert Murphy's room; there she saw Robert rocking his son and singing him a lullaby; his heart was broken.

Ms. Betty convinced Robert to let her wash the baby's little face and hands. The blood on Robert Murphy belonged to his mama. Ms. Betty got Robert Murphy all cleaned up, and she dressed him in a pair of pajamas. When May woke, she was in a lot of pain, but not so much that she couldn't ask Robert to bring Robert Murphy to her. Ms. Parthina gave her a tablespoon of laudanum to help manage her pain. Robert Murphy was brought to her.

The Ward children one by one went to the bedroom to see May and Robert Murphy. Don and Dolly thought Robert Murphy was sleeping, and they talked very soft so they wouldn't wake him. The older children had been told Robert Murphy was gone, but May couldn't deal with his death at the moment. In her mind, the baby was sleeping. The children were not to say anything to the contrary; Robert Murphy was sleeping.

May cradled Robert Murphy the same as she did when he was first born. She made sure his little blanket was right there for him to hold. She touched his curly blond hair; she kissed his once rosy cheeks. She whispered softly his name…Robert Murphy. May was in and out of consciousness all through the night; Robert never left her side, and Robert Murphy never left her arms. The dawn of a new day brought a clear mind to May.

May knew Robert Murphy was gone; Coley had died trying to protect them. She marveled at the joy she had experienced with Robert and their child. Even now her heart was full of joy and happiness for the life she had lived, she wouldn't change a thing. May told the family she would be going to be with Robert Murphy and Coley. When it was time, she wanted to be buried next to her brother Alvie. She also wanted to be laid to rest just as she was right then, holding her baby in her arms. May was calm when she expressed her wishes.

Shortly after noon, May looked around the room and gave a sweet smile. "Robert Murphy and Coley are waiting for me…I have to go." May closed her eyes and went to be with Robert Murphy and his four-legged friend, Coley on November 16, 1929.

Robert fell into a deep depression. Ms. Parthina wanted to cover May and Robert Murphy, but Robert would not let it be done. He wanted more time with his wife and son; he screamed to have them back. The family gathered throughout the rest of the house while Robert stayed with his family. Robert loved May and Robert Murphy with every ounce of his being.

Robert lovingly tucked the covers around his wife and son to keep them warm while they slept. He gently closed the bedroom door behind him as he left them. Robert was a broken man on the inside, but he knew he wasn't the only one hurting. Ms. Betty guided Robert to the kitchen to have a cup of coffee. Robert watched the steam from his coffee until it was no more. He sat at the table rocking from side to side; he didn't say a word.

Mr. Will sent Seaburn and Clanton to buy lumber for a coffin. On their way home, the boys stopped by to see Rev. Vanderburg. The funeral arrangements were not complete, but the family would like him to perform the service. "A drunk driver is the cause of their deaths," said Seaburn. The reverend didn't ask if they knew who the driver was, and they didn't offer any more information. The boys were relieved Rev. Vanderburg didn't ask; they would sure hate to lie to a reverend.

It was too late in the day to start building a coffin, but it was not too late to start hunting. Ms. Parthina and Ms. Betty would see that May and Robert Murphy was bathed and dressed for their funeral. Coley was lovingly wrapped in an old blanket and brought to the Cartwright house. He would be laid to rest with his little buddy, Robert Murphy.

Mr. Will, Seaburn, and Clanton had been keeping an eye on Walter's old truck; it was still in the ditch. Now was the time to go hunting—hunt for Walter. Coley had done some damage; that was evident by the blood in the truck. Because the grass and weeds were brown, it would be easier to spot any kind of a blood trail. The three men separated to cover more ground. Finally, a yell rang out. "Over here." Clanton found Walter.

Walter seemed to have weathered pretty well overnight. He had his arm wrapped with his shirt, and he was sucking on his bottle of whiskey as usual. Walter was surprised to see Clanton; he wondered who else might be out combing the brush for him. Mr. Will and Seaburn showed up right away. When Mr. Will went hunting, he always took his rifle and a good rope; the animal was hung by its hind feet and field dressed on the spot. Walter was the animal that was being hunted and now found.

Clanton didn't give Walter a chance to go for his pistol—the pistol used to kill Coley. Since Walter was leaning up against a tree, Mr. Will thought that would be a good place to tie him while they had a nice little talk. Walter knew what he had done; he wanted to blame the do-gooder's daughter for walking on the wrong side of the road: "Your dog attacked me so I killed him. That damn dog never did like me." Mr. Will just let Walter run on about whatever he was saying. Mr. Will sent Clanton to the house to get Robert. Mr. Will and Seaburn sat patiently waiting for Clanton and Robert to arrive.

For some reason, Walter thought Robert would be coming to his rescue. "Son, killing that girl was an accident and that dog attacked me." Robert already knew Walter laid blame on the do-gooder's daughter. "If it was an accident, why didn't you try to help them? The dog was dead. You were not in any danger," shouted Robert. "Them. That scrawny do-gooder was alone." Robert lowered his voice; he sat down on the ground face-to-face with Walter.

Walter watched as Robert tried to hold back the tears; he showed no empathy. Anything that could be done to inflict pain on another person was exactly what Robert wanted to do to Walter. Physical pain would be too good for Walter; that pain would stop sooner or later.

Robert calmly told Walter about the scrawny do-gooder. "Her name was May, and she was my wife. We had a son, Robert Murphy was his name. He would have been one year old in December. Robert Murphy had a wagon he loved to ride every day to go see his Grandma and Grandpa Ward. Yesterday, Robert Murphy was a happy little boy going to see his grandparents when you chose to run them down because you didn't like the do-gooders."

Robert had delivered a pain more powerful than any kind of physical pain. Robert grabbed Walter's injured arm to give him more pain. "I wish I could kill you, but you're not worth the guilt I would carry with me for the rest of my life," cried Robert. Walter started to speak, but he was stopped with the butt end of a rifle. Mr. Will asked Robert and the boys to go back to the house and be with the family. "Not that I care what happens to Walter now, what are you planning to do?" asked Robert.

"I'm going to make sure he is securely tied to this tree. I'm going to walk away and never look back. If he manages to get loose, he will never come back to this area. I will kill him if I ever see him after this night."

Robert, Clanton, and Seaburn went back to the house as Mr. Will asked of them. Mr. Will sat with Walter until he was sure the boys were home. Walter's front teeth were on the ground instead of his mouth; Mr. Will was happy to give them back. "Let's pretend you have a headache, your teeth are aspirins, and your whiskey is water."

When Mr. Will was sure Walter no longer had a headache, he decides to take him for a little walk. "You said you were going to leave me here, and if I could get loose, I would leave and never return," questioned Walter. "I'm just changing the location of where I'll be leaving you tied up. Everything is going to be the same, except the location."

Walter was a little worried about the location, but he was sure he could get loose and run for his life. Mr. Will was now ready for Walter to shut up; he gagged him with his own bloody shirt. Walter's bloody shirt was the only thing that could be used as a gag. Walter was gagged, his hands were tied behind his back, and a lead rope around his neck so he could be controlled. Now they were ready to travel.

Mr. Will felt Walter was still a threat to his family; he couldn't leave him so close the Cartwright house. With the safety of his family in his mind, Mr. Will led Walter away from his family. Walter had brought such pain and suffering to his own son. Mr. Will cried with each step he took while looking for a good place to leave Walter. Before leading Walter away from the Cartwright house, Mr. Will thought about stripping him of his clothes, knocking him out, and dumping him into the hog pen. He knew the hungry hogs would devour him, leaving nothing to be found.

Feeding Walter to the hogs sounded like a good idea. However, he told Robert, Clanton, and Seaburn he would leave Walter tied to a tree, giving him a chance to escape and run for his sorry life. The deeper into the woods, the darker it became; there were no houses, farms, or people for at least five miles in either direction. Mr. Will had found the perfect place to leave Walter. No one would be coming to his rescue; if he got loose, he would have to do it alone. Since Mr. Will had refrained from feeding Walter to the hogs; he saw nothing wrong with hog tying him when he left him in the woods.

Mr. Will did bring Walter's whiskey bottle with them, just in case Walter needed a little something to drink. Before Walter was hog tied, Mr. Will held the whiskey bottle so Walter could have a couple big swigs. Mr. Will was worried debris may have made its way into Walter's wounded arm; of course he didn't want him to die from an infection or lose his arm. Mr. Will disinfected Walter's arm by pouring a little whiskey on it.

Walter was still gagged so he couldn't say if it hurt or not, but Mr. Will thought maybe it did hurt him. Mr. Will offered him another swig of whiskey, and Walter was happy to nod yes. "Now that you're all liquored up, I think I better check that wound to make it ain't going to get infected." With the last little bit of whiskey, Mr. Will poured it over his pocketknife.

Mr. Will used his disinfected pocketknife to conduct a thorough examination of Walter's wounded arm. Just to be on the safe side, he checked it again. Mr. Will found no signs of infection, but he did find that Walter's arm was bleeding again. Of course, Walter was too drunk on his whiskey to care. Mr. Will changed his mind about hog tying Walter; he figured firmly tying him to a tree would do just fine, which is exactly what Mr. Will did.

Walter was tied to a tree in the middle of nowhere. Mr. Will sat and cried for the loss of his daughter and grandson. Before Mr. Will left for home, he took a stick and banged on the tree that Walter was tied to; Walter looked to be still under the influence of his whiskey. Mr. Will walked away and never did he look back. On his walk home, Mr. Will cried for his lost. He remembered how happy May was the day of her wedding, how excited she was to be going to New Orleans for a honeymoon, all the fun she had with Grandma and Grandpa Baker, taking the train home, and able to bring gifts home for the family. Then he remembered the joy of Robert Murphy—all the love and joy he brought to everyone who knew him.

Just at the edge of the Cartwright place, Mr. Will sat on the ground his heart was broken in many pieces. He didn't want to bring any more sadness into the house. He wanted to be strong for the family, but he didn't know for sure if he could be the strong one. No questions were asked about Walter when Mr. Will returned. Ms. Parthina met Mr. Will with an embrace that was heartfelt by both. She knew there was the possibility that Walter would never been found, much less alive. Ms. Parthina would like to think the black hearted Walter got his self loose and high-tailed it back to Louisianan.

Effie and Lizzy took the little ones home to sleep in their own beds. Mr. Will and Ms. Parthina stayed with the Cartwrights. The next morning, Mr. Will and Seaburn would make a coffin for May, Robert Murphy, and Coley. Robert and Clanton went to Oak Grove Cemetery to prepare a grave for his family. May once called the Oak Grove Cemetery a peaceful cemetery. The large oaks provided plenty of shade; the concrete benches welcomed the visitors to sit and rest a while; the trees were haven for many beautiful birds. Just outside the fence, honeysuckles were growing, sending the sweet aroma all through the cemetery. May was right; this is a peaceful cemetery, thought Robert.

The following morning, May, Robert Murphy, and Coley were laid to rest. Rev. Vanderburg performed the service at the cemetery. His words were sweet and tender when he talked about May and Robert Murphy. He called Coley a hero. "Coley gave his life trying to protect his family—that made him a hero." Robert stayed behind as the others left the cemetery. Rev. Vanderburg stayed behind with him; he would see that Robert got home.

When Rev. Vanderburg saw the old truck in the ditch, he inquired about the drunk driver, but Robert said nothing. Robert had not spoken a word since his family was laid to rest. The reverend didn't press the matter. Ms. Cathy, the reverend's wife, encouraged the ladies of Dover to prepare food for the grieving families. Mr. Bailey and Ms. Ida offered their general store as a drop off place for the food. Ms. Cathy gathered the food and delivered it to the home of Mr. Will and Ms. Parthina...where the families gathered.

Ms. Pamela Womack delivered a pork roast to the family. Ms. Womack was an independent sort; she wasn't one to leave matters for others to do on her behalf. She wasn't one to wear out her welcome either. Ms. Womack didn't want to seem rude, so she stayed just long enough to drink a cup of coffee with Ms.

Parthina and Ms. Betty. Ms. Womack was a spinster; she had never experienced the loss of a child, but she knew her friends were heartbroken. Ms. Womack tenderly hugged her friends before leaving for home.

Mr. Will never gave the pork roast a second thought, except to ask for another slice, but now he felt differently about pork. He couldn't believe how close he came to dumping Walter into the pigpen; how easy it would have been. Mr. Will was sure he wasn't the only one to ever think about pigs as a deadly weapon. The thought of having Walter for breakfast didn't sound appetizing at all. Mr. Will told his family, "Never eat pork from a stranger."

"Most pigpens are open; anyone could dump a body in a pigpen without the owners ever knowing," said Mr. Will. He decided to put chicken wire over the top of his pigpen. There would be no Walters in Mr. Will's breakfast. Seaburn and Clanton helped Mr. Will fix the Cartwright's pens first. The pigs were safe; at least until the packing company bought them. The piglets in Mr. Will's pen would be divided with the Cartwright family.

The Pope County sheriff, Marlin Hawkins, came to talk to both families about the drunk driver that killed May and Robert Murphy. A week had passed since May and Robert Murphy had been laid to rest. The sheriff was sure Walter Cartwright was long gone by now; however, the family could still swear out a warrant for his arrest. "If Walter is foolish enough to come back to Pope County, I'll be happy arrest him for vehicular homicide," promised Sheriff Hawkins. The old truck was still in the ditch. Sheriff Hawkins suggested Robert or Ms. Betty take the truck home and slap a for sale sign on it. "He ain't coming back."

Thanksgiving was a difficult holiday. Ms. Parthina and Ms. Betty had gone all the way to Russellville to buy a turkey for Thanksgiving. Mr. Will didn't want any pork on his holiday table. Getting ready for Thanksgiving was a little therapeutic for Ms. Parthina and her girls. Ms. Parthina was determined to make a happy Thanksgiving for her little ones. She even gave instructions:

no one was allowed to be sad at the dinner table; Ms. Betty gave the same instructions to Robert and Clanton. Everyone followed Ms. Parthina instructions.

Grandma and Grandpa Baker didn't come for Christmas as planned. Ms. Betty would have loved to see her parents, but she was somewhat relieved they didn't come. Clanton seemed to be the only Cartwright that was looking forward to Christmas. Ms. Betty struggled to keep herself busy. One day, Robert refused to get out of bed; Ms. Betty called Clanton for a little help. "If you're not getting out of bed today, none of us will get out of bed," laughed Ms. Betty. Clanton and Ms. Betty crawled into bed with Robert; Clanton on one side of Robert and Ms. Betty on the other side of Robert. His bed was definitely not made for three people. Robert, Clanton, and Ms. Betty had a good laugh as they all got out of bed.

Grandpa Baker died two years after May and Robert Murphy. Mr. Will agreed to look after the Cartwright place while they traveled to New Orleans for the funeral. The longer Robert stayed with Grandma Baker, the more he dreaded going back to Dover and the home that held so much pain. Robert remembered every wonderful day he and May had while in New Orleans. Grandma Baker asked Ms. Betty and her family to move back to New Orleans. Robert never thought he would be considering a move back to New Orleans, but he was.

May and Robert Murphy had been gone six years when Robert finally made a decision to move back to New Orleans; he become a companion to Grandma Baker and the overseer to her cotton plantation. Robert was content to live with his happy memories of May and their time spent in New Orleans and his memories of their sweet baby boy. Grandpa Baker's flower garden had been maintained over the years. Robert and Grandma Baker took their evening stroll through the garden. Robert felt his love for May deep in his heart with each stroll they took through the flower garden. Robert could never love another so deeply; he never wanted to love another. Robert was never to marry again.

Ms. Betty and Clanton remained in Dover where they remained close to the Ward family. Ms. Betty still enjoyed having tea with Ms. Parthina; Clanton and Seaburn became close friends. Mr. Will never quite recovered from all that happened in the loss of his daughter and grandson. He didn't seem as happy-go-lucky as before. Velma was now a beautiful little girl.

Clanton grew to be a well-respected man in the Dover community. His heart was captured by a young lady new to the area: Martha Ruff. Clanton and Martha were married in the Dover Baptist Church by Rev. Vanderburg. Their first child turned out to be twins; Mary Margaret and William Thomas Cartwright. The Cartwright home was once again filled with love, happiness, and the laughter of babies.

Walter was declared dead after seven years. His assets were turned over to Robert his eldest son. Robert wanted nothing to do with Walter or his fortune; everything was sold. Most of the proceeds were placed into a trust for Clanton's children. A large donation to the Dover Baptist Church was made by a secret benefactor. Robert remembered Mr. Will always had high hope of owning his own place, to no longer be a sharecropper. By way of Clanton, Robert sent nine hundred dollars cash money to Mr. Will and Ms. Parthina. No matter what, Clanton was not to mention anything about Walter. Clanton agreed.

The Ward children were growing up, getting married and moving from the Dover area. Seaburn and Ms. Ruby Pruitt got married in September 1933; Effie married Isaac Shiflett also in September 1933; Lizzy married Cloud Williams in 1934; Don never married; however, he left Dover to live with Effie and Isaac while he looked for work. Mary Jane married Doyle Robinson in December 1938; Dolly married Lloyd Kinder in 1943, and then she married Joe "Sonny" Smith in 1947. Mildred Gracie Ann

"Shorty" married Marvin Young in 1939; Velma married L. G. Cochran in 1943.

Mr. Will and Ms. Parthina held on to the money from Robert for eight years before touching one dime of it. Their children were scattered over Conway and Perry County, with the exception of Effie and Don. Effie and Isaac moved to Fresno, California, and Don went with them. Isaac joined the Merchant Marines; Effie and Don got work in the shipyard.

Lizzy and Cloud bought a place in Birdtown where Cloud built them an old-fashioned log cabin, somewhat modern on the inside. Mr. Will and Ms. Parthina travel to Birdtown to look at a place that was for sale. The house wasn't as nice as their sharecropper's house, but it had possibilities. Mr. Will was more interested in the land. Mr. Will and Cloud met the owner at the Morrilton Court House; Mr. Will left the court house with the deed in his pocket.

Chapter 24

Anyone who knew Mr. Will knew he didn't pay full price or spend all his money at one time. Mr. Will wanted to raise enough vegetables so he could sell some in town. He wanted enough hogs for his family because they would *never eat pork from a stranger*. Maybe a few hogs to sell for cash money. There were many berry patches around the place; they could have jelly with their hot, buttered biscuits.

It was hard for Ms. Parthina to move away, to leave the Cartwright family behind. Ms. Betty had become such a dear friend. Clanton bought Mr. Will's hogs. Mr. Will and Ms. Parthina didn't have much furniture left after the children took their beds and chest of drawers with them when they married. There wasn't much left to do, but the Cartwright family came to help anyways. Ms. Betty helped wrap a few leftover dishes and pack them away. Mr. Will and Clanton loaded the chest of drawer and the bed. The boxes with the breakables were snugly packed between the mattresses.

Their last supper in Dover was spent with Ms. Betty and her family. Clanton's children called them Grandma and Grandpa Ward. Mr. Will and Ms. Parthina loved them as if they were their grandchildren. After supper, Mary Margaret and Thomas walked Grandma and Grandpa Ward back home. Mary Margaret wanted to hold hands with them before they left. Mary Margaret was such a sweet little girl; she had brown hair and chocolate-colored eyes. She for sure favored her mama and the Ruff side of her family. In his looks, Thomas was just the opposite; his blond hair and blue eyes for sure came from his Cartwright family.

Mr. Will and Ms. Parthina said their good-byes to the Cartwright children. It couldn't be helped; Ms. Parthina cried when the little ones walked away. Ms. Parthina wiped her tears and they went to bed. Sleeping on a pallet wasn't as fun as it use to be; the floor was hard. The pallets would be easy to roll up and put in the wagon. Mr. Will and Ms. Parthina were up and ready to leave at first light. Before they left, the Cartwright family came to say good-bye one more time. Ms. Betty and Martha were up long before daylight, making breakfast for Mr. Will and Ms. Parthina. Hot biscuits and sausage made into little biscuits sandwiches. A few hard-boiled eggs, a sack filled with apples, a saltshaker filled with salt, two thermoses of coffee with one with manly coffee and one with girly coffee. Ms. Parthina needed her coffee first thing in the morning; otherwise, she would be cranky all day long. Mr. Will was thankful for Ms. Parthina's coffee. There wasn't a dry eye when the Wards drove away.

Mr. Will and Ms. Parthina traveled from daylight to dark their first day of travel. They set up a cold camp just off the beaten path of Highway 64. They enjoyed more of their breakfast sandwiches, hard-boiled eggs, and an apple for their supper. Mr. Will saw to the livestock before anything else was done. With only a lantern for light, Ms. Parthina fixed their palettes under the wagon. The next morning, Ms. Parthina couldn't even remember if she had finished her prayers. Over the years, as the Cartwright's sharecroppers, Ms. Parthina had gotten use to sleeping in a soft bed and having a roof over her head.

Just as before Mr. Will and Ms. Parthina were on the road at first light, Birdtown bound. Lizzy and Cloud had everything ready for Mama and Papa Ward's arrival. The utilities were connected; a used icebox was installed and filled with some food. They even left the porch light on for them. Ms. Parthina was so happy to be home; she was tired to the bone.

It didn't take long for Mr. Will and Ms. Parthina to get all settled in at their new place. Ms. Parthina slapped up some new curtains before the first week was up. Of course, Mr. Will didn't see what the big fuss was with the curtains. "Ain't no-body out here but me and you," laughed Mr. Will. Ms. Parthina just shook her head and rolled her eyes at him. The plans for their new place had worked out pretty much like Mr. Will had hoped. Even though Mr. Will was spryer than Ms. Parthina, he too was beginning to slow down due to age, which was accompanied by a few aches and pains. Ms. Parthina always had a bottle of liniment handy for such aches and pains. Liniment was used for disinfecting cuts and wounds, burns, sprains, and bruises more so when the children were growing up.

Mr. Will and Ms. Parthina worked their vegetable garden together. Ms. Parthina still made homemade vegetable soup and canned it for the winter months. Most anything they grew in the garden was canned for later use. Mr. Will made shelves for displaying vegetables from his wagon. People in the rural areas still grew their own vegetables, but there was some that had become so citified they had to buy their fresh fruits and vegetables. Sometimes Ms. Parthina sent a few jars of her homemade jellies to be sold. If the apple trees were producing, Mr. Will would load up a bushel or two to sell with his vegetables.

Mr. Will set up his little vegetable stand just outside the city limits. If he wanted to sell inside the city limits of Morrilton, he would have to buy a peddler's permit. Lizzy and her boys helped Mr. Will make a sign for his stand. Lizzy had a flair for fancy writing; the boy painted her fancy writing. Mr. Will sat in the shade of his wagon waiting for customers.

As the years went by, Mr. Will and Ms. Parthina grew dependent on those with an automobile to get them to town. Ms. Parthina enjoyed going to town with Lizzy and Cloud. Besides picking up supplies from the store, they went to visit some of the families. Some weekdays, Mary and Mary Jane would come for a visit while Bill was sleeping and Jerry was in school. During the summer, Mary, Mary Jane, and Jerry would come for a day of berry picking; sometimes they would pick wild plums or maybe even a few apples.

Ms. Parthina was a little sad to see Mary and the little ones go home. She didn't have too many visits from the other Ward children. When Ms. Parthina went to town with Lizzy and Cloud, they went to visit a different family each time. Every few months, Velma and her family drove up from Pine Bluff for a visit. Danny Wayne always brought his Grandma Peppermint sticks; he brought Grandpa a bag of navel oranges.

It was hard for Effie and Don to get back to Arkansas for a visit. However, when they did come home for a visit, they stayed a whole week. Effie and Isaac might stay a night or two in Birdtown with Mama and Papa Ward; the Shiflett children might spend the night with Aunt Mary one night and maybe another night with Aunt Shorty and her children in Atkins. Uncle Don spent a night or two with Mama and Papa Ward and then one night with Aunt Lizzy and her family. Aunt Velma and her family came up from Pine Bluff, but they spent the night with Uncle L. G.'s mama. Aunt Ruby and Uncle Seaburn invited the entire family to stay for supper, at least one night. Uncle Seaburn's house was so full of family; he thought they might start oozing from the windows and doors.

The last night of their visit Aunt Effie, Uncle Isaac, Ronnie, Barbara, and Uncle Don all stayed the night with Aunt Dolly and Uncle Sonny. Everyone was invited to supper. Aunt Dolly used paper plates and other disposable dishes; she wasn't about to spend the rest of the night doing dishes when she could spend it with the family. One by one the Ward children and their children hugged, kissed, and patted each other before going home. Early the next morning, the Shiflett family and Uncle Don left for California.

While Aunt Effie and Uncle Don were home, they discussed with the other Ward children their thoughts on Mama and Papa living so far out in the country. Uncle Don asked Uncle Seaburn and his sisters to be on the lookout for a place that might be good for Mama and Papa. There didn't seem to be any place the Ward children could agree upon for their mama and papa. The cost was too much, the location wasn't convenient, the condition of the house wasn't livable, the yard was too big, and the garden space was too small.

The Ward children had almost given up the search for a place in town for Mama and Papa Ward to live…almost. They had overlooked a place right under their noses; the little gray house on Maple Street was right there the whole time. Uncle Seaburn took notice of the little house when he followed the flight of a red bird. He gave it a quick look inside and out; it wasn't perfect, but it had possibilities as some might say. One by one, the Ward children, with the exception of Aunt Velma, inspected the little house. The location was good, the yard wasn't too big, and it had plenty of space for a garden.

No one knew the property owner; that's when Mary started her search through the land records. Grandma Ward knew the children wanted to move them to town; she was happy with the thought of living in town. The little gray house on Maple Street was kept a secret until everything was complete. Grandma Ward had been dropping hints for months, trying to get Grandpa Ward thinking about moving to town.

Grandpa Ward knew Grandma wanted to move to town; he heard all the hints from her and their children. Grandma and Grandpa Ward finally sat down and had a heart-to-heart talk about the possibility of moving to town. Grandpa Ward didn't want to be a renter—not after owning his own place. "I believe selling this place would break my heart," Grandpa sadly said. "What if you didn't have to sell this place, would you consider moving to town?" Grandma hopefully asked. "If this is what you want, if we don't have to sell this place."

Grandpa Ward knew his children were scheming about something, but he didn't know what. He also knew Grandma didn't know all the facts; otherwise, she would have let it slip. Aunt Lizzy and Uncle Cloud came by for a visit, but Grandpa Ward knew it was more than just a visit. It seemed Gene was in love with Ms. Betty Ruth Gibson; he wanted to marry her. Betty Ruth said yes, but she was not going to live with his parents or hers. "Gene and Betty Ruth are going to need a place to live," Aunt Lizzy sweetly said.

Grandpa Ward wanted to see where he was moving before agreeing to let someone move into his spot. Aunt Lizzy and Uncle Cloud took Grandma and Grandpa to Morrilton to see the little gray house on Maple Street. Grandma Ward was truly surprised; she instantly fell in love with the little house. "Will, don't you just love this little place?" Grandma asked. "Now, Parthina, I'd like to inspect this place before you tell me…I love it." Grandpa lit his pipe and began his inspection. The little house was all clean and sparkly; the windows had new curtains and the bedroom was furnished with a new bed frame, a dresser, and mirror.

Grandpa Ward and Uncle Cloud came through the back door. "Parthina did you see this kitchen?" shouted Grandpa. "Ain't this the cutest little kitchen you ever saw," he continued? Besides the gas stove and the icebox, a small white table for two sat in front of the kitchen window. It had been a long time since Grandpa saw Grandma so happy. Grandpa Ward was now ready for Grandma to tell him "he loved the place." She told him; he loved the place.

One week after Grandma and Grandpa moved to town, Gene and Betty Ruth got married at the courthouse. Gene and Betty promised to take care of the place. Gene and Uncle Cloud agreed to pay Grandpa four dollars from the sale of each hog until there were no more Grandpa Ward hogs left in the pen. Occasionally, they would bring Grandma and Grandpa some fresh pork chops or bacon. Everyone was happy with their agreement. Grandma and Grandpa Ward moved to town and into the little gray house.

Each morning, Grandma watched with Aunt Ruby and Mary as the children got on the school bus. Sometimes Grandma invited Aunt Ruby, Diana, Mary, and Mary Jane inside for coffee and hot cocoa. She always had marshmallows to put on top of the hot cocoa. Grandma's hot cocoa took Mary Jane's mind off going to school and riding the big yellow school bus. Sometimes Grandpa let Mary Jane walk with him in the garden. Picking tomatoes with Grandpa was fun; he always took a saltshaker with him to test the tomatoes. Grandpa and Mary Jane sat on the ground, picked their tomato, wiped it off with their shirt, and licked the tomato so the salt would stick to that first bite. Warm tomatoes eaten with salt and Grandpa was Mary Jane's favorite way to eat tomatoes.

When the aunts, uncles, and cousins came to see Grandma and Grandpa, the street was full of cousins. Sometimes, Mama let Mary Jane play outside with the big kids, as long as she didn't get in the street. If the big kids got in the street, Mary Jane would find another cousin to play with; there was plenty. One day, Jerry, Kay, and Harold got to walk to the little store on the next block, Collins Grocery. Mr. and Mrs. Collins had a daughter, Freddie Sue Collins. Freddie Sue was in high school, and she rode the same bus as the other kids.

Jerry, Kay, and Harold found a shortcut coming back from the store. The grass was covering up a trail that went from the street down to Grandpa's old smokehouse. Grandpa already had a trail from his smokehouse to the house. Grandpa took his sling blade and cut the grass covering the trail. The kids now had a shortcut to and from the store.

Grandma liked living in town—better than she thought she would. Grandpa wasn't much for living in town, but it made Grandma happy. He figured the hardship of living out of a covered wagon; being dragged from pillar to post for all those years, she deserved to live in comfort surrounded by her children and grandchildren. He just wished it hadn't taken so long for her to get the life she deserved. Grandpa knew Grandma's life of comfort came from their children; more so for her than him. Grandpa knew he was a hard man to love.

Grandpa spent most of his days at his little smokehouse. He had a bed, a little wood-burning stove, an old coffeepot, and a few old ten cups. Winter or summer, Grandpa kept his self busy at his little smokehouse. He grew his own tobacco just outside the smokehouse door. Sometimes Grandpa could be found taking a nap inside his smokehouse.

Grandpa took a large burlap bag and added a long red strap. Grandpa took his burlap bag and walked all over, picking up empty soda bottles. Some bottles he found were clean as a whistle, and others were full of dirt and mud. As long as they were in good shape, Grandpa Ward picked them up. Back at his little smokehouse, he washed each bottle. He had a coat hanger with a piece of old cloth tied on the end to reach down deep in the bottles. At the end of the week, when the bottles were ready to be sold, he took them to Mr. Collins; five cents a bottle was the going rate. If any of the grandchildren were handy, Grandpa Ward paid them one cent to help carry his bottles to the store.

Mary Jane, Jerry, Kay, and Harold were always available to help with the bottles. Diana was too little to carry any bottles, but she got to walk to the store and get candy too. According to Grandpa, it wasn't Diana's fault she was so little; she would help with the bottles when she grew a little more. Everyone was happy when they left the store; Grandpa had cash money in his pocket; the kids had candy. Mary Jane, Diana, and Grandpa Ward skipped down the trail going back home. It was funny to see Grandpa skipping; Kay and Harold didn't know Grandpa could skip. When Grandpa sold his bottles, he always brought home a chocolate bar for Grandma. Chocolate bars cost five cents; he loved her a lot.

The confirmed bachelor, Scooter Humphrey, across the street from Grandma and Grandpa Ward, paid Jerry and Harold five cents each to clear the broken limbs from his yard. Scooter sent the boys to see if Grandpa wanted the wood for his stove in the smokehouse. Grandpa was happy to have the wood. He returned with the boys to thank Scooter for the wood. Jerry and Harold dragged the wood to the back where Grandpa and Scooter cut it and stacked it in an old wagon. The boys pulled the wagon of wood to Grandpa's smokehouse where they neatly stacked it with his other wood. For their hard work, Scooter placed a shiny nickel in each boy's hand. Neither boy had ever had a whole nickel before.

Harold asked Jerry if he wanted to go to the store; Jerry asked Harold if he wanted to go to the store. Both boys wanted to keep their nickel for a little while before going to the store. Each went straight home to show their nickel off to the others. Jerry let Mary Jane hold his nickel; she was very excited for Jerry. "What are you going to do with your nickel?" asked Mary Jane.

"I don't know how much food cost, but if Mama needed my nickel to buy food, I'm going to give my nickel to Mama. If Mama doesn't need my nickel for food, I think candy for me and you would be very nice," said Jerry.

Jerry held on to his nickel for two whole days, but as Mama called it, it was burning a hole in his pocket. Jerry wanted to go to the store with Harold because they earned their money together. Jerry promised to get Mary Jane the kind of candy she liked. Jerry headed down the street with his nickel in his hand. He took the trail from Grandma's house to Uncle Seaburn's house. Their screened door was latched, and the big door was closed. That usually meant no one was home. Jerry went to the front door and knocked. Uncle Seaburn was home taking a short nap on the couch. Harold was not home.

Collins' Grocery was just around the corner from Uncle Seaburn's house. As tempting as it was, Jerry knew he wasn't allowed to walk on the busy streets by his self. He went back to Grandpa's little trail leading to the store. Jerry stopped by the little smokehouse to visit a minute with Grandpa, to see if he needed anything from the store. Grandpa didn't need anything from the store; Jerry went happily on his way.

Just a few minutes passed when a loud boom sounded, followed by the sound of squalling tires. Grandpa couldn't tell exactly what was going on, but he could hear Mr. Collins yelling something. Grandpa ran toward the sounds of screams; Mr. Collins was talking but it was all muffled. Mrs. Collins was putting a blanket on Jerry to keep him warm. Mr. Collins sent Freddie Sue running to fetch the family. Mr. Collins sat Grandpa down to hold Jerry's little hand, to softly talk to him. Mama and Grandma arrived just before the ambulance; the street was blocked by police cars and flashing lights. Mama rode with Jerry and Grandpa in the ambulance. A blanket was put around Grandpa; they said he was in shock.

Grandma went to find Seaburn; she needed to get to the hospital. "Jerry was hit by a car and Papa is in shock. They took Papa to the hospital too," sobbed Grandma. Seaburn knew all too well the thoughts that went through Papa's mind: May and Robert Murphy. Twenty-eight years later, the pain and horror of that day came rushing back. Grandma and Uncle Seaburn entered the hospital by way of the emergency room. St. Anthony's Hospital was a Catholic hospital; most of the nurses were also nuns. If the nuns gave Grandma their usual "Have a seat and someone will be right with you," she was prepared to box her jaws.

Guess what? Grandma got the opportunity to box a nun's jaws, but Uncle Seaburn was there to intervene; he gently moved Grandma from her boxing range of the nun. Once Uncle Seaburn was sure the nun was safe, he and Grandma quickly slipped through the double door leading to the hospital. They made their way to the lobby of the hospital. The information desk was being manned by a much younger nun. As much as Uncle Seaburn hated to ask, he had no choice. The hospital was too big to be aimlessly searching.

The much younger nun was very pleasant and helpful. The surgery waiting area was on the sixth floor; the young nun called the nurses' station to make sure someone from the family was there. Grandma was much calmer; she no longer felt the need to box someone's jaws. Although, she did feel the need to ask a question "The nun's in the emergency room are so rude and you're such a pleasant nun...how can that be?"

"The nuns in the emergency room get paid more to be rude," said the young nun. Uncle Seaburn let out a big snicker and Grandma's eyes bugged out. The young nun apologized for her witty answer.

Uncle Seaburn and Grandma left the hospital lobby with a bounce in their step and a smile on their face—just what they needed. The hospital lobby smelled of disinfectants and who knows what else; the deeper into the hospital you went, the stronger the smell. Mary and Grandpa were sitting in the waiting room on the sixth floor. Grandpa had a blanket draped around him; his face was still pale. "Mama, physically there is nothing wrong with Papa, but he is in shock," said Mary. "Papa thinks we're here for May and Robert Murphy."

Grandma and Mary went to get some stale hospital coffee; Uncle Seaburn stayed with Grandpa. "Papa, can I get you anything?" asked Seaburn. Papa didn't need anything; he was just waiting to hear about May and Robert Murphy. Uncle Seaburn knew Grandma would be the only one that could bring Grandpa back. "They were all out of stale coffee, so we had to bring back fresh coffee," said Grandma. Grandma watched Grandpa drink his coffee before asking him any questions. Grandma squatted so that she would be face to face with him.

"Will, do you know who I am?" she asked.

"Parthina, you're Parthina." Slowly, Will came back to his Parthina and their family. He knew they were waiting to hear about Jerry.

Jerry's little body had been put back together as best it could, but he had slipped into a coma. The doctors couldn't say how long he might be in the coma, or if he would ever come out of the coma. Mary and Grandma went to the intensive care unit to see Jerry. Grandpa wasn't allowed to see Jerry right then—Grandma's orders. Grandma stayed at the hospital with Mary. Grandpa spent the night with the Robinson children. Little Mary Jane wouldn't let Grandpa Skippy out of her sight, and since Mama wasn't home, Mary Jane let Fuzzy Dog come inside; she was sure Fuzzy Dog was sad too.

Grandpa stayed with the grandchildren for two days; Fuzzy Dog slept inside with Mary Jane. Doylene started to make Mary Jane's bed, but that was not possible; her bed smelled just like a dog. "Mary Jane, you and Fuzzy Dog need a bath, ya'll stink," said Doylene. "Fuzzy Dog, we stink, and Doylene said we need a bath…come on." Fuzzy Dog followed little Mary Jane as if he knew he was about to get a bubble bath.

Mary Jane had Fuzzy Dog jump into the bathtub; she couldn't lift him. She tested the temperature of the water just like Mama did for her. When the water was just right, she squirted liquid soap from the kitchen right under the running water. She also used her plastic cup for rinsing the soap out of her hair. When the bubbles were big, Mary Jane got into the tub with Fuzzy Dog. "We ain't going to stink anymore." Fuzzy Dog quietly stood in the tub with its mountain of bubbles while Mary Jane attempted to bathe him. Mary Jane lathered Fuzzy Dog the best she could; she washed his face with a washcloth—just like Mama washed here face. She took extra care not to get soap in Fuzzy Dog's eyes.

The house became all quiet and that worried Doylene. Mary Jane quickly answered when called: "We're taking a bath." Doylene and Kim went to see "we." Fuzzy Dog and Mary Jane were shivery; their bathwater was no longer warm. Kim offered to help with Fuzzy Dog's bath. The cold soapy water was drained from the tub, and fresh, warm water was run. It took a while, but bath time was over. Mary Jane and Fuzzy Dog didn't stink any more.

Chapter 25

Mama and Grandma came home after two days at the hospital with Jerry. Mama came home just long enough to bathe and change clothes. Mary Jane thought Mama would be coming home with Jerry. She didn't understand the severity of his injuries. "Jerry has two broken legs, so he has to stay at the hospital until he gets well," explained Mama. "I'll draw him a picture so he will have something happy to look at. Tell Jerry I gave Fuzzy Dog a bath. I'm taking good care of him until Jerry comes home," said Mary Jane.

When Mama went back to the hospital, Grandma didn't go back with her. Mama told Grandma she needed to rest because she might need her help later. Grandma was tired to the bone, so she didn't fuss too much about staying home. Uncle Seaburn and Aunt Ruby volunteered to check in on the Robinson children. Aunt Ruby made some of her fried pies, and Uncle Seaburn brought them down. Mary Jane was very appreciative of the fried pies; especially the chocolate fried pies, but she missed her mama and Jerry.

Uncle Seaburn explained as best he could; Jerry was sick and Mama was there to help get him well. Uncle Seaburn took Grandma and Grandpa to the hospital a few times, but Grandpa didn't want to see him while he was in the intensive care. Aunt Ruby sent some of her fried pies for Mama to enjoy; Mama shared them with Grandma and Grandpa.

Jerry was in intensive care for two weeks before he was moved to a regular room. According to Dr. Mobley, Jerry wasn't out of the woods just yet. Dr. Mobley had a cot brought in for Mama to sleep on. Jerry remained in a coma. Mama was so afraid Jerry would wake up and no one would be there with him. Members of the family took turns sitting with Jerry while Mama went home to be with the other children.

Everyone knew little Mary Jane had a vivid imagination; she enjoyed playing pretend. She called it "play like." On rainy days, she liked to play like she was having a tea party. So when Mary Jane told Mama she had talked to Jerry, Mama of course thought she was playing like she talked to Jerry. Mama tried keeping Mary Jane busy, but it didn't always work. A few times, Mama and Mary Jane went to visit Aunt Ruby so Mary Jane could play with Diana. Since Jerry was sick at the hospital, Mama and Mary Jane didn't wait for the big yellow school bus.

Mary Jane still looked forward to going to school and riding the big yellow school bus. "When Jerry gets all better and I get big enough to go to school, Jerry's going to hold my hand while I climb the big steps to get on the school bus and then we can sit together on the bus...every day. Ain't that right, Mama?" asked Mary Jane.

"Yes, honey."

Mary Jane continued to draw happy pictures for Jerry's hospital room. Every day Mary Jane wanted to go see Jerry at the hospital. She promised Mama she would be quiet as a little mouse. Mary Jane was not old enough to be anywhere in the hospital except the lobby. Finally Mama agreed Mary Jane could go to the hospital with her, but she could only go as far as the lobby. "You can tell Jerry I'm in the lobby wishing I could come see him."

Mary Jane and Hannah Polly sat in the hospital lobby waiting for Mama to come down in the elevator. The hospital had a gift shop with pretty things to buy for sick people. May Jane was sure if she didn't touch anything, it would be all right to go inside. Mary Jane struggled with the door to the gift shop; one of the nuns offered to help. The nun had a pretty face, but her dress made her look a little scary. The pretty nun talked to the lady behind the counter as Mary Jane slowly looked around the shop.

After a few minutes of looking, Mary Jane asked the lady behind the counter if they had sunglasses and how much they might cost. The gift shop didn't have sunglasses. Mary Jane and Hannah Polly went back to the lobby to wait for Mama. The pretty nun soon followed; she was curious about why Mary Jane needed sunglasses. Mary Jane was somewhat reluctant to tell why she needed sunglasses. "My brother Jerry is sick, and he is the one who needs sunglasses," said Mary Jane. Sister Agnes, the pretty nun, didn't understand about the sunglasses either. "Mama thinks I'm playing like I talked to Jerry because I miss him."

"Every night when I say my prayers, I ask Baby Jesus to help me get sunglasses for Jerry. If I know how much they cost, I can go find empty soda bottles and get money for the bottles." Mary Jane didn't mean to tell Sister Agnes all that she did. Sister Agnes wanted Mary Jane to see the hospital's chapel where they could pray together for sunglasses. Sister Agnes introduced Mary Jane to the Virgin Mary, Baby Jesus' mother.

Together, Mary Jane and Sister Agnes prayed for sunglasses for Jerry. Mary Jane finally told Sister Agnes everything. "Jerry told me he is in heaven. The beautiful light in heaven is so bright that he needed sunglasses. He said it was easy to tell who would be staying in heaven from those who were just visiting, just passing through. A woman and her little boy were ready to show Jerry around in heaven. If Jerry doesn't get sunglasses, he will have to stay in heaven," sobbed Mary Jane. "I want Jerry to stay here with us."

Mama was just getting off the elevator when Sister Agnes was walking Mary Jane back to the lobby. Mary Jane introduced her new friend, Sister Agnes, to her mama. "Mary Jane and I went to the chapel to say a prayer for Jerry. I hope you don't mind," said Sister Agnes. Mama was grateful for the prayers. Mary Jane was all excited that she met the Virgin Mary. "Mama, did you know the Virgin Mary is Baby Jesus' mama?"

Mama smiled and took Mary Jane's little hand; together they walked to the car. Mama and Mary Jane saw Aunt Lizzy and Uncle Cloud in the parking lot. Aunt Lizzy was planning to spend the night with Jerry.

Mary Jane had talked to everyone she could about Jerry and the sunglasses, but everyone thought she was just making it up. If she had talked to Grandpa, she was going to ask him again. Mama was busy—keeping herself busy. Mary Jane slipped out the back while Mama was busy; she and Fuzzy Dog walked to see Grandpa. They went straight to the smokehouse where Grandpa spent most of his days. Mary Jane asked Grandpa, "Don't be mad at me until you know why I came to see you." Mary Jane's determination caused Grandpa to listen and hear what she was saying about Jerry and his need for sunglasses. Of course, she had to start from the beginning and tell him every little detail; she told it just the way Jerry told her.

Grandpa walked Mary Jane back home where he asked her Mama if she could go to the store with him for ice cream. Just as Grandpa said ice cream, he shot a quick wink to Mary Jane. Mary Jane knew Grandpa was keeping the sunglasses for Jerry their secret. He was also keeping the secret that Mary Jane walked all the way to his smokehouse by herself. Mama gave her permission. Mary Jane was told not to be sassy, and Grandpa was told to hold Mary Jane's hand there and back. Grandpa and Mary Jane smiled and said yes.

"Grandpa, are we really going for ice cream?" asked Mary Jane. "Well, I figured if Mr. Collins didn't have any sunglasses, we might need a little cheering up," replied Grandpa. Mary Jane and Grandpa had no idea if Mr. Collins's store sold sunglasses; they never needed any until now. Mary Jane held Grandpa's hand tighter and tighter the closer they got to the store. Grandpa assured Mary Jane they would get some sunglasses for Jerry *somewhere*.

Mr. and Mrs. Collins were happy to see Grandpa and Mary Jane. They were hoping to hear good news about Jerry's condition, but nothing had changed. Mary Jane stood on her tippy toes to see over the counter. She blurted out, "Mr. Collins, do you have sunglasses? How much do they cost?" Mr. Collins was sorry to say he didn't sell sunglasses. Mary Jane immediately started to cry.

"Grandpa, Jerry is going to stay in heaven with May and Robert Murphy if we don't get him some sunglasses real soon," cried Mary Jane.

Grandpa's heart jumped straight up to his throat. He lifted Mary Jane and sat her on the counter. Grandpa wanted Mary Jane to say that again. Mary Jane sniffled, "Jerry told me the people with sunglasses were just visiting heaven. The people without sunglasses were staying in heaven. A woman and her little boy were there to show him around heaven. May and Robert Murphy are their names. Grandpa turned white as a sheet; he knew Mary Jane was telling something that he and the others had never believe until now.

Mr. and Mrs. Collins thought Grandpa was going to faint. Mrs. Collins took his arm to help steady him. "Grandpa, don't cry...we'll find some sunglasses," Mary Jane softly said. "I have some old sunglasses, but one of the legs is ready to fall off. I have a new pair if ya'll want the old ones," Mrs. Collins happily said. Grandpa and Mary Jane instantly became happy. "Yes, please, yes, please," they shouted. Mr. and Mrs. Collins's home was connected to their little grocery store; Mrs. Collins didn't have to go far to get the sunglasses.

Grandpa's knees were still a little wobbly; Mrs. Collins brought him a chair when she returned with the old pair of sunglasses. "Fred, go find some tape. Let's see if we can fix these sunglasses for that sweet little boy," bossed Mrs. Collins. The only tape Mr. Fred could find was black electrical tape or butcher's tape. Mrs.

Collins didn't hesitate when she chose the black electrical tape; she said it would hold better. It didn't matter what color the tape was or that the sunglasses were white; Grandpa and Mary Jane were just happy to have sunglasses.

Grandpa's fingers were too big and clumsy to work with the tape; Mary Jane's fingers were just too little. Mrs. Collins took charge of the tape and sunglasses. Mary Jane tried on the sunglasses once they were repaired. "These will work just fine," said Mary Jane. Mr. Fred put Jerry's sunglasses in a small paper bag for safe travel.

Before leaving the store, Grandpa offered Mary Jane ice cream. Mary Jane was too happy for ice cream. "Chicken leg ice cream always makes Grandma happy. Can we take one home to her?" asked Mary Jane. Mary Jane and Grandpa left the store with sunglasses and chicken leg ice cream. Mary Jane carried the bag with Jerry's sunglasses, and Grandpa carried the bag with Grandma's ice cream. Grandpa made sure to hold Mary Jane's hand all the way home.

Grandpa presented Grandma with her chicken leg ice cream. Grandma did appreciate her ice cream, but she knew Grandpa was up to something. "Did you get Mary Jane into mischief or did Mary Jane get you into mischief?" asked Grandma. Grandma could always tell when Grandpa was up to some kind of mischief; he smiled like the cat that ate the canary. "Now, Parthina, you know I wouldn't do anything to get this little child in trouble," Grandpa sweetly said. Grandma almost believed him—until he started laughing.

"Eat your chicken leg ice cream while I walk Mary Jane home," said Grandpa. Later the same day, Mama was taking Grandma and Grandpa to see Jerry at the hospital. Mama had already said Mary Jane could go too. Grandpa had the little bag with the sunglasses tucked away in the bib of his overalls. Now Grandpa had to find a way for Mary Jane to get past the hospital lobby and the nuns walking the halls. Grandpa felt Mary Jane should be the one to give Jerry his sunglasses because he asked her for the sunglasses.

Grandpa volunteered to get Mary Jane settled before going up to see Jerry. Once again, Grandpa and Mary Jane were up to something; Grandma was sure of it. When the coast was clear, from Grandma and Mama, it was time for Grandpa and Mary Jane to hatch a plan to get her upstairs and into Jerry's room. Sister Agnes came by to say hello to her new little friend. Even Sister Agnes thought Grandpa and Mary Jane were up to some mischief. Mary Jane showed Sister Agnes what was in the little bag. "What can I do to help?" asked Sister Agnes. Grandpa, Mary Jane, and now Sister Agnes were hatching a plan.

Grandpa asked for ten minutes to get upstairs and start his part of the plan. Sister Agnes and Mary Jane waited five minutes before they started to the stairwells. Rarely were the stairs used; Sister Agnes was sure they wouldn't be seen. Sister Agnes and Mary Jane climbed six flights of stairs; there they would wait for Grandpa. Soon after Grandpa got to Jerry's room, he casually mentioned how cold the hospital was kept. After about ten minutes, Grandpa started pouring it on: how cold he was and how good a fresh cup of hot coffee would just hit the spot. Grandpa knew Grandma would offer to go down to the lounge for some hot coffee; he also knew Mary would go to the lounge with her.

Finally the coast was clear…well sort of clear; Grandma and Mama were down the hall getting coffee. As the nuns went in and out of the rooms, Grandpa had to time it just right to get Mary Jane and Sister Agnes out of the stairwell and into Jerry's room. Sister Agnes used the fullness of her dress to help hide little Mary Jane. Grandpa, Mary Jane, and Sister Agnes made it to Jerry's room without being caught. Mary Jane's heart was pounding.

Little Mary Jane was not prepared for what she was about to see. Mama didn't want Mary Jane to see Jerry looking so pitiful; Grandpa knew it, but getting the sunglasses to her brother was more important. Grandpa raised Mary Jane so that she could see Jerry; she placed his sunglasses just right on his face. She whispered something in his ear.

Grandpa, Mary Jane, and Sister Agnes hadn't thought about how they would explain Jerry's new sunglasses to Mama and Grandma. Well, that would have to wait.

Dr. Mobley came strolling into the room—oops! Dr. Mobley pretended he didn't see anyone, but he couldn't pretend he didn't see the ugly pair of ladies sunglasses on a comatose little boy. Now, Dr. Mobley enjoyed a good practical joke from time to time; however, if this was a joke, someone had gone too far. Dr. Mobley started to remove Jerry's sunglasses; Mary Jane yelled, "Don't take his sunglasses off!" Dr. Mobley did not.

Dr. Mobley promised Mary Jane he would put them right back; he just needed to look at Jerry's eyes. Jerry's sunglasses were put back just the way they were found. Dr. Mobley pulled up a chair to talk to Mary Jane about the sunglasses. Mary Jane sat straight and tall as she told Dr. Mobley the things Jerry told her. Grandpa let Dr. Mobley know: "I know who May and Robert Murphy is; Mary Jane does not. Sister Agnes believed the child to be earnest. "Will you tell Mama and Grandma that Jerry has to keep his sunglasses on until he gets back from heaven?" asked Mary Jane. Dr. Mobley agreed the sunglasses were necessary; he even wrote it on Jerry's clipboard hanging at the end of his bed.

Mama and Grandma were pretty surprised when they saw Grandpa, Mary Jane, and Sister Agnes having a nice visit with Dr. Mobley. They were more surprised to see Jerry wearing his sunglasses. "I knew you two were up to something," growled Grandma. "Mama, Dr. Jack says Jerry's sunglasses are good for him," bragged Mary Jane. "The sunglasses will do no harm to Jerry, but to take them away would be harmful to Mary Jane. She desperately needed to do this for her brother. Whether we believe or not, she does."

"Dr. Jack, I think I should visit Jerry every day, don't you?" said Mary Jane. Mama was surprised when Dr. Jack agreed with

Mary Jane. Dr. Mobley and Sister Agnes left the family to visit with Jerry. A few minutes later, Sister Agnes returned with a visitor's pass for Mary Jane. She clipped the visitor's pass to Mary Jane's collar. "Dr. Jack says you have to wear your visitor's pass every time you come to see Jerry. With this visitor's pass, you can ride up in the elevator with your Mama," Sister Agnes softly instructed. Mary Jane couldn't help herself; she gave Sister Agnes the biggest hug. Sister Agnes smiled.

With each visit to the hospital, Mary Jane stopped by the hospital chapel to thank the Virgin Mary and Baby Jesus for helping her and Grandpa find sunglasses for Jerry. If she saw Sister Agnes, she was greeted with a big hug. Grandpa had a dark, sad feeling about him before he knew May and Robert Murphy were happily together in heaven. Mary Jane had an Aunt May and a little cousin, Robert Murphy, that she never knew mostly because they lived in heaven. Grandpa's sad heart was no longer sad; he found joy in telling Mary Jane and Jerry stories about May and Robert Murphy.

Mary Jane went every day to visit Jerry in the hospital. His white sunglasses remained until he returned from just passing through heaven. Jerry didn't remember much about heaven, but he did remember May and Robert Murphy being with him. He also remembered hearing Mary Jane whisper, "It's time to come home now."

It took six months for Jerry's broken little body to heal well enough that he could go home. His body cast was removed, but he would still have a cast on each of his legs. The day before Jerry was to go home, Sister Agnes and some of the other nuns brought cake and ice cream for Jerry and his family. Sister Agnes and Dr. Jack both signed Jerry's cast before he left the hospital. Little Mary Jane got to draw a flower on Jerry's cast.

Despite his injuries, Jerry grew straight and tall.

THE END

Endnotes

1   Property information from the last will and testament of Mrs. Parthina Ward, dated May 5, 1959.

2   Information from Lt. Mauldin's great-great-great granddaughter, Shannon Hamilton.

3   From www.findagrave.com.

4   Pope County Arkansas Marriage Records

5   Varina Howell Davis Chapter 2559, United Daughters of the Confederacy Certificate, December 30, 2008